No Substitute for Mistrust

No Substitute for Mistrust

Carolyn J. Rose

No Substitute for Mistrust

Cover design by Dorion D. Rose, Broken Cork Photography

Interior design for print edition by Boulevard Photografica/Patty G. Henderson

Digital editions (epub and mobi) produced by Booknook.biz

Paperback edition ISBN: 978-0-9995310-4-4
Mobi edition ISBN: 978-0-9995310-5-1
Epub edition ISBN: 978-0-9995310-6-8

Chapter 1

Slamming the front door of our condo behind her, Allison stomped toward the living room, continuing a heated discussion with Mrs. Ballantine.

I didn't look up. When Allison was in a snit, it was better—if you had a choice—to remain on the sidelines and refrain from making eye contact. So I kept my head down and went on paging through a book claiming to be stuffed with hundreds of quick and easy recipes anyone can make.

"Now, Allison," Mrs. B said in a soothing voice, "I'm certain if you replay our conversation in your mind, you'll realize I didn't use the word 'loser' when referring to your ability to master rudimentary driving skills."

"Maybe you didn't say it. But that's what you thought. And it's your fault I ran the stop sign. You kept grabbing the handle thing over the window like you didn't trust me to stop when I was supposed to and I got all nervous."

The sound of feet clomping up the stairs told me Allison had veered off and was headed for her bedroom, a place otherwise known as sulking headquarters.

"I'm never driving with you again," she shouted just before the door slammed. "Never ever ever."

1

Mrs. B, her silvery hair standing up in tufts and her silk blouse marred by clutches of wrinkles where I assumed she'd gripped the fabric in spasms of fear, hustled to the kitchen. She flung cabinet doors open like a woman in search of an antidote.

"We're out of everything except beer," I told her.

"Beer it is." She opened the refrigerator and seized a bottle from Dave's stash, clutching it the way a drowning woman might grab a rope.

I laid the recipe book aside and sat up straight, taking more interest. Since Mrs. B prefers vintage wine or expensive liquor, and since she takes only a sip or two of designer beer on the hottest of summer days, and since the bottle she held contained off-brand cheap swill, and since her condo and her liquor cabinet were right next door, the situation was serious.

"I admit I grabbed the roof handle. But that was pure reflex, not a sign of mistrust. Not of Allison herself. Although her driving . . ."

"It was an unconscious act of self-preservation," I agreed. "I've clutched that handle a dozen times on every drive. Allison isn't big on anticipating stoplights and signs and letting up on the gas."

"Exactly. She stomps the brake like it's a black widow spider. And she shoots away from intersections like a rocket." She unscrewed the cap from the bottle and tossed it in the garbage can in the cabinet under the sink. "There were many things I wanted to say to her, Barbara, but I held my tongue. I never called her a loser."

As if to punctuate that claim, she flopped on the other end of the sofa.

Yes, flopped. Mrs. B, former showgirl, the queen of serene, the princess of posture and poise, the empress of etiquette, flung herself on the cushions. Next she sprawled like a starfish, plunked her feet on the coffee table, and guzzled beer straight from the bottle.

Yikes.

Forget serious.

The situation was dire.

"I'm sure you didn't say she was a loser," I assured her.

"I never said anything that wasn't couched in the most positive way. Honest."

I leaned over and patted her arm. "We all know Allison has a tendency to take things the wrong way and . . ." I paused, searching for a kinder way of saying "go off the rails," but came up with nothing as descriptive and accurate.

"But I was trying to help," Mrs. B moaned.

"In Allison's book, good intentions don't earn you an exemption."

"I thought perhaps a gentler approach to her driving lessons would make a difference." She finished the beer in a few swallows and, not even glancing around for a coaster, set the bottle on the table. "I thought perhaps her driving was so erratic because Dario frightened her."

Dario O'Brien frightened plenty of people. Mrs. B's squeeze was a big man with a gruff voice and the demeanor of a paid thug who enjoyed doing what it took to be an enforcer. But anyone who knew him—and that included Allison—knew he was more of a Teddy bear than a grizzly bear. And many of us also knew the thug act was simply that—an act.

"I thought perhaps stress might be contributing to her failure to fully grasp the basics and build a skill set." As she fingered her five-strand pearl choker, I noted she also wore a pair of pearl earrings, two bracelets, and three rings. Mrs. B was all about pearl power as a way to pave the road to success. But today it seemed either pearl power had failed, or the project had required more jewelry than she'd decked herself out in.

"I'm not a quitter, dear, you know that. But when I noticed the gas gauge was in the red, my heart fluttered and soared like a captive bird freed from a cage." Her fingers did a fluttery dance in the air. "Of course, I didn't let Allison see how relieved I was when I pointed to the gauge. I offered to let her use my card to fill it up, but she said she was tired of driving anyway and gas stations were dirty and smelly and she didn't know where the gas went or how much to put in and—"

"And why couldn't we move to Oregon?" I guessed. "Where people pump gas for you?"

"Yes. Exactly. I offered to explain how everything worked and help her fill the tank, but she said she was tired of driving anyway and wanted to quit." She groaned. "And now I feel terrible because she must have sensed my relief. I should have handled the situation better. I should have been more patient."

The beer didn't seem to have done much to lighten her mood, so I dug Cheese Puff from the crevice between the seat cushion and the arm of his favorite chair and set my entitled mutt in her lap. He grunted, checked her hands to see if she had a dog cookie, licked her chin, opened his mouth to display the gold-capped tooth she'd paid for after he'd chomped on a roulette ball, and then curled up to resume his snooze. Mrs. B scratched the top of his knobby head and rubbed the soft skin behind his ears. She followed that up with a series of strokes along his spine. "Is it my imagination, or is his hair getting thinner?"

"Not your imagination. He's shedding his winter coat. With a vengeance." I eyed a drift of orange hair in the corner of the kitchen and wondered if it was my turn to vacuum or whether that chore fell to Dave or Allison. My live-in boyfriend, in

4

training to be the homicide and major crimes detective for the county, insisted he had an amazing memory so there was no need to write a chore rotation on the calendar tacked up near the phone. His daughter Allison, on the other hand, probably didn't know the calendar existed because it was definitely old school and wasn't where she'd notice it—like taped to the center of the mirror she used to apply her makeup. Having the ability to overlook an entire calendar, I had no doubt she could also fail to take note of a particular square with her name in it.

As I did several times a day, I wished Jim, my second-favorite neighbor, wasn't busy with his part-time job and his full-time love life and still came in a few times a week to wipe, sweep, vacuum, and even mop downstairs. Immediately, as I also did several times a day, I wondered when my friend Paulette would drop by and notice that, while cleaning, he had also taken it upon himself to rearrange several pieces of furniture she'd placed with great precision when Dave and I moved in together last year. Granted, Jim had shifted things only a few inches and changed angles only a few degrees, but that would be enough to set off fireworks. Major fireworks.

When I'd mentioned the incendiary nature of the situation, he'd been unconcerned, saying he hadn't altered the arrangement much. When I suggested we simply restore the old order, he'd claimed he couldn't remember exactly where things had been, contended that his arrangement was superior, and fell back on the theory that Paulette wouldn't notice. I'd bet him five bucks she'd know in a minute and asked how he intended to handle the fallout. He'd shrugged it off, saying there were plenty of women scarier than Paulette and, tiny as she was, she could hardly work up a good head of steam. I'd reminded him that Wilhelmina Frost, the current woman of his dreams, was every bit as tiny and probably two decades older. Known as Big

Chill, she could make me tremble in my sneakers without breaking a sweat, and I was sure she managed to do the same to him. He'd blanched a bit, allowed that I might have a point, and left with a promise to give some thought to the situation.

That left me in a rock vs. hard spot position. I preferred Jim's arrangement, but valued my friendship with Paulette. I also couldn't remember where she'd placed each piece and feared I'd make things worse if I rearranged. On top of that, Mrs. B had added a rolling cabinet/shelf arrangement for me to use as a mini office. Needless to say, she hadn't checked with Paulette before making the purchase.

"It hardly seems that we should be only a few days from the official start of summer already." Mrs. B interrupted my thoughts. "Time doesn't simply fly as you get older, dear, it moves with the speed of a meteor falling to earth."

Thanks to great genes, an exercise program, a wizard of a hairdresser, skin creams, makeup, and a dearly departed husband who left her a pile of dough to smooth the financial worries that contribute to wrinkles, Mrs. B seemed to have stopped the process of aging in its tracks. Not that anyone knew the exact location of those tracks. Not one of us in the circle of friends residing at 90 Columbia Lane in Reckless River, Washington, had the gumption or gall to ask. Our best guesses all landed in the vicinity of seven decades.

"Were you hunting up a recipe for dinner?" She pointed at the book on the center cushion of the sofa.

"Hunting. Not finding."

(For the record, my unproductive search was largely due to the fact that the recipe I had in mind would make use of ingredients on hand, pass the basic level of good nutrition set on a sailing ship in the year 1750, taste better than a chunk of carpet, and involve no more than 10 minutes of prep time.)

"Perhaps your search has been futile because you've limited it to dishes topped with crumbled cheesy snacks?"

Ouch!

Yes, I admit I have a cheesy snack habit, a *bad* cheesy snack habit. I always had at least one bag in the pantry. And, sure, there were times when I'd crushed a few to top my serving of a salad or casserole. And, okay, once—but only once—I pulverized and sprinkled a few to add flavor and color to steamed cauliflower.

But I wasn't an addict.

At least not a hard core, do-anything-to-get-a-fix addict.

And I wasn't a pusher!

I would never force others to munch on those crunchy globes and twists and puffs of corn and air and—perhaps—even a small percentage of real cheese.

Where did my neighbor get off making snarky comments? She, after all, frequently returned from shopping trips with sacks of new types of cheesy snacks she'd spotted. She enabled me. She fed my habit.

Before I could verbalize any of that, Mrs. B slid closer, moved the cookbook to the coffee table, and patted my shoulder. "You know I'm only teasing, dear. Forget making dinner. I'll order out. We deserve a night off from cooking."

This from a woman who seldom had a night *on*. Especially lately. Dario's hours as the manager of the radio station she'd purchased a few months ago were long. And, during the past few weeks, they'd hosted a series of dinners for potential advertisers. Each dinner had been preceded by several cocktails, washed down with wine, and topped off with rich desserts.

Planning and hosting the dinners helped the station, but the project also filled Mrs. B's spare time. Fortunately for me, she hadn't tried to use her free hours to plan the aisle walk she hoped Dave and I will take soon. After my last close call with death in the Columbia River, Dave and I had agreed to think seriously about setting a date. But the date depended on the demands of his new job and how fast he settled into it. And it depended on whether I landed a teaching position or would spend yet another year as a substitute. Subbing allowed me to take time off at will—although without pay. Landing a job would increase my income, but also require me to put in many more hours.

When Mrs. B agreed there was no point in planning until all the dust settled, she'd jumped into a number of hobbies. The knitting craze ended when, with the help of Cheese Puff, she made a hopeless tangle of seven skeins of high-quality yarn, and an even more hopeless tangle of the scarf she attempted.

The painting interlude came to a halt when, again with the help of Cheese Puff, several open tubes of paint landed on her living room carpet. A bad day for her became a good one for a carpet salesman and an installer.

Finally, her desire to become a birdwatcher cooled the day her car mired deep in the mud when she sighted an eagle at a nearby wildlife refuge and pulled too far off the road. When I say "deep in the mud," I mean so deep we couldn't open the doors and had to climb out the windows. In addition to having to arrange for a tow and pay to have the car cleaned, she was out the cost of a pair of designer boots and the camera, complete with a long lens, that slipped from her chilled hands and into a ditch. I'd been wearing rubber boots, old jeans, and a jacket that was even older. I lost only my cool.

Perhaps Mrs. B had sensed that because she'd stuck to reading and shopping for the past two weeks. But this afternoon she'd volunteered to take the passenger seat—or, as

8

Dave referred to it, "the suicide seat"—while Allison prepped for her driver's test. Since my own experiences with Allison were hair-raising enough, I had no intention of asking what transpired on her excursion. Like it or not—and, because of the cost involved, he didn't—Dave would soon have to hire a professional driving instructor. If he didn't, we'd run out of friends, and out of nerves that weren't frayed. We'd also be stuck providing transportation for Allison until . . . well, until who knew when.

"I'm surprised you can think about eating after the ride you had."

"I confess that when we came to a stop and I slid out of that land whale of a vehicle Dario bought for her to learn on, I nearly lost my lunch. But after she said she'd never drive with me again, I miraculously felt better. In fact, I've developed quite an appetite." She patted her flat, firm stomach. "But I'll order something light."

"That will go over like a lead balloon. Dave believes light meals are a form of torture. And with the mood Allison is in, a salad won't play." I glanced toward the staircase. "Not that I think we should cater to her."

"I agree. But it would be wise not to cause the current crisis to escalate." Mrs. B tapped a finger against her lips. "Chinese? Crisp vegetables and brown rice for us? Meat and noodles for the others?"

"Works for me. Have them throw in extra crunchy noodles for Dave and Dario."

"And extra fortune cookies. To increase the chances of Allison getting one she approves of." She checked her diamond-studded watch. "What time do you expect Dave?"

"I have no idea. He's been playing a waiting game with Harvey Goodspeed so he isn't the first to leave and doesn't get the lecture about the job being 24/7. Not that Dave thinks of law enforcement as having set hours."

"Of course not." Mrs. B smoothed her blouse. "Well, fortunately, Harvey Goodspeed is a man who has never missed a meal. And, more fortunately, today is Tuesday."

Chapter 2

I swung my gaze to the calendar and tried to figure out the significance of the day after Monday. "Tuesday?"

"That new all-you-can-devour buffet place on the other side of town has roast beef and stuffed baked potatoes on Tuesday."

"Ah." And Harvey, who shouldn't have much of either since his heart episode, would surely be in line with the largest plate available. Probably more than once. He ate as if his brush with death never happened. Was he in denial? Or was he trying to kill himself with calories and go out doing what he loved?

Mrs. B patted my shoulder again. "Harvey will be out of Dave's way in a few weeks."

"He's supposed to be halfway out of there now," I groused, "but he doesn't seem to give a fig about what the doctors say. Or about the reduced schedule HR set for him. He's at his desk when Dave gets there in the morning, and most days he hangs around until early evening."

"Well, the job has been his life for a whole lot of years," Mrs. B mused.

"And he doesn't see any reason to change a thing. He's got a hundred little rules and systems. Dave is bogged down doing things Harvey's way to avoid confrontation, plus catching up on

11

all the paperwork Harvey got behind on. He doesn't have time to work on anything else. And even if he did, Harvey squelches ideas that aren't his."

"How frustrating," Mrs. B sympathized. "And what a shame for the sheriff's office and the community. I'm sure Dave has some fine ideas."

"He does. While he was catching up on the monthly reports he noticed a rise in crimes targeting seniors. Mostly theft and cash machine withdrawals and mostly small amounts. Dave has ideas about proactive educational programs and working with other agencies, but Harvey doesn't get it. He says the crimes aren't 'major' enough to fit the description of what his office handles."

"I'm sure Dave believes something should be done before those small crimes multiply."

"Right. He also thinks a lot of seniors don't realize they've been victimized or don't say anything because they're embarrassed about mislaying their credit cards or going off and leaving their doors unlocked. He thinks the reported incidents are the tip of a crime iceberg. But unless he goes over Harvey's head and appeals to the sheriff—and he doesn't want to do that—he's stuck until Harvey retires."

"Poor Dave." Mrs. B sighed. "Poor Harvey."

"What? Now you're feeling sorry for him?"

"A little. I bet he didn't have a single plan for his retirement before his heart seized up."

I hadn't thought about that. Harvey had no family and probably—given the in-your-face personality of an enraged badger—few friends. Letting go of his job might feel like watching his home burn. Maybe he'd hoped to push retirement back indefinitely.

"Perhaps my next project should be finding a project for him." Mrs. B sat up straight and twisted a ring with a pearl the size of a garbanzo bean. "Yes, I've been muddling about for too long. I think that's exactly what I shall do."

Did you notice the use of the word "shall"?

I did.

I also saw sparks in her sapphire eyes.

And I cringed.

When Mrs. B steamed into a project, others were often "enlisted" to join in, or were carried along in her wake. One of those others was likely to be me.

The impending battle of the furniture placement between Jim and Paulette might be nothing more than a tiny puff of air compared to the storm a collision between Mrs. B and Harvey Goodspeed would generate.

But I had no time to consider the magnitude because a voice boomed along the hallway. "What's for dinner?"

Crap!

My sister!

This called for more than a cringe.

This called for assuming the fetal position and sucking my thumb.

"Sorry, dear," Mrs. B whispered. "I forgot to lock the door."

"That's okay," I murmured. "She would have hammered on it until I opened up."

Or hammered until the hinges or the lock gave way. My sister Jeannine Reed, who went by the name Indigo Zephyr, was a large and forceful woman with an attitude to match. She generally wore cargo pants with numerous pockets, most bulging. Some contained granola bars or chocolate. Others—since Iz never carried a purse—probably held her wallet and keys. But the remaining ones? I had no idea.

13

Recently, when Iz did a two-day stint as my bodyguard—not an experience that would make me write a glowing letter of reference, although she distinguished herself in the final moments—she'd patted a pocket and insinuated she was packing. But packing what exactly? A gun? A knife? A salami sandwich so far past its prime it would be as effective as pepper spray if she unwrapped it?

Mind thoroughly boggled, I took a deep breath and prepared for the onslaught.

"Hello, Iz," Mrs. B chirped with a bright smile I knew was mostly authentic. My neighbor was a benefit-of-the-doubt kind of person who tried—amazingly without tying herself in mental knots—to look for the best in everyone. Usually she found something to like or admire, or at least discovered a redeeming characteristic. And, despite her know-it-all bombast and her conviction that men were inferior beings and largely unnecessary, my sister had several of those. Recently she'd stepped up to help our neighbor Verna after her stroke. More recently, she'd rescued me from a killer set on sending me to the bottom of the river.

Iz grunted a reply, sat in Cheese Puff's favorite chair with all the grace of a water buffalo in high heels falling off a fashion runway, and scooped up the cookbook. "Ha!" She pointed to the "anyone can make" part of the title. "That's a lie. What are these, fake recipes?"

Mrs. B giggled. "Like fake news?"

"Right." Iz dropped the book on the table, drawing a yip from Cheese Puff. "Anyone *can't* make these concoctions. Not unless they crack the code."

"What code?" I asked, cursing my curiosity. I hadn't intended to enter the conversation, but the words popped out.

14

"The code that translates all those nonsense words like sauté and coddle and baste."

"Ah," Mrs. B said. "Cooking terms."

"Sometimes the definitions are in the back of the book," I said. "Or in a section in the front. And sometimes there are illustrations. But you could go on the Internet and look them up and probably find videos."

"Yes." Mrs. B clapped her hands. "There must be thousands of cooking videos. They show you all the cookware and utensils you need and how to measure and chop. They demonstrate how to mix and stir and blend and—"

"Nobody told me cooking would be part of the job." Iz picked up the book once more. "It's not a big part of the job, and not part of every job, but I didn't know before I signed up for the course. They didn't tell me about the cleaning, either. That's not honest."

Mrs. B and I exchanged a glance that said we were both refraining—with great difficulty—from rolling our eyes at the use of the word "honest." My sister, you see, had been far less than honest on her application to the home health care aide program. She'd left out her many official warnings and arrests for things like parading without a permit, disturbing the peace, inciting riots, and generally being a pain in the backside to police, elected officials, and men in general in at least six states.

Before she met Penelope and decided to ditch her magenta Mohawk hairdo and settle in Reckless River, my sister had attempted to snatch her 15 minutes of fame on a daily basis. Couch-surfing her way around the country, she spoke at women's conferences on everything from her views on feminine myths to practical magic to hidden messages in children's literature to the need for women to realize their potentials and fulfill their destinies.

15

Thanks to Angus Drummond, a retired attorney who came out of retirement whenever Mrs. B crooked her index finger, the program director had been persuaded that my sister's disruptive exploits could be overlooked in exchange for establishing a fund for students who otherwise couldn't afford the training. But she'd insisted Iz enroll under her real name, a name my sister loathed. That led to a long hour of acrimonious outbursts before Mrs. B suggested Iz enroll as J.T. Reed instead of Jeannine Theresa. Being far more evolved than I am, my wealthy neighbor never reminded Iz of her claims to a high level of intelligence and asked why she hadn't thought of that herself.

"I'm sure the literature spelled out the details of the job," Mrs. B said.

Iz waved that aside with a twist of her wrist—probably the same kind of twist she'd used to consign the brochure and other information to a trash can or recycling bin. She'd never been a detail person. When she'd been on the conference circuit, she'd always managed to attract a platoon of minions to take care of the nuts and bolts of housing and transportation.

"They just assume we know how to cook," she complained.

I hid a smile. If my culinary skills were rudimentary, my sister's could be described as crudimentary. As in crude. Or perhaps crud. When my parents checked out emotionally after my brother's death, Iz pitched in to provide basic care and get my 10-year-old self raised up to what approximated adulthood. That basic care included yelling at me to do my homework or take a bath, combing tangles from my hair with little regard for whether strands remained attached to my scalp, and heating up a variety of frozen meals generally featuring potatoes or noodles and generous amounts of gravy. And even though those meals came with specific instructions for heating, they were often either cold in the middle or burnt on the edges. In the course of a year, I mastered the microwave, oven, and stove burners and took over. I also became adept at making cocoa, grilled cheese sandwiches, and English muffin pizzas. I had the good sense, however, to realize Iz would turn me into her personal chef if I admitted to doing more than heating up, so I restricted my adventures in cookery to the hours Iz wasn't at home.

"I expect most of their students have a great deal of cooking experience," Mrs. B said. "But, of course, those students haven't had careers as colorful as yours."

Iz, who had been working up a world-class glower, curved her lips and transformed the expression to a smug smile. "Most of them have never been out of Reckless River. A few never had a real job."

I held myself back from asking how she defined that. From long experience I knew her definition of "real job" would include everything she'd done that could—by counting tasks requiring only a few hours of effort and stretching imagination to the outer limits—be defined as work.

"Well, you have to give them credit for taking on this challenge," Mrs. B said in a soft voice. "As you must realize from your experience with Verna, it's not easy taking care of someone who is ill and in pain. And it's more difficult when that person is angry because she can't do everything she's used to doing, and because asking for help hurts her pride."

Iz nodded.

"And while others may have more experience in the kitchen," Mrs. B went on, "I bet not many have the natural talent we all saw you display in working with Verna."

Iz, to my surprise, had displayed quite an ability to gently turn aside Verna's arguments and maneuver her toward healthy choices. But when it came to steering and maneuvering with flair and finesse, few could hold a candle to Mrs. B.

(For the record, since the invention of electricity and the light bulb, candle holding has pretty much disappeared from the workplace. Apprentices now are more likely to hold flashlights or shine beams from their cellphones. But the expression lingers on. And the point is that Mrs. B has this manipulation stuff down.)

"You think I should cut them some slack?" my sister asked, her tone halfway between scornful and belligerent.

Mrs. B sidestepped a direct answer. "I'm sure you haven't been overtly critical of other students."

Note the use of the word "overtly" in that sentence. Iz had a whole range of contemptuous expressions, and I was willing to bet every dime in my wallet—all three of them—that she'd employed many of those expressions before noon today.

"Should I cut the instructors and the director slack too?"

"Perhaps the slack you cut should be for yourself." Mrs. B worked up a sugary smile to help the medicine go down. "I've noticed you're inclined to get angry and obstructive when you feel you don't have a firm grasp of things—like cooking, for example."

At the speed of rage, the scowl on Iz's face morphed to a glare.

Mrs. B held up a hand. "There's nothing wrong with a little healthy anger, dear. It can make us stronger and faster and more willing to take on what we ordinarily wouldn't. But sometimes it has the opposite effect."

The glare slipped back to a scowl.

"And I've noticed that when you feel you don't have control you occasionally allow your anger to lead you to try to subvert a project, or lead you away from it instead of leading you on to complete it."

Yow!

Mrs. B called out my sister.

I crossed my arms and braced for the explosion.

Iz opened her mouth.

And closed it.

And opened it again.

I gritted my teeth and drew my arms tighter against my chest. This was going to be a big one. Perhaps I should take cover behind the sofa or make a run for it.

"You don't have to say anything," Mrs. B said in a breezy voice. "I know you know I'm right."

Whoa!

Not only had Mrs. B lit my sister's fuse, she was sloshing gasoline around the room. No way would I escape the coming blast with all my extremities intact. And running might only draw attention to me.

Closing my eyes, I tried to sink into the sofa cushions.

I heard Iz breathing and snorting out bursts of air the way a bull might in the seconds before it charged a matador.

I heard Cheese Puff grunt and turn in Mrs. B's lap, his claws scratching against her cotton slacks.

I heard my sister's fingers drumming on the cookbook, drumming faster and faster.

I heard the whisking sound of Mrs. B smoothing her silk blouse. The motion seemed measured and calm. Perhaps, after driving with Allison, she had less fear of the verbal havoc Iz could wreak.

I heard the cookbook land on the table. Not quite a slam, but definitely a drop from a height of a foot or more.

And then my sister spoke, the words hard enough to serve as paving stones. "Are you telling me I shouldn't try to change parts of the program that are terminally dumb? Are you telling me I shouldn't walk away from it?"

"Not at all. What I'm saying is that the program has been established for years and is highly thought of and you should examine your motives for wanting to alter or omit even small parts of it. What I'm saying is *if* you walk away, I would hope you had carefully examined your reasons and were completely honest with yourself beforehand. And the fact that I arranged for you to get in and paid your tuition shouldn't influence your decision."

That was a tall order. Iz was all about prodding others to stand in the harsh spotlight of honesty to examine their actions and beliefs, but she seldom turned the lamp on herself.

"Cooking and cleaning aside," Mrs. B said, "is the program beneficial?"

I opened my eyes to see my sister shrug. "I suppose it's good to know first aid and what to do in emergencies. And the stuff about communicable diseases and medications and food allergies. And the right ways to help people get up and down."

"Of course it is," Mrs. B agreed. "It's a very comprehensive program. Probably more than you'll need, but it's a good foundation if you decide to go on to a nursing program."

I couldn't imagine Iz as a nurse, even a nurse on a par with the sadistic woman in *One Flew Over the Cuckoo's Nest*. And I certainly couldn't imagine her jumping through all the educational and training hoops necessary to get there. School had never been her thing.

But people change.

Some people.

Under some circumstances.

"I guess. But I refuse to believe the dress code for training is necessary." Iz plucked at her dark green T-shirt. Like others in her collection, it bore a message insinuating that men were lesser life forms. "If I don't start wearing shirts with collars tomorrow I'll lose points. I've got one, but it has a bullet hole and a bloodstain. And most of the buttons are gone."

Such was the cost of making herself a target at a rally to see justice done for an abused woman.

"I'll have to go shopping." She made that sound like going shopping was about the same as going to prison.

Mrs. B, who loved shopping even on days when nothing was on sale and she came home empty-handed, took command. "I'll swoop to the stores the first chance I get and lay in a supply for you. In the meantime, you're welcome to go through the closet in my spare bedroom. There are a number of shirts Dario has tired of. Of course they'd be too large—"

"I like my shirts large," Iz said. "Large is more comfortable."

"Well, then, there's one problem solved." Mrs. B dusted her hands. "What other concerns do you have?"

"Suspending my First Amendment rights while I'm on the job."

"Suspending in what way, dear?"

"We're not supposed to talk about politics. Or religion."

"I see." Mrs. B tapped a finger against her cheek. "I know that must be difficult for you. You have such potent views on those subjects."

Potent?

Try explosive. Incendiary.

"I hope you understand why they ask you to steer clear of those topics."

"Sure I do." Iz opened a pocket of her cargo pants, pulled out a clipper, and sliced off bits of her thumbnails. "It's because their minds are locked so tight they're blind to reason."

Before Mrs. B could attempt to dilute that opinion, my sister said, "Tomorrow should be more interesting. We start to shadow."

"Shadow?" Mrs. B asked.

"Go with someone who went through the program and has been working for a couple of years. Go out on a few jobs to get a feel for what it's all about."

"That should certainly be more interesting than classroom work. And I know once you meet some of the people in need of help you'll be better able to focus on the aspects of the job you don't particularly feel drawn to."

While Iz was considering that, Mrs. B nudged me. "Now, Barbara, don't you have a menu somewhere for a Chinese restaurant?"

Silly question.

She knew darn well I had the menu. And a host of others. And not just "somewhere." I had so many menus I'd recently slid them into plastic sleeves and put them in alphabetical order in a three-ring binder stashed beneath the phone on the kitchen counter.

Maybe I could be charged with the "crime" of ordering out way too often, but I couldn't be accused of sloppy handling of the evidence to be brought against me.

Chapter 3

Armed with a lunch of leftover Chinese food and an attitude that was as good as it gets for a substitute teacher facing kids long past ready for a vacation that would mean no paychecks for me, I entered Captain Meriwether High School the next morning. With dragging feet, I made my way to the office of the head secretary. Big Chill was a tiny tornado of a woman in high heels, gem-studded eyeglasses, and short white hair, today tinted springtime green.

"I changed your assignment," she said as I signed in.

This was potentially a good thing. I'd been assigned to horticulture and wasn't looking forward to an encounter with the boys who launched a mud ball fight when I subbed in March. Being teens, and having put me on the ropes once, I suspected they'd try again. Sure, they'd been disciplined, but more than two months had passed. The letters of apology and promises to be better students were ancient history.

On the other hand, having my assignment changed could be a bad thing. There were worse places than horticulture—the gym, for example.

"Diplomas," Big Chill said. "Graduation program. Discrepancies."

23

While I wondered what that meant and what I was supposed to do about it, she added two more words. "Theodora Fitch."

I dropped my school bag and—never mind that the chair in front of her desk was about as comfortable as an ice floe carpeted with broken glass—sat. Following the death of Jerome Morrow, longtime Captain Meriwether principal, Theodora Fitch had been brought up from a district elementary school to serve as an assistant administrator. Not—to say the least—a good fit. Theodora wasn't used to playing to a tough crowd and reacting at a faster pace. "She resigned two months ago. Right after the food fight in the cafeteria."

"And every day since has glorious," Big Chill said with a heavenly smile.

I rolled my eyes. Never have I used to word "glorious" to describe a day in high school—no matter how well that day had gone. "If she's gone, what does she have to do with the diplomas?"

Big Chill's smile altered to the kind of expression that could curdle milk. "Before she left, she managed to mangle the list of graduates."

"Mangle?"

"Names spelled incorrectly. Names left out. Names added on. Juniors mixed in with seniors. Kids who graduated last year on the list. Names of kids who moved out of the district not deleted."

I groaned. This was shaping up to be hours of tedium broken only by bouts of drudgery, fatigue, boredom, ennui, and hair-pulling frustration. And then there would be the strain of trying to come up with new words to mutter under my breath.

"I'm sorry," Big Chill said in a tone that indicated she almost half meant it.

"I'm sorry too," Principal Tremaine Scott said from the doorway to his office. "I'm sorry the list is a mess and sorry you always get saddled with these chores. But we go to you because you're—"

"So good at it?" I asked. "So easily persuaded to take one for the team? So needy? So eager for a teaching position that I'd do almost anything to suck up?"

"I didn't say that." Tremaine grinned, his teeth flashing bright against his dark skin. "You did."

I had. And it was true. I *did* want a teaching position at Captain Meriwether. And I *was* willing to do almost anything—except sub in PE or chemistry. PE because the gym and locker rooms had the gamy stench of sweaty clothing and the reek of jokes that weren't funny. Chemistry because things might get out of hand and create a stink far more toxic and perhaps even lethal.

He crossed the few feet of carpet between us and handed me a white envelope. "I don't have a job to offer you at the moment, but this might help ease the pain until something opens up."

I peeked inside and spotted a gift certificate to the popcorn shop at the mall, a certificate hefty enough to keep me stuffed with treats for a long weekend of indulgence. "Thanks."

"No problem." He tipped a thumb up and headed for the cafeteria to help supervise until the first bell rang.

I tucked the gift certificate in my school bag. "He knows bribery isn't necessary, doesn't he?"

"He does, but he seems to enjoy recognizing and rewarding good work."

That was a far cry from the approach of Jerome Morrow, a man I'd referred to as the invisible principal, a man I'd spotted only at a distance in more than a year of subbing at Captain

25

Meriwether. He'd communicated mostly by e-mail or through Big Chill.

"Everything you'll need is in the conference room," Big Chill said.

"And the deadline is?"

"Yesterday," she said with a wince. "Graduation is Saturday."

Three days off. But programs would have to be printed. "So I should take my time?" I teased.

"Only if you're tired of being on my good side."

As I've mentioned before, the bad side of Big Chill is a vast and scary place. Just thinking about the possibility of ending up there conjured mental images of winter at the North Pole, alone, without food or shelter, in the middle of a storm, on the darkest day of the year.

"Not tired of that at all." I stood and hefted my school bag. "Nope. No way. I'm wild about your good side. It's paradise. It's—"

"It's time you got to work." She pointed toward the conference room.

"Exactly what I was about to say."

She rolled her eyes.

I scuttled off to spend the morning with files and lists.

By the time third period ended, I felt as if someone had poured sand under my eyelids and then forced me to blink 100 times. Eye drops didn't help. Neither did the tears I manufactured by thinking about homeless kittens, raw onions, and my bank balance.

"You look like you were spit out of a sandstorm in the Sahara," Doug Whitman said as I entered the teachers' room where I usually ate lunch.

"Or chased for three days by a rogue moose," Aston Marsden suggested.

I stuck my bowl of leftovers in the microwave and didn't ask whether it was possible for a moose—even a rogue one—to chase someone for three days. Aston, after all, played the part of a mountain man in historical reenactments all over the Northwest. It was possible he had first-hand experience with at least one moose. It was also possible he was exaggerating.

"If a moose chased Aston, it was probably female," Brenda Waring sniped. "Considering his aversion to soap and water, she'd think he smelled like a male moose with a big set of—"

"Don't say it!" Gertrude Suttle and Ardette Johnson chorused.

"Antlers?" Brenda feigned surprise. "What's wrong with saying that?"

Aston aimed a rib bone at her, a large rib bone. "That wasn't what you intended to say."

"You're right," she admitted with a smirk. "And I also intended to say that poor female moose would be sadly disappointed if she caught you."

"Not as disappointed as a man would be if he chased you expecting—"

"Enough." Gertrude slapped a spoon on the table. "I wish you two would either get together or get far enough apart that the rest of us don't have to listen to you shoot each other down."

"Amen," Ardie and Doug said in unison.

"You're less mature than most freshmen," Ardie added.

Aston jabbed the rib bone in her direction as if he intended to impale her. "Brenda started—"

"I don't care," Gertrude said. "You can't pay me to care. You can't pass a law to make it illegal for me *not* to care. I doubt you have the stamina and endurance to torture me long enough to *force* me to care."

"Ditto," Doug said.

"Same here," Ardie added. "And poor Barbara needs a little care and concern instead of an overdose of aggravation."

Brenda clamped her lips and plunged a fork into a container of something that resembled woven potholders layered with beets, something that smelled like a compost pile on a humid day in late August. Aston gnawed on the rib bone. I tried not to wonder about its origin or how he got it.

Doug peered at my eyes as I took the empty chair between him and Aston. "What did the Chillster assign you to, sweeping the parking lot with a whisk broom held between your teeth?"

"I wish. I'm checking the list of names for the graduation program and checking the spelling on the diplomas. Somehow Theodora Fitch messed things up."

"Somehow?" Ardie snorted. "You shouldn't use that word in reference to things she messed up. You should reserve it for when you're speaking about anything she did right."

From what I'd seen and heard, there had been darn little of that. "Like what?"

"She usually got here on time," Doug said after a long moment.

"When she ran a meeting," Gertrude offered, "it ended when it was supposed to."

"Mainly because she couldn't wait to get out of the building," Ardie added.

"Some of her outfits were interesting," Brenda offered after another pause.

"She made strange noises when she got in over her head," Aston said.

"Which was on a daily basis," Doug said.

"Hourly," Gertrude corrected.

"Kind of like distress calls," Aston added. "Or maybe mating calls. Should have recorded some to play in the mountains so I could see what kind of critters came running."

"Could be hungry critters," Doug suggested.

I imagined Aston surrounded by coyotes and cougars, bears and wolves.

"Nothing I couldn't handle," Aston bragged. "I'm a crack shot."

"You're a crackpot," Brenda snarked.

"Change of subject," Gertrude commanded.

"Let's talk about something more upbeat," Ardie suggested. "Anyone have big plans for the summer?"

"Not *big* plans," Doug said. "Going to spend a few weeks visiting college buddies, do some fishing, catch up on movies and reading."

"Living history," Aston said.

"Pretending to be someone who's dead," Brenda muttered, "shouldn't be called *living* history."

Gertrude silenced her with a frown. "I suppose you'll be taking culinary classes again."

Brenda tossed her hair, now down past her ears but still not a shade I could readily describe, especially since the fluorescent bulbs above us added tinges of green and blue and yellow. "No. By rights I should be teaching a cutting-edge class through the community college continuing education program. But the short-sighted head of the department turned me down."

Like the others around the table, it took me several seconds to manufacture an expression of surprise. And, like the others, I went overboard and came up with a reaction more appropriate to news the earth had jumped out of orbit and was hurtling toward the sun.

"What about making a pitch to that specialty grocery store over on the other side of town?" Doug suggested. "They offer classes. I took one all about potatoes."

"Potatoes," Brenda scoffed. "Potatoes are simple."

"Didn't seem simple," Doug whispered to me. "At least the recipes we followed weren't. Ten ingredients. Two pans. Half an hour of prep time."

I reached across the corner of the table and patted his hand to show I felt his pain. I excelled at microwaving potatoes and was pretty good at baking them in the oven. But my mashed potatoes were characterized by lumps so hard they'd make dandy slingshot projectiles, my potato soup and stews were noted for being mealy and/or mushy, and don't even get me started on the scalloped potatoes where the sauce never thickened and tasted like envelope glue.

"There's nothing wrong with simple," Ardie said. "Lots of people don't have time to make complicated and fancy dishes. And some don't have the correct tools, or the money for ingredients."

"I'm aware of that," Brenda huffed. "But I feel everyone should be exposed to what's possible, what they can create with a few out-of-the-ordinary ingredients, original combinations of spices, and a little time and effort. Why go with the same old dishes?"

"Because those are the ones you like?" Doug whispered.

"Why go for bland flavor when you can blast flavor," Brenda cried. "I have some fantastic recipes designed to get cooks out of their ruts."

My lips betrayed me. "Such as?"

"I've created a six-week course around eels," Brenda rhapsodized. "Catching, cleaning, and cooking. You all know I'm famous for my eel Alfredo."

"More like infamous," Aston muttered. "That stuff makes pig swill taste like ambrosia."

I snorted a laugh, earning a glare from Brenda.

"Sorry." I coughed, pointed at the Chinese food, and reached for my water bottle. "Hot pepper. Under a pea pod. Didn't see it."

Brenda gave a mammoth sigh. "I don't know why I attempt to lead any of you philistines toward an appreciation of culinary artistry. You're as bad as the administration, wanting me to stick to the basics and have kids cook the same things every year. You obviously don't have the least interest in broadening your horizons."

"My horizons are plenty broad." Aston jabbed the rib bone toward Brenda once more. "Elk. That's what this is. Shot it, dressed it, and cooked it myself over an open fire. And I didn't have to dump on Alfredo sauce to kill the taste."

"I don't dump—"

"Stop," Doug commanded. "Just stop. Now."

In the silence that followed, he turned to Gertrude and Ardie. "You haven't told us what you're doing this summer."

"I'm going to Guatemala to help with a medical program," Gertrude said. "Ever since the thefts from the Family Support Room, I've become painfully aware of all the suffering in the world. We may think our lives are difficult and our problems are huge but, trust me, they're not."

"Do you need donations?" I asked. "For supplies and travel expenses? I could toss in a few bucks. And Mrs. Ballantine would probably toss in a few hundred." Or more. My wealthy neighbor never hesitated to write a hefty check to help a worthy cause.

"That would be wonderful. And while she has her checkbook out, tell her abut Ardie's project at the rec center.

31

They need funds for swimsuits and sneakers and snacks for the kids who take part."

"And money for arts and crafts materials. But we also need volunteers to lead activities and help herd kids. And tutor kids in danger of falling behind over the summer." Ardie fixed her gaze on me. "What are *your* plans for the summer?"

"Dental work. The day after school is out."

Doug winced. "A lot of dental work?"

"Two root canals, caps, and work to excavate and remove a wisdom tooth that finally decided to come in—sideways." Thank goodness the pain so far had been little more than occasional throbbing. And thank goodness Mrs. B was footing the bill. As a sub, I had no insurance through the school system. And the coverage I purchased on my own didn't run to dental work. In fact, it didn't run to much in the way of garden-variety ailments. What it did was kind of limp along, sucking monthly withdrawals from my bank account and claiming it would be there if something catastrophic happened. And, come to think of it, when I'd nearly drowned in the river, it had come through with just enough coverage to convince me to continue the policy.

"Could you help out after that?" Ardie asked.

"Probably. When I get back from Missouri."

"You're going there in the summer?" Brenda fanned herself with a napkin. "Do you know how hot it will be in Missouri?"

"And how humid?" Gertrude asked. "I hear it's so damp you can keep tropical fish without an aquarium. You should go in the winter."

"I know, but I'm overdue to visit my parents. I didn't go last winter. Or last summer. Or the winter before."

And the truth was, I didn't want to go at all. When my parents checked out emotionally after my brother's death, they checked *way* out. Oh, they worked their jobs, paid the bills, and provided cash for my sister to bring home a load of groceries each week—mostly bread, baloney, cereal, milk, and frozen meals. The rest of the time they were like zombies, sitting in the living room, the shades pulled, the lamps off, and the TV blaring out programs they didn't seem to watch. Once I got established at college, they sold the house in Omaha and moved to a gated community in Missouri. There they were reborn into another kind of life, one as manic as the zombie phase had been sedentary. They joined every club in the vicinity. They hiked, played cards, took up golf and tennis, croquet and painting. They went to movies and potlucks, acted in plays, and learned to square dance. What they didn't do was show much interest in having a relationship with me or my sister.

Iz, being made of tougher stuff, wrote them out of her life script every bit as far as they wrote her out of theirs. She'd been 15 when my brother died, and already of an independent bent. I'd been 10 and clingy. And I still was. But my parents offered nothing to cling to. They demonstrated a polite interest in my life, but asked only stock questions and seemed impatient for phone calls to end. Visits were like spending a few days picking at the edges of a wound that would never heal.

Ardie knew enough of the story of my early life to smile in a sympathetic way and gently turn the conversation. "Well, maybe when you get back you can cool down helping out with the swim program."

"Sure."

"I can help some," Doug said. "I'm pretty good at kickball."

"I could lead a nature walk," Aston offered.

"Probably through a snake-infested swamp," Brenda said.

"Why not? Teach those kids life isn't easy. You should come along," he retorted. "If we run across an eel you can show the kids how to wrestle it into a frying pan."

"If you don't make it into a belt or a pair of boots or eat it raw before the pan gets hot."

"I'm outta here." Doug crumpled the aluminum foil from his sandwich. He bowed to Ardie and Gertrude and then to me. "Thank you for this pleasant interlude." He aimed a finger like a gun at Brenda and Aston. "And thank you for making it possible for me to look forward to an afternoon spent dragging my sophomores kicking and screaming through another chapter of *To Kill a Mockingbird*."

"What did he mean by that?" Brenda asked as the door closed behind Doug.

Aston shrugged. "Didn't make a lick of sense to me. Not a whole lot of mockingbirds in this part of the country. And if you wanted a decent meal you'd have to shoot more than one."

Gertrude, Ardie, and I all opened our mouths.

Then we shut them again and exchanged a group shrug.

From experience we knew explanation was pointless.

Oddly, I'd soon hear that last word a lot.

Chapter 4

"Pointless," Mrs. B said for the third time. "Talking to Sybil about her gambling addiction is pointless." She aimed her index fingers at one ear and then the other as she circled my dining room table. "My words don't linger more than a nanosecond inside her brain. If they linger that long."

(For the record, since a second is about as long as it takes to snap your fingers, and a nanosecond is a billionth of that, I was pretty sure Mrs. B was exaggerating. Given the mood she was in, calling her on it would likely result in a recitation of all the times I'd blown things even a little out of proportion. Given my mood after a day of checking names and lists, that was an experience I could live without. Especially since, by now, you must know I'm prone to embroider, enlarge, or expand on a fairly regular basis.)

"You're calling it an addiction now," I noted as I removed my glasses, tipped my head, and pressed a damp washcloth against my eyelids. "Is it still just slot machines?"

"Yes. And only penny slots. But she's hooked. And she plays more than one line, so it's 15 cents or more a spin. When she's not playing, she can't go an hour without talking about a new system or how she if she tries another casino, or gives the current one another day or two, she'll win back all the money she's lost."

"How much *has* she lost?"

"I have no idea."

I suspected she actually had *some* idea, and likely an idea that was close to the mark. But Mrs. B had been raised in an age when it wasn't polite to discuss money in specific terms or ask others about their income levels. From what I'd gleaned over the years based on Sybil's condo (the smallest available in our complex) and the fact that her best friend Verna bought her a TV and paid her cable bills, I suspected her income was probably lower than mine. And that was low. Low with a capital L. I often thought of myself as clutching with my fingertips at the bottom rung of the section of the income ladder assigned to the middle class. If Sybil brought in less each year, she was clinging to a string attached to the lowest rung, and clinging by only three or four fingers.

I flipped the compress to the cool side. "Do you think she's lost her savings?"

"Savings? If she had more than a few hundred set aside for emergencies, I'd be surprised. No, I'd be stunned. Sybil isn't one to look down the road and anticipate what might be around the next curve."

True. Sybil lived for the day. Plus, she was an airhead. The combination wasn't ideal for the development and implementation of sound money-management skills.

"If she had an emergency fund, I expect the money is gone by now. And I expect she rationalized her decision to spend it by telling herself she'd win twice as much and build the fund well beyond the original amount."

I was a pro at rationalization, so that sounded accurate. "Has she borrowed money from friends?"

"Not from me. And not from Verna."

She didn't say neither of them would have loaned even a dime for gambling. She didn't have to. Verna was risk-averse and Mrs. B, having spent many years in Las Vegas as a showgirl, had witnessed too many financial train wrecks, too many huge losses by people who couldn't afford even a relatively small income dent. She doled out thousands for dinners and vacations and gifts, she underwrote businesses, and she gave a boatload to charity. But she didn't believe in dropping more than a few dollars at a casino.

"Her son?"

Mrs. B shook her head. "He helps her out with car repairs and medical expenses and additional condo assessments. Oh, and he set up a fund to cover her power bill—set it up so she can't tap it for anything else."

"She tried?"

"A few months ago. Complained for days about how sad it is when a son doesn't trust his mother to handle her own finances."

We shared a laugh at that. Sybil's son was a prosecutor in Idaho, a nice guy who turned up at least once a year and never forgot Mother's Day. I bet he made a decent salary. I bet he also had experience with cases involving problem gamblers. And I bet he had additional experience with Sybil's freewheeling approach to finance.

"What about Dario?" I asked.

"She's hit him up for $20 now and then. But we discussed my concerns and he promised to cut her off."

I ran through a mental list of our friends. "Jim doesn't have much to spare. Neither does Lana. And Dave's been at work so much I doubt they've crossed paths. Besides, he seldom carries much cash. That way he can tell Allison to buzz off when she asks for an advance on her allowance."

"My guess is she's 'advanced' into the next decade already," Mrs. B said with a laugh.

"And probably into the decade beyond. Dave tries to be tough, but she's an expert at wheedling. And when she plays the mother card, he caves."

The mother card had a silhouette of a woman who hadn't been in Allison's life since she was tiny. Part of the reason for not being there was because she'd been behind bars on drug charges—the first time because Dave arrested her to insure the health of his child. After Allison was born, he'd paid Rayanne $25,000 for custody. But after her fourth—or perhaps fifth—stint in jail, she'd started extorting monthly payments by threatening to get back into Allison's life even if she had to kidnap her to do that. Dave eventually confessed all and, to our relief, Allison announced that Rayanne wasn't a "real" mother and she wanted nothing to do with her. But Dave's fears lingered. No matter how crazy his daughter made him at times, he loved her deeply and wanted her with us.

Dave also loved his friends. And had a soft heart. "He might have written a check to Sybil on his private account, but it wouldn't have been huge." Dave's finances were in better shape than mine, but not by much.

"Well, by my reckoning, even accounting for occasional wins, Sybil is spending more than she's got." Mrs. B sighed. "And if she's not borrowing from friends, I'm afraid she's going to some high-interest sources for funds."

"Meaning?" I lifted the compress and put my glasses on. "Loan sharks?"

"Most likely businesses that provide cash to tide people over to the next paycheck."

Or, in Sybil's case, the next monthly Social Security payment. A payment that wasn't what you'd call substantial. Sybil had held down a variety of jobs in her life, but they'd all been in the retail arena and hadn't paid big bucks.

"When she's exhausted those possibilities, I don't know what she'll do." Mrs. B wrung her hands, the diamonds in the three rings she wore today flashing in the sunlight streaming through the sliding glass door to the deck.

My mind churned up images of Sybil, a designer scarf covering her nose and mouth, her hand in her coat pocket to simulate a gun, waltzing into a bank to demand money. I saw her panhandling on a downtown street corner, picking pockets at the mall, lifting credit card numbers from others during lunch at the senior center. Each image dissolved to a picture of her behind bars, dressed in orange and without a trace of makeup, the roots of her dandelion fluff hair growing out gray. "Maybe she'll come to her senses. Maybe she'll realize she's in trouble and join one of those anonymous groups."

Mrs. B clenched her fists and gave me a look that was part pity and part annoyance. "And maybe political parties will stop squabbling and put money into helping people instead of creating attack ads."

I didn't respond, and after a moment Mrs. B sat beside me and patted my shoulder. "I know I can go too far sometimes. I know I'm guilty of crossing the line from helping to meddling now and then."

Remembering how she'd jumped that line to bring me together with Dave, leaped across it again to buy my present condo, and regularly crisscrossed it with suggestions about a date, venue, and guest list for my wedding, I rolled my eyes.

"All right." She raised her hands in surrender mode. "I admit I may insinuate myself more often than many others might. But I—"

"You can't help it?" I asked with a laugh. "Does that mean you have a problem? That you're addicted to meddling like Sybil is to gambling?"

"It's not the same thing," she huffed. "And I intended to say that I always mean well."

An argument that could be made by plenty of people for actions that turned out to be less than positive.

Mrs. B seemed to sense where my thoughts were headed. "Call it meddling if you must, but if we don't do something soon, Sybil's problem will continue to get worse. If she gets deep in debt to the wrong people . . ."

She could lose everything. She could get hurt.

I sighed and abandoned my argument against meddling. "Okay. What are we going to do?"

(For the record, as evidenced by my use of the word "we," I assumed that whatever was to be done—and I had little doubt Mrs. B already had something in mind—would involve yours truly in some way. As I said before, when my wealthy neighbor leaped at a project, I generally found myself pushed off the decision-making cliff and falling right behind her.)

Mrs. B pried Cheese Puff from the crevice between the cushion and the arm of his favorite chair and cuddled him as she sat. "I think an intervention is in order."

Eeekkk!

That sounded ominous.

"What kind of an intervention? Taking her to a place hundreds of miles from a slot machine and keeping her there for weeks?"

Mrs. B considered for a moment. "I doubt there is such a place, dear. I also doubt if a few weeks would be enough."

"Aversion therapy? Like making her play a slot machine until she collapses of exhaustion."

"Interesting." Mrs. B tapped her lips with a forefinger. "Unfortunately, I think Sybil has more staying power than it would appear at first glance."

"Kidnapping and reprogramming?"

More tapping. "Kidnapping seems a little extreme—at least at this point. But reprogramming . . . yes, we definitely have to rearrange her brain and short circuit her desire to gamble."

She stood and plopped Cheese Puff on my lap. "I'll toddle on home and do some research and discuss it with other members of the Committee."

(For the record, in case you've forgotten or have just joined my adventures, the Committee is the Cheese Puff Care and Comfort Committee. Its members are all neighbors, all recruited by Mrs. B to provide snacks and walks and amusements for Cheese Puff during the long months when I subbed and also took graduate classes in order to acquire a teaching certificate. My schedule is no longer quite as jammed, but the Committee hasn't disbanded. Members still let themselves in and out of my condo now and then to deliver treats or provide outings for my entitled mutt. I've gotten used to it because mostly they remember to knock—or at least arrive at civilized hours. Mostly.)

"Once I've consulted with the group," Mrs. B said as she went out the door to the deck, "we'll make plans and take action."

See what I mean about getting pushed off the cliff? I only hoped the fall wouldn't be a long one and the action wouldn't be all that severe. I also hoped that after we'd taken said action,

Sybil would realize it was for her own good and would still be part of our circle. She was flighty, she was an airhead, and conversations with her took bizarre turns, but she was kind and sweet and funny. My life would be less interesting if she wasn't part of it.

I jerked off my glasses, slapped the compress over my eyes once more, and tried to remember a time when my life had been, well, *my* life.

What I recalled didn't make me feel exactly strong and independent. Unless you counted my college years, the days of going my own way in my own time and at my own speed were limited to short periods when I wasn't married to Albert, married to Jake, living with Dave and Allison, or being herded by my sister, Big Chill, Mrs. B, and/or members of the Committee. And then there were the hours and days dealing with feelings of guilt and obligation. Sure, I'd had bursts of self-determination and even defiance, but overall I'd gone with the flow or taken the line of least resistance.

I flipped the compress and considered how that had worked out. My conclusion was results had been mixed. The flow had carried me into a comfortable marriage to Albert, but over a gut-wrenching waterfall when he died. From there I'd floated into the emotional swamp of my marriage to cheating Jake, through the whitewater of job downsizing, and deep into the rocky canyon of loneliness and financial despair. Now I bobbed along on what seemed like a relatively placid rippling stream, encountering only occasional eddies to rock my boat.

Would I be here now if I hadn't gone with the flow?

Who knew?

Maybe, instead of continuing a mental debate on the issue, I needed to get out for some fresh air, walk along the river and rest my eyes by focusing on something in the distance. Snow-capped Mount Hood would be perfect.

I popped Cheese Puff into his harness, locked up, and headed off. My intention was to walk east up the riverfront trail. But before I could relax, I had to get past the upstream end of the complex where the office was located, the office that was the lair of Bernina Burke. I lacked the power to make myself invisible, so I hunched my shoulders, ducked my head and studied the ground a few feet in front of me. Then I crossed my fingers and hustled Cheese Puff along, hoping I wouldn't be spotted.

If you've been following my story, you know that Bernina and I interact with each other in the same way an enraged cobra and a territorial mongoose might frolic together in a phone booth. Bernina, who manages (and I use that term loosely) our condo complex, has definite ideas about the job. They're mostly bad ideas, so fortunately there aren't many of them.

One idea seems to be that, as a manager, her role is to boss others and do as little actual work as possible. Members of the condo board would dearly love to fire Bernina, but they don't have quite enough cause. They're also scared that Bernina might sue since "Confrontational" could be her middle name. So they've adopted a two-pronged policy of looking the other way when they can and hoping one of her resumes will rise to the top of a heap at a larger complex in need of a manager. They also hope that complex, if not in a galaxy far away, will at least be in a city more than an hour's drive from Reckless River.

Personally, I think the resume may rise, but Bernina's personality—or lack of it—will sink the interview phase of the hiring process.

43

Lately, Bernina had been dealing with straightening out condo finances in order to proceed with the clean-up and repairs necessitated by a near-record flood in March. High water and a strong current peeled away landscaping and sections of concrete steps and walkways, and left debris along condo property abutting the public trail. When the water receded, residents turned out with wheelbarrows to carry off debris and disassemble the sandbag dike many of us had pitched in to build. Along with others, I'd raked and scraped and shoveled to make cosmetic repairs, to even out the slope, and save the few plantings that hadn't floated off. It was up to Bernina to find and hire experts to do the rest, but so far the process had been contentious. The condo board wanted at least three proposals, each to include specific details about work to be done and total cost. Unfortunately, only one of those who assessed the situation submitted plans. That lone proposal came accompanied by a note making it clear Bernina wasn't to speak to workers and was to keep a distance of at least five yards at all times. If she didn't, the note went on, the price would escalate.

See what I mean?

Condo board members were now considering the merits of buying replacement shrubs and plants, ordering two dozen cubic yards of bark mulch, and leaning on residents to do the grunt work while hiring out more difficult jobs piecemeal. Before any of that, however, they wanted an accounting of funds on hand, what insurance might cover, and what kind of assessments residents would face in the weeks ahead.

So far, they'd received a jumble of numbers and a string of complaints about the difficulty of the task. Even Sybil had been able to tell from the mishmash that Bernina's books didn't balance. And Verna, after a few minutes perusing previous monthly reports, found things had been out of whack since before Christmas and probably well before that. With board members breathing down her thick neck, the condo manager was hip-deep in paperwork and in a mood that could best be described as venomous.

So I was delighted when I passed the upriver end of the condo complex without spotting her. I felt lighter and happier. I raised my chin, worked the kinks out of my shoulders, and swung my arms. In a few moments I found myself smiling at the sky, at passing birds, and at others on the trail.

I'd gone a quarter of a mile when the trail took a turn and I spotted my nemesis squatting on a bench with a stack of papers beside her. On the other side of that stack, leaning toward Bernina and making marks with a pencil on a notepad, was one of the last people I expected to see sharing a bench with the condo manager—Sybil.

I reeled in Cheese Puff and pivoted.

Too late.

Chapter 5

"Hi, Barbara," Sybil called. "Hi, Cheese Puff."

Hearing his name, my ten-pound mutt yanked at the leash. Sybil, who was the poster child for forgetfulness, somehow always remembered to put a dog cookie in her pocket each morning.

I tried to reel Cheese Puff in once more. "Don't want to interrupt you," I called.

"You're not," Sybil said.

Bernina's expression indicated the opposite. But then, I'd never seen her glance in my direction without looking as if she'd just spotted something with green and purple dots, ten legs, and pincer-like jaws—something that was about to take a bite out of her big toe.

Barking, Cheese Puff scrabbled at the asphalt in an attempt to reach the cookie Sybil drew from the pocket of her light jacket.

I let his leash play out. "We'll be off as soon as he gets his treat."

Bernina's scowl said that wouldn't be soon enough. She loathes Cheese Puff. First, despite several catlike characteristics, he's a dog. Second, he's cute (in a weird and scruffy way) and cuddly (when he wants to be). Third, most people like him more than they like her. Way more.

I approached their bench, wondering about the stack of papers between them. It was an untidy stack and some of the bits that stuck out clued me that they were financial statements. Were they discussing condo business, specifically the cost of repairing flood damage? Sybil was on the board—mostly because no one else wanted the position—so that was possible. But as you've already gleaned, her grasp of financial solvency was as firm as my grasp of geometry. And, while Bernina was no genius, she was no dummy either. If she wanted financial advice, there were other board members she'd turn to long before Sybil. And she'd do that turning in her office or in the community room where board business was conducted—not along the trail where there was little privacy and where the wind scything down the Columbia Gorge could carry off documents.

My curiosity shifted into overdrive, but I tore my gaze from the stack and pretended interest in a goose bobbing along on the current. Cheese Puff, meanwhile, snatched the dog cookie from Sybil's hand. He chewed and swallowed as if he hadn't eaten for a week, and whined for more.

Sybil patted her pockets and shook her head. "I'm all out. Sorry."

Bernina's expression said she'd apologize to a dog when hell registered temperatures approximating those on a winter day in Antarctica.

"You'll get another when we get home." I pulled at the leash and took a few steps along the trail.

"Wait a minute," Sybil said in a chirpy voice. "I want you to see our plan for making money to pay for the flood repairs and lots of other stuff."

Bernina slapped one hand on the stack of papers. "We said we'd keep it between ourselves."

47

Sybil and Bernina had a plan to raise money for the condo association? A plan Bernina wanted kept secret?

Forget overdrive.

My curiosity jumped to hyperdrive.

"But it's such a great plan," Sybil burbled. "We'll make so much money board members will stop getting all hissy about a few dollars here and there and a few columns that don't quite balance."

Bernina planted the other hand on top of the stack as Sybil held up the notepad, revealing the logo of her favorite casino on the Oregon Coast. "See! I wrote it all down right here. If we stick to just these slot machines and we hit them in the exact order starting an hour after dinner, we can't lose. It's foolproof."

The last few words told me Mrs. B was right. It was time for an intervention. In fact, it was past time.

But until a plan was in place, we had to keep Sybil in the dark. So I smiled and feigned interest and even excitement as she prattled on about how she would parlay the meager contents of the condo contingency account into a massive slush fund that could cover not only flood repairs, but a new roof, pool furniture, and fresh holiday decorations.

Bernina's eyes sparkled when Sybil mentioned platoons of inflatable cartoon characters, and she chipped in with her thoughts about a ton of plastic snow and lights for every hedge and shrub. Somehow, even while mentally reliving her decorating debacle of last November, I kept my smile in place.

I was delighted when Cheese Puff, miffed at the absence of additional treats, faced downstream and pulled at the leash.

"The little prince must be tired," Sybil said. "You should take him home."

"Yes," Bernina said in a caustic voice. "Take that spoiled little excuse for a canine out of my sight."

Cheese Puff snarled at her but then, with head high, trotted off. As soon as we were out of their sight, I broke into a jog. Panting and gasping, I kept it up all the way to Mrs. B's condo.

"You're right," I wheezed as I closed the screen door behind me. "We need an intervention. And we need it yesterday."

Mrs. B looked up from her laptop. Dario O'Brien folded the sports section of the *Reckless River Roundup* and dropped it on the rug by his chair.

I gulped air and leaned against the kitchen counter. "Sybil and Bernina are plotting to siphon off the condo contingency account and take the money to a casino."

"Sybil and *Bernina*?" Dario asked.

"Yes."

Mrs. B moaned and her hands fluttered like butterflies trapped in a net.

Since my neighbor is a take-charge person and seldom flustered, her reaction made me more than a little nervous.

Apparently it also distressed Cheese Puff. He leaped to the sofa and from there to the arm of her chair. Whining, he pawed at the sleeve of a silk blouse the color of a morning sky.

"Sybil *and* Bernina?" Dario followed the question with a laugh and a hopeful look. "*Sybil* and Bernina?"

"I'm not kidding." I got a glass from a cabinet and ran water from the tap. "Sybil and Bernina."

"If you're not lying, water isn't strong enough. You need a real drink. We all need real drinks." Dario levered himself from the chair and lumbered to the liquor cabinet where he mixed up a trio of rummy drinks. He shoved one along the counter in my direction, and carried another to Mrs. B whose fingers, to my dismay, were still fluttering. "Snap out of it, Muriel," he ordered.

She shook her head like someone emerging from a dream, set her laptop aside, and pulled Cheese Puff against her chest. Then she snatched at the glass, and downed half of it. "This is dreadful. We must do something."

"We will." Dario aimed a meaty index finger at me. "Sit."

I sat on the sofa. Although I'd recently learned that Dario was never a professional thug, and although I know from experience that he has a soft heart, he's a large unit. A large and imposing unit. I tend not to argue with him.

"Tell us all you know, dear," Mrs. B prompted after another long pull at her drink. "How did you come by this information?"

"I wasn't snooping in Bernina's office, if that's what you're implying."

At least I hadn't been snooping this time. I'd been guilty of that in the past. Not that I considered it full-bore snooping. Bernina made notes with large letters and plenty of underlining. She also left folders open and papers piled here and there. Anyone stopping by her office to check the bulletin board or ask a question could spot all kinds of things. Okay, sure, it helps if the person attempting said spotting has perfected the ability to read upside down and is able to create distractions at a moment's notice, but still . . .

I took a swallow of my drink and felt it burn its way to my stomach. Even by Dario's standards, this was one strong mix. I sucked in a few breaths to cool my throat and said, "I saw them huddled on a bench up the river. Sybil waved me over and flashed a notepad with the can't-fail system she worked out. She's convinced she's going to save the day for the condo association."

"Even Bernina's not dumb enough to believe that will work," Dario said. "They could be charged with—I don't know—embezzlement, misuse of funds, or something."

"Maybe Bernina won't go along when she has time to think about what could go wrong, but she wasn't putting the brakes on when I saw them."

"Oh dear." Mrs. B fingered her double strand of pearls, a sure sign she was about to take action. Two short strands wouldn't deliver the pearl power punch of some of her other necklaces, but they'd be enough to get things moving. "I was hoping to have a few days to find an expert to guide an intervention, but it appears we can't delay."

She tucked Cheese Puff beside her in her chair, slid the laptop to her knees, and tapped a few keys. "I've been reading up on some of the steps they recommend and it all makes sense. We let her know she's loved and valued, we lay out how she's painting herself into a tight corner, we recommend what she should do, and we present the consequences."

"Consequences?" Dario clenched a fist and studied his knuckles.

I laughed then slapped a hand over my mouth. "Sorry. But the image of you punching out Sybil is funny in a not-so-funny way. It would be like a wolf taking on a baby chipmunk."

"She might blind me with footwork," Dario offered.

I laughed again and Dario joined in, but Mrs. B closed her laptop with a snap. "That's a good point."

Dario raised one eyebrow, making me envious enough to vow to try once again to master the art. When I try, both brows jump toward my hairline. "What's a good point?"

"That, unless we wait and catch Sybil stealing condo money, we have no legal way to force her to get help. She could dance around us and go on gambling." She fingered her pearls

51

again. "And the other thing is, even if we hold an intervention and succeed in persuading her to try to kick her habit, we have nothing to offer to fill her time."

When she said that, I realized how much time Sybil must have to fill. She was retired but, unlike Jim and Verna and others, hadn't picked up a part-time job or taken on a volunteer position. Her tiny condo wouldn't require much in the way of daily cleaning and straightening, and her friend Verna was coming back strong from a stroke and needed less assistance every week.

"It's not just the time," Mrs. B said. "We must meet the need gambling fills."

"You're not talking about giving her money," Dario said. "Because that would be—"

"Counterproductive," I blurted. "I mean, she needs money now, but she didn't start playing the slots because she needed money. She started because it was exciting, and because she thought she could come up with a system no one had thought of yet. And maybe she thought she'd be a little famous."

"Exactly," Mrs. B said. "So we'll need to present her with an alternative, something exciting and stimulating and social, something that lets her feel important."

"Sounds like you want us to think." Dario headed for the liquor cabinet. "That calls for seconds."

"Not for me." I set my drink—still three-quarters full—on the coffee table. Since I wasn't home where the furniture was mostly previously owned, I used a glass coaster decorated with a photo of Cheese Puff in a tiny tuxedo and sporting a top hat. "There's enough alcohol in this one to hold me until the end of the week."

"I'll pass as well," Mrs. B said. "We need sharp minds if we're to come up with something interesting and satisfying to take the place of gambling."

I thought about the hobbies Mrs. B had pursued in the past two months. They hadn't satisfied her, so there was no point in pitching them to Sybil. There had also been start-up costs for wool and needles, boots and binoculars. Sybil, already or soon to be in debt, didn't need more expenses.

Dario returned with his fresh drink and flopped in his favorite chair. Granted, it was a heavy-duty reclining model Mrs. B had purchased specifically for him, but the springs still groaned and the wooden framework creaked. "Gotta be something she'll want to stick with," he said. "Something with a purpose."

Mrs. B pondered that as she stroked Cheese Puff's little head. "Excellent point."

"Right," I agreed. "If she feels she's part of something and making progress toward a goal and making a difference, she's more likely to continue."

"There's certainly plenty of volunteer work needing to be done," Mrs. B mused. "She could make a difference working at a food pantry or an animal shelter."

Dario shook his head. "Can't see Sybil lifting cartons of canned goods. Or sticking to guidelines for handing out food. And if she can't keep hold of Cheese Puff's leash when he pulls on it, no way could she handle a bigger dog."

True.

Sybil was petite and slight and in the same age range as Mrs. B. It was a range somewhere north of six decades and possibly even north of a decade beyond that. As I've mentioned before, I've never asked. And I don't intend to. First, I see no reason to know an exact number. And second, if Mrs. B or Sybil

53

wanted to broadcast—or even whisper—the information, they would have done so by now.

"And Sybil feels so much sympathy for others," Mrs. B said with a nod. "She'd invite strangers to sleep on her sofa, and bring home dogs and cats that didn't find homes."

I got a mental image of Sybil's condo full of barking dogs and yowling cats. Bernina Burke would go ballistic. "She'd have to learn to distance herself."

"She's better at getting closer than at distancing."

"And she's not all that great at following directions." With a grimace I recalled culinary detours in her attempts to make potato salad and apple pie.

"She's certainly a free spirit," Mrs. B agreed.

"She's an airhead," Dario amended in a low growl.

Mrs. B's sapphire eyes flashed in his direction and he raised his drink like a shield. "Just sayin'. And a lot of those jobs aren't all that fulfilling once you get them down and it's all repetition. Stock the shelves. Fill the boxes. Stock the shelves again. Clean up poop. Feed the dogs. Clean up—"

"We get it," Mrs. B said in a voice as tart a not-ripe-yet grapefruit. "I think we've covered the negative aspects of volunteering and the reasons Sybil might not be a good fit for certain positions. Now let's see what we can put in the positive column."

What we put there first was silence.

A long silence.

And then I remembered Ardie and her summer project at the rec center. Ardie didn't make much money as a classroom aide, and she didn't possess many worldly goods. But she was rich in spirit. And the love and respect and caring she doled out to her friends and the kids she worked with came back to her with interest. Kids looked forward to working with her. Teachers fought to have her in their classrooms.

"You appear to have an idea, dear," Mrs. B said.

"I do. But I don't know if it's something Sybil would like."

I told her what little I knew about the summer program.

Mrs. B's eyes sparkled. "Sybil knows Ardie."

"And Ardie knows Sybil," Dario said. "A fact that could cancel your plan. Taking Sybil on could be like taking on another child."

"When Ardie told me about her project," I ventured, "I got the impression she'd be grateful for any help she could get. And I bet Sybil would have lots of ideas."

"All of them off-the-wall," Dario countered.

"Nonsense." Mrs. B shut him down. "Sybil loves the theater. She could get kids to put on plays. And make costumes and scenery." She aimed a finger at my nose. "You talk to Ardie just as soon as you can and see if she'd be interested. Tell her I'm prepared to make a sizeable donation to her project."

"Can I be honest about what we're up to?"

Mrs. B thought for a few seconds. "Yes. Ardie may have had experience in this area and may have some helpful ideas. And the more people who know Sybil needs nudging in the right direction, the better."

"She needs more than nudging," Dario muttered. "She needs a kick in the pants."

"Well, it may come to that," Mrs. B told him. "But we'll try a firm but gentle approach first. Now, you clean up while I phone Jim and Verna and other members of the Committee and ask them to come by this evening."

I handed Dario my glass, pried Cheese Puff from beside Mrs. B, and took off on the torturous journey across about four yards of deck from her door to mine. Halfway there, the bleat of a smoke alarm pierced the air. A string of curses followed.

The door to my condo whipped open.

Smoke billowed out.

Chapter 6

I halted, thus escaping injury from the cookie pan that emerged from the smoke.

The pan clattered to the deck, contents falling loose in steaming brown clumps that smelled like nothing I can describe, but exactly like something I hoped never to smell again.

Cheese Puff barked and clawed to get down. When I released him, he bounded back to Mrs. B's condo. For a moment I thought of following him, but then I heard Allison's wail. "Dad, the whole house stinks like a sewer and— OMG, the sink is running over. Turn off the water."

"I'm trying."

That was my cue.

Waving my hand in front of my face to clear the smoke, I darted through the door and peered into the acrid haze. Dave stood by the sink, trying in vain to hold back a mini Niagara with a dish towel while struggling to pry loose a metal bowl jammed under the single handle by the side of the faucet. The bowl was putting up quite a fight while doing a dandy job of holding the control in the ON position.

"Push the handle all the way up," I ordered in a voice I hoped would carry over the shrilling of the smoke alarm.

"That turns on more water."

"Right. But if you don't do it, you won't have room to work the bowl loose."

He released the bowl and shoved the handle. "It won't move."

"It will if you get the other bowl out of there," Allison howled.

The other bowl was glass, wedged on its side in the tight space between the handle and the backsplash. A glossy brown substance I hoped was chocolate icing slopped over its rim.

"The bowl won't move." Dave reached for a small saucepan crusted with something the color of bile. "I'll have to break it."

"No breaking." I snatched a wooden mallet from the container by the stove and tapped the bowl loose.

Allison caught it before it rolled off the counter.

Dave raised the handle, freed the metal bowl, and turned off the water.

I flipped on the exhaust fan over the stove and scooted along the hallway to the smoke alarm, yelling more words of wisdom as I went. "The mop and bucket are in the pantry."

"Yeah, Dad," Allison taunted at top volume. "It's cleanup time."

I popped the cover and pried out the battery. The smoke alarm emitted a final strangled bleat and went silent. My ears, however, rang like they longed to be mentioned in that famous Edgar Allan Poe poem about bells.

When I returned, Dave had liberated the mop and bucket from the pantry. He held them out and gave me the hopeful look I'd found so endearing when we were dating.

"Not my mess." I strolled to the living room, plopped on the sofa, and rubbed my ears.

"Not mine either." Allison set the glass bowl on the dining room table and plopped beside me. "Why did you use so many bowls and pots?"

"The first ones I tried were too small."

Ah, a version of the Goldilocks defense.

"And why are you home at this hour?" I chimed in.

Dave tossed the dripping dish towel in the washer and dragged the mop through the kitchen lake, creating a wave that sloshed against the base of the stove. "Harvey had a bunch of medical tests over in Portland, so he left early."

"Bet he flunks them all," Allison said. "He eats more junk food in an hour than most kids I know do in a whole day."

"And his idea of a stress test is stressing out other people. Like you."

"Yeah." Dave squeezed the sopping mop over the bucket, water spraying out the sides and back on the floor. "And he won't be thrilled with what the doctor has to say when the results are in. That's why I thought I'd make him some healthy cookies."

I gazed through the open door at the cookie pan and the contents now fusing with the deck. "What did you put in them?"

"Stuff from the health food store downtown."

"What kind of stuff?"

"Fish oil, yeast, powdered seaweed, flax seed, brown rice, and some little envelopes of herbs."

"You found a cookie recipe that called for all that?"

He squeezed the mop again with a shade more proficiency. "No. I used a package of brownie mix for the base and added extra oil and water and chocolate chips and things."

Things? Part of me wanted to know what those things were. A larger part of me hoped to remain ignorant.

"How did you know how much to put in?" Allison asked.

59

"I guessed." He stabbed the mop at a lagoon by the refrigerator, splashing water on the lower cabinets. "Cooking isn't rocket science."

"No, it's *harder* than rocket science." Allison laughed and pointed at the mess on the deck. "And *your* rocket burned up."

Dave went on shoving the mop in silence.

I surveyed the kitchen counters, the spills and glops, the piles of seeds and rice, the drifts of yeast and substances I couldn't identify and didn't want to. "Did you cook the rice before you mixed it in?"

Dave shot me his that's-a-stupid-question look. Then his eyes flared and he winced. "Uh, no. Was I supposed to?"

"Even I know you cook rice before you eat it," Allison hooted.

"Can't you sometimes bake it in a pudding or something?"

Since my culinary skills aren't what you'd call advanced, I hedged my bets with a vague answer. "I suppose you could. If that's what the recipe called for and you mixed in lots of liquid."

"And followed directions," Allison added.

I was about to tell her it was time to lay off, when I heard a shout.

"No, Lola, no. Don't eat that. No. Sit."

I bolted for the door and spotted Verna attempting to pull her Golden Retriever away from the dietary disaster on the deck. Normally the model of obedience, Lola paid no attention to the commands. Tall, thin, and still unsteady on her feet thanks to a stroke, Verna was losing the battle until I got a grip on the leash. Together we yanked Lola back a few feet.

"Thank you," Verna said. "She was intent on eating those brown lumps. And I was afraid they . . ."

"Afraid they're what they look like?" I asked with a chuckle.

She grimaced. "Yes."

"They're not. They were supposed to be cookies. Healthy cookies for Harvey Goodspeed."

Verna sniffed the air. "They smell like some of the debris the river's been leaving behind as the level drops. Was this a recipe you got from the Internet?"

"Hardly." I gave Lola the hand signal to sit. She did, but continued to lean toward the so-called cookies. "Dave made it up as he went along."

"What *is* that smell?" Mrs. B emerged from her condo with Cheese Puff in her arms. "It reminds me of the time Jake shorted out the pressure washer and about fried himself to a crisp."

"It does," Verna agreed with a smile. "But Barbara says Dave was trying to make cookies for Harvey Goodspeed."

Mrs. B surveyed the remains. "It appears he didn't succeed."

"Not even close," I said.

Verna bent to study the debris. "Most of them didn't break. Sometimes when cookies are imperfect, a little icing will salvage them."

I suspected that, depending on what Dave added to the icing, it might not be able to save itself, let alone the cookies.

"It was nice of him to try," Verna said. "I imagine Harvey doesn't have many friends."

"And there are sound reasons for that sorry situation," Mrs. B said in a tone that implied the discussion of Harvey Goodspeed was finished. "Let's go inside and hope this smell doesn't follow us."

They turned toward Mrs. B's place, and I released my grip on Lola's leash.

Lola took a few steps along with Verna, then turned and plunged toward the mess, yanking the leash handle from Verna's hand. Too late I snatched at it. "No, Lola," we all called.

Lola paid no attention.

She lowered her head and nosed one of the clumps. Then, just as I was imagining the emergency veterinary clinic bill for making her regurgitate what surely couldn't be good for a dog to ingest, she flopped and rolled.

"Eeewwww," we chorused.

Cheese Puff barked, wriggled from Mrs. B's grasp, and joined his best friend in coating himself with pungent crumbs.

Mrs. B called for him to come to her, but then thought better of it and hustled to her condo, tugging Verna along. "The dogs are all yours, dear," she called over her shoulder. "And Dave's."

That's why, a few minutes later, Dave and I were in the master bathroom with both dogs. In the small space, the odor was even more noxious and the vent fan was no match for it. The dogs, however, seemed to consider burnt cookie residue akin to expensive perfume and kept sniffing at and rubbing up against each other, tails wagging.

"Lola didn't balk when you led her up the stairs. I think she's forgiven you for setting her up to be assigned to another drug-squad partner and all that happened when she ran off." I lined up a variety of stink-stopping remedies gleaned from a few moments of research on the Internet. "If, indeed, dogs understand what forgiving is all about."

(For the record, although I understood the concept, and although sometimes I could excuse someone's behavior, I had a lot of trouble letting go of anger and resentment. I could never completely forgive my ex for cheating on me and draining my bank account, but I got the money back and karma caught up with him, so my anger wasn't as hot. As for Lola, once she'd been rescued from the meth dealers who captured her when she ran from the police station, she'd found a good home with Verna and a new mission as a companion animal. And karma came into play once more—to avoid being busted back to patrol, Dave had sacrificed his job with the Reckless River police to join the county force.)

"Let's hope that what we're about to do to her won't set us back to where we were." Dave surveyed the bottles and boxes on the vanity. "We mix the vinegar and the baking soda?" he asked.

"Only if we want to conduct a science experiment. I didn't have time to read all the blogs and opinions about getting rid of odors, but I say you use the vinegar first on the spots that smell the worst. Then rinse if off and move on to baking soda and shampoo and follow up with a lemon rinse."

"Me?"

"You."

Dave eyed the tub. "You're smaller. It would be easier for you to get in there with Lola."

"Except I'll be washing Cheese Puff in the sink."

"How about I wash—?"

"No."

He dug in the pocket of his jeans. "Flip you for it."

"No."

"Rock-paper-scissors?"

"No."

He gave me the pleading look he'd tried before. I didn't waver. Cheese Puff, who hated to be washed and was apt to shake water all over me and the bathroom, claw at my arms, and roll on my pillows to dry himself, was still the lesser—as in

63

smaller—of two evils. And besides, I wasn't the one responsible for the culinary disaster that led us here.

"No," I repeated. "Thanks to this, I'm missing water aerobics class, so I'm not in the mood to make your life easier."

"All right." He kicked off his running shoes and shucked his T-shirt and jeans, an act that always made my pulse pound. And he knew it. Leering, he flexed his muscles. "Sure you won't reconsider? In exchange for certain 'favors' to be performed later."

"Positive." I flashed him a smug smile. When the lights went out in our bedroom this evening, I was confident I'd get those favors whether I washed Lola or not. Unless he was tired to the point of exhaustion, or boiling mad at me, Dave never passed on a chance to do favors.

I scooped up Cheese Puff who promptly growled and launched his flying squirrel routine, legs splayed and stiff. In that position, there was no way he'd fit in the sink. "The more you fight, the longer this will take," I warned.

I wasn't the least surprised when he didn't listen.

Dave, meanwhile, got Lola's front legs into the tub and, careful of the fragile right rear leg, hoisted her hind end. After one more pleading look on his part, and one more head shake on mine, he got in himself and went to work with the spray bottle of vinegar. Lola took it patiently, tail tucked.

Cheese Puff, meanwhile, howled like a young coyote. I eyeballed the sink, decided it was too small, and considered my options. Allison's bathroom sink was no larger. The kitchen sink was full of pots and bowls. Those pots and bowls were the source of the smell. The sink in the downstairs powder room was smaller than this one. And much as I'd like to toss him in the washer, I didn't relish being charged with cruelty to animals. Clearly, much as I detested the remaining choice, I had to go for it.

Keeping a firm grip on Cheese Puff, I shucked my jeans and climbed in the tub with Dave and Lola.

All in all, and compared to some of what was to come, it was relatively relaxing.

Chapter 7

As you know by now, my sister isn't one to take social cues. Heck, I doubt if she even notices social cues. In fact, I'm pretty sure a social cue would have to be armed with a lethal weapon and holding it to her head before she'd notice it, let alone get it. So, much as I try to make it clear that I don't look forward to her visits with anything even remotely resembling anticipatory joy, she still drops in. And the next afternoon there she was, thumping at my door hard enough to riffle the bits of paper pinned to the bulletin board where members of the Committee left notes about Cheese Puff's walks, treats, and upcoming activities.

(For the record, if you think my dog makes the scene at more restaurants and events than I do, you're right. Members of the Committee have smuggled him in to plays and concerts, on board excursion boats, and to spas and high-class dining establishments. And they wonder why he's so spoiled and entitled.)

I halted my never-ending battle against smears of jam, peanut butter, barbecue sauce, and guacamole dip on the kitchen counter and cabinet doors. Since Dave and Allison complained that I was "too picky" and "always on their cases" about these smears, I'd taken to launching my deep-cleaning attacks when they weren't at home so I could mutter without interruption. Since I was alone, except for my faithless canine companion, I could do that muttering at a level that sometimes approached a shout. For that very reason, I'd closed the sliding glass door to the deck. If Mrs. Ballantine heard me, she'd rush over to see if I was okay, and probably deliver a lecture about relationships not being perfect and how it would be healthier if I learned to accept a few warts without feeling the need to vent at volume.

"You're home," Iz shouted, pounding once more. "I know it. And you know I know it. Open the door."

After three deep breaths, I put my wad of paper towels aside, and opened the sliding glass door to the deck to catch the breeze. Even though I was wearing shorts and a sleeveless T-shirt, smear scrubbing was warm work. And I wasn't about to turn on the air conditioning; Dave and I had agreed to wait until the official start of summer to watch our power bill skyrocket. Shoving my damp hair behind my ears, I savored a few more seconds on my own, then trudged to the end of the hallway, and turned the knob.

"Hinges seem a little loose," Iz said as she barreled past me headed for the refrigerator.

"I wonder why," I said in my snarkiest tone.

"Cheap products and shoddy construction," she responded.

"Not constant pounding? Almost daily pounding?"

She frowned as she popped the top on a can of ginger ale. "If I had a key, I wouldn't have to knock."

No way! I'd buy new hinges and longer screws or have a steel door and frame installed before I gave Iz a key and allowed her unsupervised access to my condo. Not that supervising her visits had any effect, I thought as I watched her eat a quarter pound of pepperoni slices and top them off with half a bag of pretzels seasoned with honey and mustard.

67

"Did you miss lunch?" I asked in a sugary tone, betting myself a quarter the answer would be negative. I'd asked this question many times before while Iz was vacuuming up what she considered a snack, and a small one at that. Never had she missed a meal prior to her assault on my provisions. I'd begun to assume that her forays into my supplies were more about convenience (Iz often contended she swung by when she was on her way somewhere close by, and occasionally that was true), compensation (for the years she put in getting me to what passed for adulthood), and cost (free for her, but often expensive for me).

"I had lunch. But it was—"

"Hours ago and not very good and there wasn't very much?"

Iz narrowed eyes that already appeared too small for her face. "Yeah. For your information, Miss Smarty Pants, it was at 11:00, it was a grilled cheese sandwich, and it was the size of a postage stamp."

"No fries on the side?" I needled.

"Only a few," she grumped. "Maybe half a potato's worth if you smashed them together."

"Wow. I'm surprised you made it through the afternoon without fainting."

She narrowed her eyes once more, but I breezed on. "Unless you ate an emergency granola bar. Or two."

Her lips pressed together and her squint got squintier.

Direct hit!

And not a lucky hit. Iz generally wore cargo pants. And the bulging pockets generally contained enough food to provision her for several hours—approximately the same amount I'd need for a long weekend. As you know, I also suspect, based on a few comments she'd made, those pockets contain various forms of weaponry. During her last rabble-rousing event, Iz had taken a bullet, so I couldn't blame her for packing. But, given her many arrests for inciting riots with incendiary speech, I doubted she was legally allowed to pack anything more lethal than a water pistol.

"Maybe I *did* have a snack," she muttered. "But I had to. I was starving."

Not, I suspected, starving in the same way early pioneers were when they ate their horses to stay alive through the winter.

"I shadowed today. With Sharlene Lutz." Iz swilled the remainder of the ginger ale, tossed the can in the recycling bin in the pantry, and got out a carton of orange juice. "We went to two places in three hours. Woman's skinny as a piece of string and moves like her feet are on fire."

I smiled at the contrast to my sister. She hadn't been considered skinny even on the day of her birth, and often moved like her feet were encased in cement.

"I bet the only time she holds still is when she's in a tanning bed. And I bet she does that once a week or more. She looks like a walking piece of toast, except for the circles around her eyes."

I grabbed for the carton as she raised it to her lips. "Glass. Please. You're not at home."

Not that Penelope, my sister's partner and a woman as sleek and neat as a house cat, would let her get away with drinking from the carton at home. If Penelope caught her, that is. Iz, for all her bulk and bluster, could be stealthy.

Iz glanced around as if to say she thought the rules didn't hold at my place. There were several reasons for that. First, my sister had as strong a sense of entitlement as my dog. Second, the fact that she stepped in to raise me when my parents

69

checked out emotionally reinforced that entitlement. And third, during years of traveling and couch surfing she'd perfected the art of ruling the roost she roosted in.

Grudgingly, she got a glass and waved it within an inch of my nose. Just as grudgingly, I shoved the carton of juice at her. At the rate she was stuffing herself, I'd have to make an excursion to the supermarket this evening and drop a good portion of this week's earnings. Hoping to distract her with conversation, I asked how her day went.

"Rocky. Sharlene doesn't like me. Speaks to me like I'm nine eggs short of a dozen. Thinks I'm not committed to the training." Iz filled her glass. "The instructors think the same. That's why they assigned me to her."

I mulled that as she drank. "Because she's not the greatest? Because they don't want to waste the time of someone who really knows her stuff?"

"No." Iz gave me the smug look she laid on to show I wasn't as smart as I thought I was. "She's one of the best. She's fast, efficient, and thorough. And she drives trainees like cattle."

"Ah. So they expect you to bolt from the herd."

"Yeah. But I won't."

I knew she meant that. When my sister made up her mind and set her course, it would take more than a hundred trainers with negative views to stop her. "What's your game plan?"

"Ignore her snide comments as much as I can. Concentrate on the needs of the clients."

Color me impressed. This was miles from her usual strategy of sabotage and/or outright rebellion.

"First client was a man. Perry Walker. Old and frail. Not exactly sure what day it is or what planet he's on. Skin almost transparent. Big house out in the county. Lots of collections."

"Collections?" The word made me think of Verna's "collections" of old newspapers and broken bits of furniture and kitchenware—the junk we'd hauled to a storage unit when it appeared her stroke had wiped out all memory of her accumulations and cleared her mind of her need to acquire. "What kind of collections?"

I moved to the living room, hoping Iz would follow and abandon the refrigerator before she emptied it.

"Knickknacks, figurines, and clocks." Iz refilled the glass she'd emptied and, for once, put the juice back where it belonged before trekking to the sofa. "Stamps and coins. Books."

"Sounds like his collections might be worth a lot of money." I sat in Cheese Puff's favorite chair, careful to take the side away from the crevice between the arm and the seat cushion where he'd wedged himself, head toward the rear of the chair. The Puffster had as little use for my sister as she did for him.

"Probably." Iz set the glass on the coffee table, missing the coaster by half a foot, and flopped full-length on the sofa. "But I doubt he'd know. He's off in a fantasy land with a ghost."

"A ghost?"

All ears, I leaned forward. I'm a sucker for ghost stories, as long as the stories aren't too ghoulish or frightening. And I'm all for ghosts in movies, those glimpsed from the corner of the eye, and occasionally rattling chains in the attic. I'm not in favor of cinema specters locking doors, leaving trails of blood, or pursuing the protagonist into dungeon-like basements.

Outside of books and movies, I've never encountered a ghost. And I don't quite trust the reports of people who claim to have seen, heard, or felt them. I've been shown fuzzy pictures, and once listened to an audio recording of what sounded like

71

hoarse whispering, but my unscientific mind questioned whether those proved anything.

And—you know what?—if someone invited me to an encounter with a certified ghost, I doubt I'd go.

"Ghost is his son. Died in Iraq, Sharlene says. The old guy claims he visits a lot, late at night." Iz made a creepy woo-woo noise.

"And you don't believe that."

"I believe the house is old and the wiring may be faulty and that could cause the lights to get dimmer and brighter and make shadows seem to move. I believe the poor guy has Parkinson's and he's hallucinating or sundowning or both. I believe his cleaning service might rearrange things so he thinks the ghost took them. And I believe Sharlene encourages him to believe he sees his son." Iz frowned. "She says it comforts him."

"But you're not sure it does."

"Seems more like it agitates him. And it might not be policy—or at least not the best policy—to go along with it unless a doctor suggested that. But Sharlene says he doesn't trust doctors and hasn't been to one for years." Iz glugged down half the juice. "He was talking nonsense about the ghost telling him he needed money to pay some guy with a ferry."

Ferry? The word rang a faint bell far in the back of my mind.

Then Iz rolled on and the bell stopped.

"The woman we saw is something else again. Mavis Dupree. Must weigh 300 pounds. Getting from her bed to a chair takes about an hour and she can't remember what happened five minutes ago, but isn't bothered because she's also living in a fantasy world. Makeup put on like the stuff you use to texture walls. Scarves and shawls and silk robes. More jewelry than Mrs. Ballantine wears—but some of it looks pretty cheap and junky."

This from a woman who never wore jewelry.

"You can't always tell how valuable a piece is by the way it looks."

Iz flipped one hand as if to say I knew nothing about jewelry or much of anything else.

I changed the subject. "What's wrong with Mrs. Dupree?"

"*Miss* Dupree. Never married. Says she never met a man worth more than a few hours of her time."

That comment must have endeared her to my sister who thought along the same lines. Except Iz would say minutes instead of hours.

"Lives alone in a brick house with pink shutters. Up on that ridge with the mansions, near the place where that crazy cat woman tried to kill you."

Not an evening I wanted to relive.

Fortunately Iz, perhaps because she hadn't been the one to rescue me from that particular misadventure and thus couldn't paint herself with the heroism brush, moved along. "Sharlene says the place should be condemned. Ground is dropping away behind it, trees are leaning. Couple of big storms this winter and the back yard will be history. Maybe the house too."

"Wow. Is she planning to move?"

"Doubt it. Doubt she understands the danger. And might not want to leave her home. House has a living room as big as your whole condo and more bedrooms than I have fingers." Iz wiggled all eight fingers and two thumbs. "Gets food brought in from a couple of restaurants and the fancy market that charges double and triple what other places do."

"So you don't have to cook for her. That must be a relief."

73

"Yeah, but there's plenty of cleaning up. And we have to set places at the table for breakfast, lunch, and dinner. It's a big table." Iz spread her arms. "Breakfast setting on one end, lunch in the middle, dinner at the other end. Big plates, small plates, cups, saucers, fancy napkins, glasses for water and wine."

"She drinks wine?"

"From her own wine cellar. A bottle every night." Iz sat up and drained the juice. "Against her doctor's orders."

"She drinks alone?"

"Mostly. Sometimes a guy named John has a glass. She says he comes by a lot of evenings."

"Is he a neighbor?"

"Don't know. Sharlene thinks he's a figment of her imagination." Iz stood. "Gotta get home and get cleaned up. Penelope and I are going out to dinner. She's taking me to a new Chinese place on the east side of town."

"Ah." I'd read a review of the restaurant that claimed portions were huge. "Good thing you didn't spoil your appetite by snacking."

Iz snorted and headed for the door to the parking lot, thumbs tucked in the waistband of her cargo pants as if to demonstrate that she had plenty of room for Chinese cuisine. Or perhaps she was demonstrating that, in spite of all the stuffing I'd seen her do, she had trimmed down a little in the past few months. Or perhaps she was wearing a pair of pants that were a size too large. My sister was tall, big-boned, and muscular. Her choice in clothing—extra-large T-shirts and voluminous cargo pants—made it difficult to gauge her size and determine whether that size had increased or decreased.

Since she met Penelope, a petite electrician who walked the clean-living walk while wearing stylish clothing, Iz had been on a series of healthy-eating campaigns and fad diets. Although she lectured me about making sound food choices and demanded I stock my kitchen with organic products devoid of additives, preservatives, and faux cheese flavoring, she generally ate her way through everything I had on hand.

By now, I'd come to the conclusion that my sister was, if not indestructible, then at least darn difficult to kill. And I was glad of that. As annoying as she was, we shared a bond. I owed her, and I loved her—in a weird kind of way. So I'd mostly given up on pointing out her dietary contradictions. And, although I was still often frustrated by her behavior, I filed it under "amusing" and moved on

Right after the door slammed, and before I had time to wonder how much longer the hinges would last, the screen door to the deck slid open.

Chapter 8

I breathed a sign of relief as Verna came in, Lola at her side. Cheese Puff scrambled from his crevice, clawing his way across my legs.

"Ouch."

My entitled mutt didn't acknowledge my pain, but danced a circle around his best friend and former roommate.

"Sorry," Verna said.

"Not your fault."

"I could have called ahead to let you know I was coming." She tapped the phone compartment on the outside of her beige leather purse.

I brushed that aside with a flick of my fingers. Members of the Committee seldom called. And an unlocked door to the deck was an invitation to come in. "Not to worry." I rubbed the red marks on my thighs. "He's done worse. And it reminds me I should make an appointment to have his nails trimmed."

Cheese Puff halted in his tiny tracks and lifted his upper lip in a silent snarl.

"I'll take care of that," Verna volunteered. "Lola needs to have her nails done too. And just yesterday I received a coupon for that exclusive doggie spa over in Portland."

A spa?

I didn't roll my eyes, but only because I bit my tongue. I couldn't, however, hold back on sarcasm. "Is that the spa that sends a limousine to pick up your pets?"

Verna frowned. "I didn't see that mentioned in the ad, but I'll ask when I make the appointment."

This time I couldn't hold back on the eye roll. "I was kidding."

"Oh. Sorry. I didn't realize. Since my little episode, I can't seem to distinguish humor like I did in the past."

Since Verna was a serious sort of person, she hadn't picked up on a whole lot of humor *before* her stroke. But I let that ride. "To what do I owe the honor of this visit?"

She blushed. "To be honest, I'm here because . . . well, I guess because I'm nosy. And an eavesdropper."

Having a fair share of those qualities myself, I smiled and gave the air another brush with my fingers. "What a coincidence. Plenty of people say I'm the same. Want to form a club?"

Verna's blush deepened. "I didn't intend to. I was on my way next door to meet with Muriel about plans for the intervention when I heard your sister mention Mavis Dupree. I didn't mean to overhear your conversation, but—"

"Iz has a loud voice. The challenge isn't in overhearing, it's in *not* overhearing."

Verna nodded. "She projects well."

"She projects better than the average foghorn."

Verna giggled, the high-pitched sound contrasting with her angular frame and no-nonsense nature.

"What was it about hearing Mavis Dupree's name that made you stop by?"

77

"I knew her." Verna blushed once more. "I mean, I knew who she was. I saw her in court several times back when I was a clerk."

She paused long enough for my curiosity to heat up to a slow simmer—a process that takes about two seconds. "Was she also a clerk?"

Verna giggled again. "Hardly. She was in court because she'd been arrested."

"Arrested?" The woman Iz described—the woman with the big house and mounds of jewelry and clothing—didn't fit my idea of a criminal. And Mavis Dupree seemed more like the name of a character in a play than the name on a mug shot. "Arrested for what?"

"She was . . . well, to put it bluntly, she was a madam. A high-class madam with an exclusive clientele, but still . . ."

That explained the big house with its many bedrooms. And it probably explained why the evening visitor was named John.

"Her attorney claimed she ran a boarding house for young women who couldn't afford apartments of their own and enjoyed the dormitory atmosphere she provided."

I laughed. "That was the best he could come up with?"

"It was all he needed. She got off every time. Except once. And then the judge gave her a fine." She scowled. "A darn small fine if you ask me."

"Sounds like she greased the wheels of justice. Or had dirt on the guys in black robes."

"Court gossip said both. Anyway, I apologize again for eavesdropping, but I thought you might be interested in that little bit of Reckless River history."

"I am. But I'm not sure I'll share it with Iz." My sister, a strong advocate for the rights of women, had led many protests against abuse and exploitation. "She's already on thin ice with

78

the program director. If she goes off about Mavis Dupree or backs out of the assignment, she might not pass the course."

"Your sister has very strong ideals," Verna said. "I value that. But she doesn't always . . . well, you know."

"Think before she acts?" I suggested. "See the big picture? Check out what's at the bottom of the cliff before she leaps?"

"All of the above," Verna said as she turned to leave. "Are you coming next door?"

"For the meeting about Sybil? Mrs. B didn't ask me to." And—forget about asking—she would have commanded me to attend if she felt I was needed. Given the absence of a command, and knowing my neighbor as I did, I suspected plans were all in place and the meeting with Verna was more of a courtesy than an actual desire for input. "Why don't I walk the dogs?"

Verna considered, sliding her gaze toward the condo next door.

"I'll take my cell. Mrs. B can call if she needs me."

She didn't.

When Dave trudged up to our bedroom many hours later, I discovered that, as Allison had predicted, Harvey Goodspeed flunked his medical tests. He flunked them so badly that, right after reviewing the results, his doctor called the sheriff and recommended Harvey take full retirement. Immediately.

The sheriff, a man who generally didn't like taking orders or even suggestions, acted on this one within hours. He did that partly out of concern about Harvey's health and partly because it gave him the opportunity to rip a thorn from his side instead of drawing it out by millimeters. Needless to say, Harvey stonewalled the exit process.

"He refused to go to HR for the exit interview," Dave said. "Refused to sign any papers. Refused to pack up his personal items. Refused to turn in the keys to his vehicle. Refused to speak to me."

"That must have been refreshing," I said, attempting to lighten the mood while glancing at the clock. 9:27, a time when a high school sub who wanted to be fresh and on her toes should turn out the light. "Good thing those cookies didn't turn out because he would have refused to eat them. That would have really hurt your feelings."

"Ha. Ha." Dave unbuttoned a pale blue shirt spattered with brown spots that I hoped were coffee and not blood. "I spent six hours trying to get him to stop throwing things, stop going through files, and stop packing up cold cases to take with him. Finally the sheriff came in and threatened to call the hostage negotiator, the emergency response team, and the news media."

Dave pulled off the shirt and held it up to the light. "If I had the opportunity to retire with a good pension and kick back at home, I'd be on my way in five minutes."

"That's because you have a home to kick back in. Home to Harvey is the office." I marked my place in the latest adventures of Flavia de Luce and set the book aside. "He doesn't have a life beyond his job. Or at least not much of one."

"Well, he won't have anything if he doesn't make some changes." Dave held the shirt an inch from his eyes and examined the stains. "Think these will come out?"

"Depends on what they are."

"Coffee. Mostly. Some with chocolate creamer. Maybe catsup and grease from an old burger and fries. Possibly salsa." He tossed the shirt to me. "Harvey threw a lot of stuff."

I took a quick look and tossed the shirt back. "Put it on the washer and I'll hit it with all the spot treatment products we've got. But don't get your hopes up. I think it may become a jogging shirt."

Dave stared at me as if I'd announced I was taking up ax murder as a hobby and he'd be my first victim as soon as he bought me an ax. "No one jogs in a button down shirt."

"You're sure? Maybe someone in Iceland or Australia is setting out for a run right this minute wearing a shirt almost exactly like that."

"No." He shook his head. "Never happen. We joggers have standards."

Dave's standards seemed pretty lax to me. He jogged only occasionally and wore faded and worn T-shirts and shorts that looked like rags I'd wipe the floor with. But, wanting to avoid a defense of his wardrobe and a lecture on the importance of having the correct fabric for a form of exercise, I said nothing.

"I was looking forward to taking over the job and not having him looking over my shoulder, but I sort of assumed he'd be available to answer questions."

"Why wouldn't he be? He's retiring, not moving to the upper reaches of the Amazon."

"He might as well be moving to Neptune. I told you he wasn't speaking to me, right?"

"Right?"

"Well, when he went out the door he broke the silence. He called me a back-stabbing traitor who couldn't solve a crime if I committed it myself. Then he said he won't take my calls because I deserve the same treatment I'm giving him."

"But you didn't do anything to undercut him. And you certainly aren't responsible for the state of his health. *And* you don't force him to eat all the garbage he consumes."

Dave shrugged. "That's not how he sees it."

He removed his tan slacks and examined them. "More stains."

"If I can't get them out, you may need to go shopping."

"Shopping?" Dave uttered the word the way some of us might say "tax hikes" or "toxic waste." His eyes grew wide and wild and his hands shook. "Why would I have to go shopping? I have other slacks."

"And they have stains of their own. You're the man in charge now. You need to dress like it."

"Harvey didn't."

Good point. Harvey had been the poster boy for ill-fitting clothing combinations in need of cleaning, pressing, or—preferably—tossing.

"And that makes it a good choice?" I said, using a response that occasionally—perhaps once a month—worked in high school.

Dave opened his mouth, but apparently didn't have a ready answer. He retreated to the bathroom in silence.

When he crawled into bed he took me in his arms, nuzzled my neck, and said, "I love you. I don't know how I got along before I met you."

Something about his tone made me think this wasn't a spontaneous outpouring, but rather an application of soft soap. I kissed him, but didn't respond that I loved him too.

"You're so smart," he murmured in my ear. "So kind and generous. So supportive. So caring."

I wiggled from his grasp and rolled to the edge of the bed. "And I'm *so* not going to shop for you."

Ardie had a grin like the Cheshire Cat when I saw her the next day in the teachers' room. Lunch had gone well until Aston and Brenda launched a heated discussion about the correct way to cook grasshoppers. Doug departed gagging and Gertrude stormed out after threatening to report the combatants to Tremaine Scott saying they created a toxic work environment. That drove them to their respective classrooms, leaving us alone. "Are you involved in the intervention?" I asked.

"Possibly," she said, the grin growing wider.

"Is it happening soon?"

"Possibly."

"When?"

"Soon."

"When? Tell me."

"Can't."

"Sure you can."

"Nope. Mrs. Ballantine swore me to secrecy."

"Well, I'm sure she didn't mean you couldn't tell me. It's not like I'm a spy for Sybil."

"You may not be a spy, but you know what they say about loose lips sinking ships."

With that, she grabbed her backpack and bolted, leaving me to wonder if the reference to ships was metaphorical or whether Mrs. B had chartered a boat and intended to isolate Sybil somewhere at sea. As out-there as that seemed, it wasn't totally out of the question.

Three hours later I headed for my car, still pondering what Mrs. B was up to, congratulating myself on a day of subbing in English that went surprisingly well, and anticipating a detour to the Reckless River library on the way home. Then I heard Allison yelling for me to wait. Actually, "yelling" isn't quite the right word. The sound was more like shrieking or howling or wailing with such intensity and volume and range that a banshee would be impressed enough to ask for lessons.

My first reaction was to run.

83

But even in my teens I'd never been much speedier than a tortoise on a downgrade. I had no doubt Allison would catch me.

I stopped and waited, bracing myself for the crisis to come.

Chapter 9

The yowling continued and the volume increased.

Two fifty-something women walked past me at the rapid pace set by subs who had had all they could take and then some. Both glanced back at Allison and then walked faster.

"She's practicing for theater class," I called. "Believe it or not, the drama teacher said she wasn't projecting enough to reach the back of the theater."

Their expressions told me they'd subbed for theater classes at Captain Meriwether, knew seating for the audience was about eight rows deep, and therefore knew I was either lying or delusional or perhaps both. I aimed for an expression that conveyed a serious innocence. They didn't buy it. These were experienced subs with many years on me. They recognized a load of manure. Shaking their heads as Allison shrieked again, they accelerated.

Knowing it would do little good, I turned and put my finger to my lips.

Allison dropped the level of the shriek by perhaps a single decibel and bore down on me, backpack thumping against her spine in a way that made me fear for the integrity of her vertebrae. Her face was the color of a pomegranate and shiny with tears. Obviously, in a life filled with what she perceived as catastrophes, she was experiencing one of tremendous magnitude.

Bidding farewell to my plans for a quiet afternoon and evening, I asked the question sure to open the floodgates. "What's wrong?"

She fell against me, sobbing. "Josh is going to the senior party."

"Ah."

The senior party was an all-night affair held after graduation and designed to make sure seniors partied safely and in a supervised manner. It was, as the name implies, for seniors only. Allison, being a junior, couldn't attend, even though she was going steady with a senior.

"He told me he wasn't."

"Oh."

"But now he is."

"Ah."

I shuffled to the car making a series of sympathetic noises while Allison leaned against me, wailing and moaning. This was, I knew, no time to be rational. This was no time to point out it was just one night out of her life and it was a bonding experience for him. It could be the last time he'd hang with a lot of the kids in his class. Many of Josh's senior friends would go their separate ways after graduation and lose touch as they developed distinct interests and pursued careers.

This was also no time to make the point that if Josh had been interested in any of the girls in his class, he would have acted on that interest by now. Allison was too caught up in anger and disappointment and—let's face it—selfishness to listen. Later, maybe. But not later as in an hour from now or this evening or even tomorrow.

I unlocked the car, wondering as I always did, why I bothered to lock it. A thief would come for it only if every other vehicle in the country was out of commission. And, once I got out, there was nothing valuable inside except perhaps a few stray coins beneath the seats. "How about we treat ourselves to something special? Want to go for ice cream at that new place downtown?"

"No! I'm never eating again." Allison flung herself into the passenger seat. "When I starve to death, maybe Josh will be sorry for being such a jerk and messing up our Saturday night."

Although I pasted on an expression of concern, I wasn't worried. Not for a minute did I believe Allison would make good on that threat. Like me, she was too fond of snacking on crispy and salty snacks billed as new and improved, crunchier, tastier, or guaranteed to stay fresh longer. Not that the last claim had ever been put to a real test at our place. Four and a half days was the record for a bag of potato chips and only because the chips were chicken flavored and the bag got wedged behind a cereal box in the pantry.

I backed out of my space, wormed my way into the stream of students peeling out of the lot, and headed for home. My plan was to foist Allison and her latest crisis on Mrs. Ballantine. For one thing, I was losing patience with Allison and losing my ability to generate sympathy—even mock sympathy—for her crises. Mrs. B, despite the driving instruction debacle, would be far better at listening and saying the right things. One of those things could be, "Let's go shopping." Allison might turn down ice cream, but I doubted she'd turn down a trip to the mall if Mrs. B was buying. Granted, that wouldn't resolve the senior party issue, but it would put a temporary stop to the wailing.

"How long does it take to starve to death?"

"That depends."

"On what?"

"Well, on a person's health and age and weight and hydration. I think I've heard you can go about three weeks without food if you have water and shelter."

"That's too long."

Eeekkk.

The needle on my worry meter jumped a notch.

Allison raised her feet and kicked the dashboard. "By then Josh will be going out with some girl he stayed up all night with and he won't even remember who I am."

"Trust me, that is not going to—"

"Maybe I'll jump in the river and drown. How long would that take?"

Double eeekkk.

Even in June the Columbia was cold. And the current was strong. Allison swam, but in a pool-party kind of way. Meaning not much, and not well. She wouldn't last long.

"Or I could take a bunch of pills and drink up all of Dad's beer and go to sleep like forever."

"Not on my watch." I braked hard, pulled into the parking lot of a convenience store, and turned off the engine. "Look at me, Allison."

She ducked her head. "Why?"

I gripped her shoulders. "Because I said so."

She lifted her chin but shot me the expression I'd come to think of as the obligatory teenage defiant pout/sulk. Having seen hundreds of these during my subbing years, I was an expert. I gave this one a D+. I gave her shoulders a shake. "If we were at school and I heard you talking about committing suicide, I'd be required to report it. And I'd be required to stay with you until someone came to take you to see a counselor or the nurse or Mr. Scott."

Allison folded her arms across her chest. "Well, we're not at school. So you don't have to do any of that."

"Right." I whipped out my cellphone. "That's why I'm calling your father."

Allison sucked back a sniffle and swallowed. "But he's at work."

"Yes. He's at work. And he's under a lot of pressure learning a new job and cleaning up the mess Harvey Goodspeed made yesterday."

"So he'll be mad?"

"No. At least not at first. He'll be too worried to be mad. Like he was the time you ran away from home."

"That was a long time ago."

"Not that long. A year and a half."

Allison had been in a Goth phase then. Also a nobody-loves-me-or-listens-to-me phase. And an everybody-picks-on-me phase. After she'd ditched a dental appointment, causing Dave to lose time and money, she'd run off. She hadn't gone far. I'd found her hiding in the bushes near my favorite Mexican restaurant and calmed her with chips, guacamole, and melted cheese.

"He got mad later," Allison reminded me.

"Not very mad. Not mad like he gets at my sister when she starts ranting." I plucked a couple of tissues from the package in the console and handed them to her. "I think he had good reason to be upset with you. And I think you know that."

She blew her nose. "I guess."

"But this isn't about anger. This is about love. Your father loves you. I love you. Mrs. Ballantine and all the members of the Committee love you."

Tears filled her eyes. "Josh doesn't love me like I love him. If he did he'd—"

89

"He'd do what you want?"

"Yes!"

"No matter what *he* wanted to do? No matter if he didn't enjoy what you wanted to do? No matter if he couldn't afford it, or it conflicted with his job or cut into his study time?"

"Yes." The pout returned. "If he loved me he would."

"So, what I hear you saying is that all the time, every time, he should do what you want?"

The pout faltered.

I said nothing more, but picked up my phone and brought up the tiny picture of Dave. Even in a shot the size of my pinky, he was a fine-looking man.

"Are you calling my dad?"

"I'm thinking about it."

"What are you going to tell him?"

"I'm not sure." I traced the edge of the phone with my index finger. "Maybe I'll say he better start turning out for water aerobics with me and eating cheesy snacks, and coming along to the mall to shop for new summer sandals and stuff."

"Dad doesn't like cheese snacks all that much. And he hates shopping."

"I know. That's why I always went without him before. But from now on I expect him to suck it up and go with me to pick out clothes and shoes. I expect him to prove he loves me."

"But he has horrible taste." Allison made a gag-me motion. "If he helps you pick out stuff you'll look like a bag lady. Or a groupie for some band from the olden days."

Olden days meaning more than ten years ago.

"And he'll get all jittery and sweaty. That's how he gets when I ask him to take me shopping."

"I know." I twisted my lips in what I hoped was a wolfish grin. "And I'm planning to spend hours and hours at the mall. I'll probably go to every store at least twice."

"He'll be miserable," Allison said in a voice more sympathetic than self-centered.

"*Really* miserable." I managed an evil laugh. "But if he loves me like he says he does, he'll have to do everything I want. Right?"

Allison's puffy eyes narrowed. "Are you trying to teach me a lesson?"

"What do you think?"

"Yeah. You are." She blew her nose again and wiped her eyes. "But it's not the same thing with you and Dad."

"Why not?"

"You have cars and jobs and you make money."

"Josh has a car and a job and makes money."

"But you're old!"

Ouch.

That hurt. I was standing in the shade of 40, but no way was I old. I went on the defensive. "Not compared to Dario and Mrs. Ballantine."

"You know what I mean." Allison threw the tissue on the floor. "You've already had all your fun."

Double ouch.

Now Dave and I were not only old, we were embalmed, mummified, preserved behind glass on a top shelf in a dusty room that hadn't been opened in years.

Allison folded her arms and went into heavy-duty sulk mode. "Can we go home now?"

"I don't know. Home is right by the river. And there are knives at home. And beer. And maybe some pills." Probably all over-the-counter pills, but I imagined they'd be dangerous if she took enough. "If we stay right here and I stay right next to you, I know you're safe. But if we go home and you run upstairs and lock your door, I'll worry. So, *should* we go home?"

Allison chewed at her lower lip and thumped her heels on the muddy brown carpet in the footwell. "I'm still mad at Josh for changing his mind. Well, maybe not just for changing his mind, but for not telling me he was thinking about changing his mind until after he did it, for not *discussing* it like people are supposed to do when they're going steady."

I nodded. "That seems like a fair analysis. I'd be mad if that happened to me. Especially because graduation is tomorrow and there isn't a lot of time to make plans." I paused to let that sink in and then went on. "Plans like having a spa evening with some of your girlfriends, or shopping with Mrs. Ballantine."

A smile twitched Allison's lips and I guessed she was making a mental list of the items she'd need to buy in order to feel better.

"I'm still really, really mad at Josh, but I'm not going to hurt myself," she said. "We can go home now."

"You're sure?"

"Yes."

"Positive?"

"Yes. But only if we stop for ice cream on the way."

From our present position, ice cream wasn't on the way— unless I triangulated on Honolulu. But that was a sacrifice I was willing to make.

I turned the key and started up the engine. "Ice cream it is."

An hour later, full of sugar and chocolate and butterfat, we arrived at 90 Columbia Lane in time to see Ardie and Verna steering Sybil toward a limousine. From the way Sybil was dragging her feet and demanding that they release her, it didn't take a genius to conclude she was going with them against her will. From the way she was dressed—in bunny slippers and a fuzzy pink bathrobe—I guessed she'd had no notice and been given no time to change.

The intervention was underway.

Chapter 10

"What's going on?" Allison asked as we eased past on the way to my parking spot. "Where are they taking Sybil?"

"I don't know where they're taking her. I seem to be out of that section of the loop. But what's going on is an intervention."

"Huh? What's that?"

"It's an attempt to make someone see they're going down the wrong road and get them to change their ways."

"Sybil was driving on the wrong road?"

"I'm using the concept of a road as a metaphor." I paused, wondering if Allison paid even a little attention in English class and knew what that meant. Deciding this wasn't the time to fill a possible educational gap, I went on. "Sybil has been spending far too much time, and money, in casinos. We're afraid she's addicted to gambling."

Mrs. B emerged from her condo with an enormous picnic basket and slipped inside the limo after Ardie.

"So when there's an intervention, you get to ride in a limousine and have fancy crackers and stuff?"

"Apparently you do if Mrs. B organizes the intervention." I opened my door and eased out of the car, feeling like I'd gained five pounds since our stop for ice cream.

Allison followed suit as the limo drove off. "Is there a special place for having interventions?"

"I don't think so. Lots of people do them in their living rooms. But I'm guessing Mrs. B wanted to take Sybil away from her normal routine."

"They'd better make sure she doesn't get near a computer," Allison said. "I'm pretty sure she plays card games on line."

That could explain why she was in her bathrobe late in the afternoon. Playing on the computer meant she wouldn't have to get dressed and leave home to lose money. And that meant she could be deeper in debt than we'd imagined. "Why don't you text Mrs. B and tell her that?"

Allison, usually quick on the draw with her cellphone, hesitated.

"You won't be ratting Sybil out. It's for her own good."

I cringed inwardly as Allison sent the message. I hated that expression. I'd heard it a hundred times when I was a kid. And here I was using it. But this *was* for Sybil's benefit. Even if she wouldn't see it that way. "The intervention won't work if she's gambling while the others think she's sleeping and they aren't watching her."

And their attempt to alter her behavior might not work anyway. Sybil had to be ready to change.

I opened the door and was greeted by two tail-wagging dogs and a several pages of notes fluttering on the bulletin board. Allison patted Lola and Cheese Puff while I read Verna's message and confirmed what the sight of Lola tipped me to— we'd be dog sitting while the intervention was underway.

"It's not going to be easy to get Sybil to stop." Allison led the way along the hallway, the dogs trailing behind. "She really loves those machines. And she wins lots of times."

"But not *every* time. And probably not more than half the time. I bet if you added it up, you'd see she lost a lot more than she won."

95

Allison pondered that. "Okay, but she always says we shouldn't be stingy and not have fun, and we should live for today because we can't take it with us."

"Well, the last part is right."

At least I assumed it was. But the assumption was based on a lack of knowledge about information to the contrary.

"What about the stingy part?" Allison held up dog cookies and gave the hand command for the dogs to sit. Lola plopped her bottom down immediately. Cheese Puff eyed the cookie as if considering whether it was worth the effort, decided it was, whined, and pawed at Allison's ankle in a bid to get her to skip over his part of the deal and deliver the treat.

"No way," Allison said. "No cookie until your butt hits the floor."

He yipped and pawed again.

"No. Being cute and whining doesn't entitle you to be pushy and always get what you want." Her tone indicated she didn't grasp the irony of her statement.

He yipped once more.

Lola gave a low growl, raised a paw, and pressed it against his back.

Cheese Puff's beady little eyes widened, but he assumed the position. After Lola got her reward, he snapped up the cookie offered to him.

"Because Dad can be pretty stingy," Allison said as if there hadn't been a gap in the conversation. "Like about my allowance and clothes and stuff I need."

I stifled a laugh. If Allison genuinely needed something, Dave was on it. But she had yet to make the distinction between needing and wanting.

"Your father isn't stingy. He's cautious about what he spends and he's careful to save a little every month."

96

Wondering if I'd need it again before September, I put my school bag in the hall closet. "The trick is not to spend all your money having fun today, because when you wake up tomorrow you won't have enough for food and rent and heat."

Allison got a diet soda from the refrigerator. "Did Sybil run out of money?"

"I don't know. But I suspect things were heading in that direction. She was asking friends for loans."

"Did you lend her any?"

"No. First because I don't have much to lend. And second because I knew she'd gamble it away and want more."

Allison flopped on the sofa and got busy with her phone. The dogs, sensing no more cookies would appear in the immediate future, stretched out in a patch of sun beside the door to the deck. "Gambling's like taking drugs, huh? People get hooked."

"Some people. Not everyone."

"So I can play the slot machines when I'm old enough?"

"Yes. When you're old enough, and you have money of your own, you can do that. But if you're smart, you'll play with money you can afford to lose. Otherwise you might as well take a pile of bills and set them on fire."

"And if I lose a bunch of money, Mrs. B will stick me in a limousine and take me somewhere." Allison frowned and sipped her soda. "If she's still around when I'm old enough to go to casinos."

I felt a cold clutching in my stomach. Mrs. B had been in my life for only a few years, but I couldn't imagine life without her. She took good care of herself and could afford quality medical attention if she needed it. Still, like the rest of us, she was mortal.

"If she wants to drive with me again," Allison said in a tone indicating huge sacrifice, "I won't get all hissy so she doesn't get stressed out. Old people shouldn't get stressed. It's not good for their hearts."

To my credit, I didn't point out that stress wasn't good for anyone, including me, the woman she'd just stressed out with talk of suicide. This wasn't time to revisit that. This was time to plug in a movie and make popcorn.

Since I'd steered clear of promising Allison I wouldn't tell Dave about her latest crisis and her talk of suicide, I felt justified in sending him a lengthy e-mail while Allison was absorbed in *The Breakfast Club*. When he got home, she protested that she was over Josh and never wanted to see him again and wouldn't do anything stupid. Dave said that was fine, but sat her down for a long and wide-ranging talk about love, life, and the limits of his ability not to freak out when she threatened suicide. When he joined me on the deck to watch the sunset, he looked as tired as I've ever seen him, so tired I doubted a blood transfusion and a quart of strong coffee would have restorative effects.

"Think you got through to her?"

"No clue. She's always been good at knowing when to tell me what I want to hear, whether she means it or not." He sipped his beer and set the bottle on the deck beside his lounge chair, then took my hand. "Not like you. I can always count on you to tell me the truth."

I winced and waited for the rest.

"Except when you don't. Except when you go off on one of your little spy missions."

"They're not spy missions. They're, um, investigative endeavors."

"Unofficial and sometimes uninvited investigative endeavors."

I let that go by without a response. Yes, the detecting I'd done was "unofficial" by his law enforcement standards. And, okay, sometimes it was "uninvited" if you defined that as meaning Dave or other "official" investigators hadn't asked me to help.

Dave peered at me, squinting into the low, red sun. "You're not on a USUIE mission now, are you?"

"No."

"Are you thinking of taking one on?"

"No."

(For the record, that was not because I'd sworn off USUIEs, but because I hadn't come across a possibility.)

He squinted harder. "You'd tell me if you were, wouldn't you? So we could discuss safety issues and backup plans? It makes sense, doesn't it? After what happened the last time?"

What happened the last time was a man who'd gotten away with murder twenty years earlier tried to drown me when the victim's sister and I started taking a fresh look at the case. Shortly before my submersion, Dave discovered what I was up to and admitted he knew "snooping" was in my nature. He swore he would no longer try to stop me, even though he feared one of my USUIEs would result in me wearing a shroud. Without playing the guilt card, he said his life would be bleak without me.

Although I hadn't asked at the time, later I wondered if he hoped exposing his emotional underbelly would make me reconsider my course of action. Because it had. But reconsidering brought me to the same conclusion about that cold case—someone needed to right a wrong. And, being unencumbered by legalities and already in the act of digging for unrevealed information, it was apparent that someone was yours truly.

"I'd tell you if I was actively investigating something," I said, making sure the fingers he didn't have a grip on were crossed and out of his sight. "Of course I'd tell you."

"Yeah." His laugh was as bitter as a bowl of arugula dressed with vinegar. "What you mean by 'actively investigating' is 'up to your neck' in it. And probably in big trouble."

Obviously denying that would be a waste of time and breath, so I changed the subject without a segue and told him about what Allison and I had witnessed when we got home.

"A limo?" Dave marveled. "Trust Mrs. Ballantine to do it in style. Wonder where they went."

"My guess is someplace remote but with all the amenities, including gourmet meals."

"Sounds like a slice of paradise to a man who suffered through another day of Harvey's tantrums."

"I thought Harvey was escorted from the building yesterday?"

"He got in this morning. Twice."

"Twice?"

"Once because the guy manning the front desk hadn't read the memo. The other time he tagged along with the woman who stocks the vending machines."

"Sheesh. Good thing he's not a terrorist."

"At least I might be justified in shooting a terrorist," Dave muttered. "The second time he got in I was in a meeting. By the time I got back and found him, he'd mangled the office."

"Mangled?"

"Pulled files from drawers, knocked books off shelves, tore up papers, snapped pencils and pens, smashed the computer keyboard, and broke two chairs. Wouldn't stop. Refused to speak to me. Refused to listen to me."

"Wow. What did you do?"

"Stood back. Let him go at it. Waited for backup. Thought about how glad I am I have a home and you and Allison and our friends and even that scruffy mutt of yours."

I squeezed his fingers.

He raised my hand to his lips and nibbled my knuckles, his stubble brushing the back of my hand. Have I mentioned lately how much I love stubble? I got a chill that wasn't due to the breeze off the river, and hoped Allison would soon abandon the TV and go to her room so we could go to ours.

"If the intervention works out for Sybil, maybe we could get Mrs. B to take on Harvey as her next project."

"Someone should." He kissed my palm and folded my fingers over the spot. "He looks like he's seven seconds away from a heart attack." He squinted at the thick rind of red sun on the horizon. "It's almost 9:00 and the sun is still up. What time is sunset?"

A question many of us in the Northwest ask in June when the hours of daylight are about double those of darkness. As we approach the winter solstice, we're prone to question why the sun sets well before 5:00 PM and doesn't manage to top the eastern horizon until long after 7:00 AM. Not that we get that much actual sunlight in the winter—unless you count what filters through the clouds. And, just so you know, I don't.

"Soon," I told Dave. "A few more minutes."

"Too long." He nibbled my knuckles again. "Way too long."

"I agree. But we're responsible adults. With a teenager in crisis. We need to monitor her emotional condition until she's asleep."

"Tomorrow's Saturday, so there's no school. She could be awake for hours."

"And hours," I agreed.

Dave groaned. "I remember when I was a kid and thought when I grew up I could do whatever I wanted, whenever I wanted."

"You could if you didn't have any morals. Or a conscience. Or a caring nature."

He sighed and kissed my palm again. "Will you take a rain check?"

"From you? Always."

When I woke up and reached out for Dave, my fingers found only a sheet of paper with a scrawled note. "Went in to clean up Harvey's mess. Call if Allison needs me. Call if you need me. Call to order dinner."

That last sentence brought a smile to my lips. A day without cooking was . . . well, it was a day of eating something tasty. It was also a day without cleaning up after cooking.

I pried myself from the bed, leaving Lola stretched out on the carpet beside the dresser and Cheese Puff lounging on the dirty clothes Dave removed last night and almost—but not quite—got in the hamper. After a quick check to make sure Allison was okay, I ambled downstairs. My first cup of coffee was barely cool enough to drink when a hammering at the door clued me to the arrival of my sister.

"I'm coming," I shouted.

Then I took my sweet time.

"Good, you've got coffee," Iz said by way of greeting.

"Feel free to help yourself," I responded after she'd tromped to the kitchen and poured a cup.

102

(For the record my sarcasm, as usual, was wasted—as both you and I knew it would be. Why do I bother? Well, a sharp tongue, like a sharp knife, needs to be honed to keep its edge. And the brain that thinks up sharp remarks needs practice. And my sister makes a perfect target because I feel she deserves what I dish out and because she doesn't feel the sting of my slings and arrows.)

"Already did," she pointed out as she rooted through the refrigerator, pulling out marmalade, bread, ham, cheese, and mustard. And, yes, it all went into her sandwich along with a garnish of chopped green olives and carrot slices. To each his own, right?

"Had a strange experience last night," she mumbled as she chewed.

I made myself comfortable in Cheese Puff's chair, sipped, and waited for elaboration. It came in syllables squeezed out around another mouthful. "Thought you could make sense of it."

I felt mildly flattered until she added, "Seeing as how most of your friends are nowhere near normal and this place is oddball central."

Firing up my substitute teacher's glare, I hit her with a frosty silence. Iz didn't notice.

"So, I shadowed Sharlene again yesterday." She hunkered on the sofa. "Same two places. Same out-to-lunch clients."

"Is 'out-to-lunch' one of the official terms you learned in class?"

Iz batted that aside like it was a mosquito. "Got home and couldn't find the notebook where I've been keeping track of important stuff and techniques." She mimed writing. "Went back after dinner, early enough so they wouldn't be in bed. But it was seriously strange."

103

The words "seriously strange covered a lot of ground, but in my life and with my circle of friends, as Iz said, they were comparable to the words "business as usual." So I asked, "How strange? And how seriously?"

She raised a finger signaling the need to chew off another hunk of her sandwich. When she spoke, her voice was mushy. "Perry was all stirred up. Anxious. Stressed. Confused. Searching drawers and cabinets for more coins to give his son for the ferry. Wouldn't believe me when I told him there's no ferry from Reckless River."

Chapter 11

"There was a ferry years ago. But I bet the bridge was built before he was born. Maybe he's remembering his father and mother talking about it."

"Who knows?" Iz shrugged. "I played along. Helped him search. Even scattered all the change I had on me for him to find."

"Did he calm down?"

"Some. He said the coins I put out weren't old enough and the dollar bill I offered was worthless. But he took them anyway. Said they'd have to do until he found older ones." She wiped her mouth on her sleeve. "I'm worried about that old guy. I don't think he should be on his own. Especially not at night."

The compassion in my sister's voice both surprised and pleased me. Perhaps she had a feel for this. "Did you find your notebook?"

"No. So I went to Mavis Dupree's place. She was dolled up even more than the other morning and sitting on a sofa in the living room sipping champagne with a guy named John. Maybe he's a grandson or nephew or something." Iz chomped more of her sandwich. "While I was hunting for my notebook, she told him to go on upstairs to room number 5. And here's the strange part. She told him not to take more than an hour this time."

105

"Hmmm." I wondered whether I should reverse my thinking and share the information I'd gleaned about Mavis Dupree's past.

"Now here's another strange part. After he went upstairs, Mavis told me not to be shy about my 'proclivities' because she wasn't born yesterday and had seen it all. Told me to take a seat and tell her what I was looking for in a woman."

I didn't want to ask. But I had to. "And did you?"

"Not on your life. I'm not exactly sure what 'proclivities' entail, but I know they're personal and I'm not talking about them with strangers. And, besides, I stopped looking when I met Pen—" Iz dropped the crust of her sandwich and jumped to her feet, rattling the mug I'd set on the coffee table. "I'm late. Call Penelope and tell her I, uh, lost track of the time while we were talking about, um, our parents."

"Nope."

"Please."

"Not happening." I crossed my arms. "Not lying to Penelope for you."

Iz glowered.

I smiled. I'd seen more potentially explosive expressions on the faces of freshmen instructed to take their seats and put their phones away.

"After all I've done for you," she said in a tone that implied sacrifice and suffering on a level that would qualify her for sainthood.

"I'm not lying to Penelope," I repeated. "She deserves better."

Before Iz could ask exactly what I meant by that and whether I was implying she wasn't good enough for Penelope, her cellphone rang. "We'll have this out later," she informed me.

"I can hardly wait," I murmured to her retreating backside.

Two seconds later the long-suffering front door slammed and I sighed with relief. I hadn't divulged what I knew about Mavis, so Iz hadn't felt compelled to deliver a lecture on the exploitation of women. And she'd split before the conversation had come back around to Perry's need for coins for the ferry.

Although the city of Reckless River is right on the Columbia, and although there are boats aplenty on that wide river, as I'd told Iz, there hasn't been a ferry close by in many years. And, as Iz had told me earlier, Perry's son was dead and wouldn't be paying for a ferry ride across the Columbia, or any river—except perhaps for that mythological waterway, the Styx.

I fired up my laptop and did a quick search to refresh memories made in middle school when I'd been assigned a report on the topic. Charon was the ferryman and he had to cross the Acheron as well as the Styx, to get souls to the world of the dead. He collected a coin from each passenger, an obolos or a danake. (Don't ask me how to pronounce the names of those ancient coins.) No coin, no passage. Your soul would wander for a century.

I read it all again, taking in the section about relatives putting a coin in the mouth of the deceased. One coin. A single coin. That's all Charon seemed to require. So why was Perry giving out coins almost every night and hunting for more?

Not for one minute did I believe his son's ghost was prowling around telling him to cough up money.

Okay, to be honest, the thought crossed my mind, but it lingered for only a few seconds, not a full minute. It's not that I don't believe in ghosts, because I do. At least, I believe in the possibility of ghosts. For all I knew, it was possible our souls or our essences could get stuck between this earth and . . . well, wherever. I also believe it's possible that remnants of pain or

107

love or thought may linger and our senses may, in an unconscious kind of way, pick up on more than we can explain in a logical, rational manner. And I further believe the mind is a strange and wonderful thing and capable of creating fictions so convincing we see them as fact.

So, while I wasn't sure the ghost of Perry's son visited him often, I was sure Perry believed that. Perhaps the belief sprang from a desire to have a few more moments together, a need to wipe out harsh words spoken when last they met. Or perhaps he hoped to assure himself there was an afterlife. But if the ghostly visitations had originated from a need for soothing and comfort, they now seemed to cause stress.

As for Mavis, the man sipping champagne had been no ghost. So who was he? And why was he—?

My cellphone rang.

Mrs. B's photo popped up.

About time.

"Where are you and how is the intervention going?"

"We're at a lodge on the underside of the left foot of nowhere. The last mile of road was so narrow I thought the driver would have to remove the fenders. But the view is stunning, the rooms are exquisite, and the food is marvelous. Unfortunately, we're not here on vacation. More unfortunately, the intervention is going slowly."

"How slowly?"

"Extremely similar to the rate of progress Allison is making toward driving in a safe and sane manner."

"So, not only slowly, but erratically."

"Excellent word choice. Sybil doesn't perceive that her gambling is a problem." Mrs. B sighed. "Yes, I knew that getting her to recognize and accept would be the first hurdle, but I didn't imagine it would be such a *high* hurdle. She's denying and arguing in a very loud voice and making nasty comments about everything and everyone, including the cuisine and the poor chefs and waiters. I've doubled my usual rate of tipping, but I fear that won't be enough."

Since Mrs. B's usual rate of tipping was at least 50% more than the high end of what was recommended, I imagined the service staff would be willing to put up with a few hateful remarks. And, knowing Sybil, I doubted they were as caustic as some I've overheard in the hallways at Captain Meriwether.

"I hate to admit it, because I've always thought of Sybil as a flighty person without a great deal of backbone, but she's wearing us down. Last night Ardie made a bed in front of the door from our suite into the corridor and I took the sofa beside the door to the bedroom Verna shared with Sybil. Verna normally wakes up if a bird drops a feather, but she didn't hear a thing when Sybil tied her sheets together and tried to escape over the balcony. She was in her nightgown." Mrs. B lowered her voice to a whisper. "Without a stitch on under it."

I tried to stop my brain from creating a mental image of the scene. I couldn't. I suspected I'd require many days and several adult beverages to erase the picture from my gray cells. "When did you realize she was gone?"

"When she called for help." Mrs. B chuckled. "Sybil's always been a poor judge of distance."

While I pondered what that meant, Mrs. B said, "A rope made from only two sheets doesn't reach from the third floor to the ground."

I chuckled along with her. "At least Sybil wasn't determined enough to escape that she let go and dropped."

"Small mercy. Perhaps there's hope. Did I mention she's having withdrawal symptoms?"

"What kind of symptoms?"

109

"Finger twitches. Eye twitches. Arm twitches."

"Like she's playing a slot machine?"

"Exactly. But I've called for a doctor to check her over. And I'll ask him to give her something so she can sleep tonight. So *we* can sleep."

"Good idea."

Notice that I didn't ask where and how Mrs. B found a doctor willing to make a house call on a Saturday in such a remote area. "Persuasive charm" was practically her middle name. And money greased the wheels that charm alone couldn't turn fast enough.

"Now, before I return to trying to reason with someone who doesn't seem to listen, what's new with you, dear?"

In the interest of freeing her to get on with the intervention, I left out my sister's report on Perry's ghost and the man Mavis was entertaining, and unloaded details of Allison's crisis and Harvey's meltdown. Mrs. B murmured surprised or soothing comments at appropriate intervals. I wound up with Dave's wish that she'd stage an intervention for Harvey.

A long silence followed that remark and then she said, "That idea isn't completely without merit."

Sometimes Mrs. B can make a simple statement sound complex, so I wasted a few seconds trying to parse it. "Huh?"

"You don't happen to have his phone number, do you?"

I scrambled for the low-tech address book buried in a stack of well-worn to-do lists on a corner of the counter. Sure, Dave and I had cellphones, but he believed in backing up systems with other systems. I flipped to G for Goodspeed and found a blank page. I flipped to H for Harvey and found a list of hamburger stands. I flipped to N for Nospeed, Harvey's nickname, and there it was. I reeled it off and, before I could ask what she had in mind, Mrs. B disconnected.

Before I could do much wondering, Cheese Puff and Lola demanded, in their unique doggie ways—Cheese Puff by shoving his food dish against the base of the stove and Lola by sitting and fixing a longing gaze on the sack of kibble on a pantry shelf—to be fed. I'd taken care of that and escorted them across the deck and down the short flight of wooden steps to the tiny rose garden to leave deposits on the bark mulch, when I spotted Jim jogging toward me on the trail along the river. He'd dressed for summer in a T-shirt and khaki shorts, but from the neck up he was a vision of winter holidays with his flowing white beard and hair, his pink cheeks and twinkling eyes.

"Heard from Muriel?"

"Just a few minutes ago. She—"

"Got coffee enough to share?"

Silly question. Jim was a founding member of the Committee and therefore a person to whom I owed a debt of gratitude I'd be paying back for the rest of his life. "If I don't, I'll make a fresh pot."

"Don't need much." He followed me across the deck. "A little jolt should do it."

I eyed the pot. "Coincidentally, that's all I have."

"Plenty." Jim poured, filling a mug to the halfway point. "Feel like I'm running on fumes this morning."

That was pretty much how I felt every morning—or at least those when I had to haul myself to a subbing assignment. If I lived to be Jim's age—whatever that might be—I expected I'd be thrilled to have fumes. And then, of course, there was Jim's definition of "fumes," a definition I bet squared with my definition of "tank full of high-powered gas."

111

Jim raised the coffeepot, sniffed it, and peered through the glass. "Need to run some vinegar through and clean it up."

And, because he was a get-right-to-it kind of guy, he got right to it, pulling a gallon of white vinegar from the pantry and filling the pot to the halfway point and adding water. As he dumped it into the well on the coffeepot, someone knocked at the door. My initial reaction was to wince and cringe, but then I realized the knock had been an actual knock, not the kind of battering ram thud favored by my sister.

"Not Iz," Jim said. "Saw her walking to her car. Heard her telling Penelope she'd be there soon. Not Bernina. Past few months she's been tossing in a little kick with her knocking."

"Good to know," I called as I trucked along the hallway. "I'll listen for that and hide in the pantry if necessary."

So, without peering through the peephole, I flung the door wide.

Chapter 12

"Strawberries." Paulette offered a cardboard carton of plump berries. "Fresh, ripe, red, and delicious."

My mouth watered. "I'll buy the whole box."

"No buying. They're yours. I traded a little decorating advice for enough to fill the back seat of my car."

Since Paulette's car was as small and sleek as she was, that didn't seem like a great trade. "What was the advice?"

"Burn everything and start over." She laughed. "Their farm is a vision. The layout is stunning. The use of space for crops is amazing. The barn is beautiful. But their house . . ."

She shoved the flat of berries into my hands and brushed past. "I need coffee."

Uh oh.

I raced after her, staying on the living room side, blocking her view and herding her toward the deck. "Jim's cleaning the coffeemaker. Why don't we sit outside until he's done and I can make a fresh pot?"

Paulette turned toward the kitchen. "Good morning, Jim."

"Morning." His voice cracked in the middle of the word and I saw he was looking over her shoulder at the furniture he'd repositioned. "This is, uh, going to take a half hour or so and the smell of hot vinegar isn't right up there with the finest perfume. Why don't you run over to the little bakery on the south end of downtown? They have great coffee. And croissants."

I couldn't remember ever hearing Jim run off at the mouth like this. A sure sign he hadn't worked out a plan to control and/or contain the explosion sure to occur when Paulette spotted what he'd done.

"Well . . ." Paulette cocked her head, considering. "I've been wanting to check that place out, but we should clean the berries first. And pack and freeze the ones you can't eat in the next few days."

"Leave the berries." Jim practically shouted. "I'll take care of them."

"Great." I set the flat on the dining room table, staying between Paulette and the living room. "I'll get my purse while you warm up the car."

"It's June," Paulette reminded me. "It's 75 degrees. And sunny."

"Oh, right. Silly me." I edged around her toward the staircase. "I'll get my purse while you cool down the car."

"It's a convertible."

"Oh, right. I forgot."

From the corner of my eye, I spotted Jim waving a couple of twenties. "Forget the purse. I don't need the purse." I snatched the bills. "Look. Here's money. Let's go."

Paulette didn't move. "What is wrong with you?"

"Nothing. I'm fine. Fine and dandy." I tugged at the strap of her designer purse like I'd tug at a leash. "Hunky dory. Rarin' to go."

Paulette pressed one hand against my forehead. "You're feverish. Your face is flushed and your eyes are too bright. Lie down on the sofa and I'll make some iced tea."

"I don't feel like lying down." Especially not on the repositioned sofa. "I don't have a fever."

"She was outside," Jim added. "With the dogs. Waiting in the sun while Prince Cheese Puff decided where to lift his royal leg."

Cheese Puff, who had jumped to a dining room chair and was sniffing at the berries, yipped and followed up with a snarl. In Puffster language he was calling Jim a beard-faced liar.

"Well, lie down for a few minutes," Paulette instructed. "Cool off before we go."

The coffeepot gurgled, spit, and released a hot cloud of vinegary steam.

"Sure stinks, doesn't it?" Jim fanned the air with a potholder. "And it's hot in here. You two get going. Barbara will cool off on the way."

Paulette's eyes narrowed. "You two are as jumpy as bugs on a hot griddle."

Jim choked out a laugh. "That's a good one. Bugs on a griddle. Funny. Huh, Barbara?"

I managed a lame chuckle. "Great imagery."

"That does it." Paulette clenched her fists and planted them on her hips. "Something's wrong with you. Both of you. Have you been drinking?"

"No," we protested in unison.

"Smoking?"

"No," we chorused.

"Then why are you trying to rush me out of here." As she spoke, she nodded toward the door, her gaze sweeping past me as she did. Her eyes widened. "What did you do?"

Without even a second to confer and agree on a plan, and with separate playbooks started during early childhood and added to through years of denial, obfuscation, feigned

115

ignorance and/or innocence, and verbal tap dancing, Jim and I managed to land on the same page.

"Huh?" I asked.

"Do?" he queried.

"In the living room!"

"Where?" we harmonized.

"There." She pointed. "And there. Everything's been moved."

"Moved?" Jim echoed. "Moved where?"

"What do you mean by that?" I chimed in. "It's all right there."

"It's all there. But it's all been moved."

Jim scratched his head. "Maybe it's me, but that doesn't make sense."

I tipped a thumb up behind Paulette's back, bowing to his mastery. I also made a mental note to pry for details of his childhood and compare them to my own. I took a step closer to Paulette. "Are you sure you're not the one who has a fever?"

Glowering, Paulette stomped to the sofa. Even though she wore sandals that couldn't have been more than size 5, and even though the living room is carpeted, she managed a darn good stomp. "Moved. Shifted. Angled."

"Really?" I cocked my head and squinted. "I hadn't noticed. But I don't have the decorating sense you do."

"No, you don't. That's exactly why, doing the best I could with the few decent pieces you possess and the constraints of your budget, I selected and placed everything for you in the best arrangement possible."

Ouch.

That was me, put in my place.

Jim framed his view of the room with his thumbs and forefingers and managed the kind of expression you might see on the face of a man who just found dill pickles in his wallet. "You know, it seems things possibly have shifted slightly. You could be right."

"*Could* be?" Paulette fumed. "I *am* right. Someone moved everything I arranged."

"I hadn't noticed until now." Jim tilted his frame and moved it back and forth. "Was there an earthquake this morning?"

"No." Paulette pointed to the carpet. "And if there had been, I'd see tracks where things shifted."

Jim's Adam's apple bobbed as he swallowed air. Would he crack? Would he own up to what he'd done? Would he throw himself on his sword? And if he did, would Paulette excuse me for not moving the furniture back into position when I noticed?

The answers were: possibly, possibly, possibly, and never.

To spare him, I choked out a suggestion of my own. "Poltergeist?"

"Really?" A smug smile lit Paulette's face. "Have you noticed other evidence of this spirit?"

"Um, uh, yes." I crossed my fingers, told myself this was a ghost story and not a lie, and went for it. "Things fell off the shelf in the pantry. Things that were far back on the shelves."

"When?"

"Last night."

"And the night before," Jim added. "Dave told me."

"Ah. So the poltergeist has only been around a few days?"

Jim and I nodded.

Paulette's smile went to gotcha level. She set her miniscule pink leather purse on the arm of the sofa, knelt, leaned forward with her head at an angle, and examined the area around the sofa, coffee table, and television stand. "This was moved weeks ago," she said in a voice that held not an iota of uncertainty. "Maybe months."

"Really?" I asked in a voice I pumped up with what I hoped was awed amazement. "How can you tell?"

She ran a hand across the carpet. "By the nap."

I wasn't about to question her pronouncement. If there was a TV show called *CSI: Décor*, Paulette could have been the lead investigator.

"Nap?" Jim turned off the spitting coffeemaker. "I could use a nap. Maybe I'll come back and finish this later."

I shook my head and skewered him with a substitute teacher glare. No way was I letting him escape.

"Or I could stay and finish cleaning up and nap this afternoon," he said with a whimper.

Brushing the carpet with her fingers, Paulette crawled past the TV stand to Cheese Puff's favorite chair and on to what I considered my deskette, a wooden stand on wheels Mrs. B had purchased for me when I sacrificed my space in the downstairs office so Dave could create a man cave. The stand was designed with a file drawer and two shallow shelves where I could tuck my laptop and a book or two. A lamp sat on top, and beside it was an orange ceramic gnome. I'm not a huge fan of gnomes, but Allison had given me this one for Mother's Day and insisted I place it where we could all see it. "I picked it out myself and bought it with my own money," she'd said. "Because you like cheese crackers and Cheese Puff. They're orange, just like the gnome."

Paulette got to her feet, staring at the wooden stand as if it was a termite mound and the gnome an anteater about to dig in for a feast. "What is that?"

"That?" Jim asked. "What that?"

"That what?" I asked at the same time.

118

"Knock it off," Paulette shouted. "You sound like a pair of gibbering baboons with heat rash."

"Good imagery," Jim whispered.

"Enough," Paulette said in a murderous tone.

We clammed up.

"Now." She smoothed her denim skirt and tucked her crisp pink blouse in a little tighter. "I'll ask the question again, and I'll expect a serious and honest answer. Okay?"

We nodded like a couple of those toy dogs you see in the rear windows of cars.

"What is this orange creature doing in the living space I designed?"

"Gnome one knows," Jim offered.

I stifled a snicker and poked an elbow in his ribs.

"Allison gave it to me for Mother's Day," I blurted. "She bought it with money she saved from her clothing allowance."

As the owner of an expensive and expansive wardrobe, Paulette understood the sacrifice involved in diverting funds from couture to anything less than a spa treatment. As someone who knew Allison and our family dynamics well, she understood the gesture meant far more than the actual gift. She didn't exactly stop frowning, but her muscles relaxed slightly.

"I'll, uh, move it as soon as I can without hurting her feelings," I promised.

"Good. Now, about this thing. The rolling file cabinet."

She said the final two words in the same way I'd say something like toxic sludge or fried liver or ruptured appendix. "Was this thing a gift as well?"

Ha!

I had her now!

She didn't know it, but the answer to that question would cause her to do a 180. Once I invoked the name of Muriel

119

Ballantine, Paulette would dismount from her high horse so fast she might sprain both ankles. Like the rest of us, Paulette was in awe of the force of nature that was my neighbor. But I didn't give her the full answer immediately. I let her think she was pulling the truth from my lips with a tweezers.

"Actually, it *was* a gift," I said in a halting voice as I took two backward steps toward the kitchen. "It was specially made for me. And for that spot."

(For the record, I didn't know if the deskette was a special order or not, but I figured throwing that in couldn't hurt. And I had no doubt that if Mrs. B hadn't found what she was looking for in a showroom or online, she would have commissioned something without flinching at the cost.)

Paulette's frown muscles hardened once more. "Why?"

"Because after I gave up my desk in the office so Dave could have a man cave, I needed a place to keep my laptop and file bills and other stuff."

"Man cave?" Paulette swiveled toward the tiny office by the front door. "Did you tell me about that?"

"I can't remember."

I took two more steps. When I delivered my final answer, there would be a reaction of some kind and some magnitude. I wanted to be as far from the epicenter as possible.

"Ah ha. Let me rephrase my question. And bear in mind the level of trust I feel for your answers has dropped to a notch extremely close to zero. Did you *intentionally forget* to tell me about that?"

(For the record, if you feel Paulette bullies me, go with your instincts. If you feel I roll over for her rebukes like a puppy caught peeing on the floor, go with that. But, rest assured, deep down I found this entertaining. Paulette, like Mrs. B, was a take-charge person, and letting her take charge of my living room had been an act of friendship.)

While I dithered, Jim rode to the rescue. "It happened pretty fast. Right after Dave transferred to the sheriff's department."

"You might have been out of town," I added. That was a fairly safe statement since Paulette, who was married to an airline pilot, was out of town a lot.

"And a man knows what he wants in his own space," Jim said. "And where he wants it."

"Pwah." Paulette blew air between her lips.

"And where's the challenge of decorating when what you have to work with is a desk, a big-screen TV, puffy recliners, and a mini fridge used as a side table?" Jim asked in a voice more sarcastic than soothing.

"And most of the time you can't see the desk through piles of paper." I pointed along the hallway. "I keep the door closed as much as I can, but feel free to take a look."

"Pass," Paulette said after two seconds of thought. "Who gave you the file thing? And what's your excuse for not consulting me?"

"Mrs. Ballantine," I said, answering both questions at once.

Paulette blinked. She gaped. She sucked in a breath. She blinked again.

I backed up another two steps, bumping against Jim who had retreated all the way to the washer and dryer on the far side of the kitchen. "Checkmate," he whispered.

Paulette's slender fingers curled toward her palms, driving the edges of her sculpted nails into soft flesh. She sucked in another breath, chewed her lower lip and said, "Oh."

For a moment I thought she was down for the count, but then she rallied. "So, Mrs. Ballantine moved the furniture as well?"

While I hesitated, weighing whether my karma could hold up to another fib, Jim jumped in. "Yeah. Well, I gave her some help. She's in great shape, and she's feisty, but she's not up to shifting that sofa on her own."

He sounded so convincing that I could almost see Mrs. B pointing while he shoved the sofa.

Shaking her head, Paulette took a long look at the living room. "I suppose the sofa isn't that far off. And I suppose you need that thing until you can afford a larger place. But the gnome has got to go. The sooner the better."

"The gnome will roam to a brand new home," Jim promised.

Paulette groaned. "It will take more than coffee to get that out of my head." She hitched her adorable purse on her shoulder and headed for the door. "Early lunch on the deck at the fish place across the river?"

"Works for me."

"Good, because you're buying."

"Okay," I said with less enthusiasm. The fish place Paulette had in mind was upscale. Really upscale. Granted, the food and presentations were awesome, but the prices were also awesome.

"Get your purse. And make sure you have your credit card. Jim's money won't be enough. I'm ordering the lobster."

Lobster!

I shouted the word inside my head. Lobster didn't have a price listed beside it on the menu. It said something like "market price" in that space. And who knew what that would be since the critters were flown in from Maine. My budget, such as it was, would be torpedoed, blown to bits, and sunk.

Paulette gave me that smug smile again. "Don't think for one minute that I bought the whole story you handed me. I know there's more to it. But once I'm full of fresh Maine lobster, I won't care enough to try to dig out the details."

Chapter 13

Later, after watching Paulette devour lobster dripping with butter while I nibbled on a less-than-satisfying meal of salad and breadsticks, I returned home to find the condo still smelling vaguely of vinegar and Dave sprawled on the sofa. His feet were propped on the coffee table, and I was about to remind him he'd promised to kick off his shoes before doing that when I noticed he was holding a sack of frozen peas against his jaw.

"Are you okay?" I tossed my purse on the counter and sat beside him. "What happened?"

"Harvey punched me."

"Punched you? Like with his fist?"

Dave rolled his eyes.

"Okay, that was a stupid question." I pried the bag of peas from his grip and studied the swelling. "Does it hurt?"

He rolled his eyes again.

"Does it hurt *much*?"

"Only when I laugh." He winced. "Or smile. Or talk. Or chew."

"Poor baby. Are your teeth okay?"

He nodded and I handed him the bag of peas, fast becoming more soggy than frozen. "Can you talk enough to tell me how Harvey got into the office this time?"

"He didn't. Ambushed me outside. When I went for lunch."

"Did you punch him back?"

Dave shook his head and rubbed his left shoulder. "Seemed like kicking a kitten. I let him hammer on me until he wound down. He's in bad shape, so after the second punch it was like being mugged by a marshmallow."

Like I've said before, Dave is a more highly evolved person. I would have kicked Harvey into next week.

"Anyway, he got in a few more licks and then a limousine pulled up. He grabbed a suitcase I hadn't noticed, got in, and was gone."

A limousine?

I didn't have to power up more than two brain cells to come up with the name of the person who hired the limo to pick up Harvey Goodspeed. But all my gray matter couldn't figure out what Mrs. B's plan was. So I moved on. "Will you file charges against him?"

"Man's a sad case."

"So you won't? Even though he clearly assaulted you?"

"Can't see how it would help."

See what I mean about being more highly evolved? I would have filed charges as an act of revenge and a way to humiliate Harvey. But Dave wasn't the type to try to balance the scales like that.

I filled a plastic sack with ice cubes, wrapped it in a kitchen towel, and exchanged that for the limp sack of peas. Those I tossed in the refrigerator with the aim of mixing them in a tuna casserole later. After the damage Paulette's lunch had inflicted on my credit card, we'd be eating at home more than usual for the next few weeks.

Trying not to think about that, I sat beside Dave and tried to make a little happy chat to take his mind off the pain.

125

(For the record, the technique never worked for me. Pain, after all, is pain. And pain hurts. Talking about my favorite foods never once lessened the intensity by even a few degrees. Eating a favorite food, however, sometimes knocked it down—at least until the plate or bag or container was empty.)

I told him about Paulette spotting the slight rearrangement of the furniture and how Jim and I attempted to blame that on natural and supernatural forces before transferring responsibility to Mrs. Ballantine's elegant shoulders.

Dave smiled, winced, and said, "Trump card."

"Oh, yeah." I stopped there, leaving out the part about the cost of slapping down that trump card—the part about Paulette sensing there was more to the story, and especially the part about forking out for a lunch that included wine and lobster. "And before that, my sister dropped by."

"Iz doesn't drop by." He moved the ice pack to his shoulder. "She drops in. Like a meteor. Like debris from a volcanic eruption. Like baseball-sized hail. Like—"

"I get it." I raised my hands. "I stand corrected. Iz dropped *in* to give me an update on the clients she's working with as a trainee."

Dave muttered something about Iz being as trainable as a rogue elephant with an infected tooth, two sore toes, and a bad case of gas. I gave him a sour smile and went on, "She's worried about these people. They're elderly and confused about what's real and what isn't. The man thinks a ghost talks to him and the woman seems to believe she's still in business as a madam."

"A madam?" Dave's brows lifted. "Like in a woman who runs a house of prostitution?"

"Yep." I told him more about Mavis Dupree, her lifestyle, and visitors named John, at least one of whom, according to Iz, was real.

"This is what I've been telling Harvey," Dave said. "There are a lot of vulnerable people out there—some elderly, some not thinking clearly for one reason or another, and some just not fully capable of managing their finances and their lives. They don't have relatives or close friends to watch over them, and they're being taken advantage of. Guys come to the door and say their driveways need sealing or their roofs and gutters need repairing or a tree needs to come down. They're easy targets. Sitting ducks."

He paused and transferred the ice pack to his chin again.

"What can you do? And I don't mean you specifically, I mean all of us, especially families and friends. If a person wants to remain independent and stay in their home, you can't make them move. I mean, I guess you can if you're a relative and you put your foot down and get a court order or something. Or pull a Mrs. Ballantine and stage an intervention and physically carry them off. But if there's no family and no one to step in . . ."

Dave sighed. "Then it might not end well."

We sat in silence for a few moments. "Now that Harvey's out of your hair, will you be able to do something for people like that?"

"Hope so. Increase outreach and education, get more media attention, build cases and arrest more. After I get the office straight and finish the paperwork backlog and set priorities. And find some money for educational materials."

He said that last sentence with a straight face and a hopeful tone, so I had to ask, "How do you *find* money? Isn't it all accounted for in the budget?"

"Yeah. But there might be grant money. Somewhere."

"But don't you have to *apply* for a grant? Write up a proposal and project costs and write job descriptions for staff and stuff? And wouldn't you have to survey senior agencies and others to see what's already in place?"

"Yeah."

He didn't say more and I knew what he was thinking. A survey could take a lot of time—developing questions, making contacts, compiling responses. And then he'd have to write a grant. Writing wasn't his strong suit. Oh, he was fine with a few simple sentences stuck into a few short paragraphs, but anything beyond that and he went at it like Sisyphus rolling the rock, endlessly writing, rewriting, deleting, and revising.

I took his free hand. "I'll help you."

And I meant it. I'd pitch in. Of course I had no experience writing anything other than the papers required in the educational courses I'd taken. And I'd heard that grant writing was a whole different animal. But I wasn't a dummy—at least not a *total* dummy. And I was sure I could find lots of information and helpful tips on the Internet—some of it even accurate.

Time to change the subject.

I nodded at Lola, stretched out on the carpet with her back against the sofa. "Looks like Lola stopped keeping her distance."

Dave lifted one foot from the coffee table and rubbed it along her side. "I think she knows I'm in pain. Doesn't mean she's forgiven me."

"Speaking of forgiving—" I glanced at the staircase. "Is Allison up in her room?"

"No. Out by the pool. Why?"

"We need to talk about Josh and the graduation ceremony this evening."

"Allison won't go. She made that abundantly clear last night when I tried to get her to see his side of things. She said

128

she'd been abandoned and humiliated and would never get over it as long as she lived. That was right before she told me to stuff it. I doubt she's changed her mind."

"I have the same doubt, but Josh is a good kid. He's been practically part of the family for a long time. We should go to support him."

Dave shuddered. "She'll be furious."

"Not to sound flip, but that happens on a daily basis anyway."

"Yeah, but this time she'll be really furious, seriously angry. Enraged. Outraged. Any other kind of raged there is."

I couldn't argue. Images of the 1980 eruption of Mount St. Helens came to mind. I pictured forests leveled and scorched by the blast, mudslides, and a rain of ash that went on for days. "She'll get over it," I said with about as much conviction as if I'd once again vowed to lose ten pounds by Christmas.

"If you believe that, you're kidding yourself on a major scale. She'll carry the grudge for the rest of her life."

He nailed it. She'd do just that. At her age, I might have done the same. But I didn't back down. "It's the price we'll have to pay."

"The price for an evening of torture at graduation." Dave groaned louder. "Nervous, sweaty kids in funky robes, mumbled speeches, waiting half an hour to get out of the parking lot when it's over."

"It will be good practice for next year, when Allison graduates."

"*If* she graduates."

"She will, she'll pull it out at the last minute like she always does."

"Yeah, if you define pulling it out as getting a string of Ds. With her grades, her only option will be catch-up classes at the

Reckless River Community College. And she won't get in there unless Mrs. B greases the skids with a donation."

Something that wouldn't surprise me.

"Those ceremonies are so boring." He shifted the sack of ice cubes to his shoulder. "I didn't go to my own graduation. I was hoping when the time rolled around I could bribe Allison not to go to hers."

"Fat chance. No matter how funky those robes are, you don't have enough money to get her to pass up an opportunity to walk across a stage in a pair of high heels and be the center of attention at a big party."

"And get a bunch of gifts," he added.

"Speaking of that, we should give Josh a check."

"How big a check?"

I thought of that long and expensive lunch, then put the memory aside. "At least $100."

"Can we use that to buy our way out of going to the ceremony?"

I mulled that for a moment. Two things affected the answer. "Luke's graduating too. And with the intervention, I doubt Mrs. Ballantine and the others will remember. Or be able to get back here if they do."

"So we *have* to go." Dave slapped the ice pack over his eyes and moaned.

"We don't have to. But it's the right thing to do."

"I know. I know." He moaned a little more. "Will you explain that to Allison when you tell her we're going?"

"Me? You're her father."

"So?"

I pried the ice pack from his face and gave him a squint-eyed glare. "So, having meaningful talks and tough conversations is part of the job description for a dad."

He grimaced and, if a man sitting upright could do such a thing, groveled. "But you're way better at those things. You have more experience with teenagers."

"That may be true, but—and I repeat—you're her father."

He dug in his pocket and pulled out a quarter. "Flip you for it."

"No."

"Rock-paper-scissors?"

I crossed my arms. "No."

"Cut the cards?"

"No way."

"Roll the dice?"

"Forget it."

"Arm wrestle?"

"Definitely not."

"Okay." He started to stand, grinned, and sat again. "How about I pay you?"

I hesitated. After shelling out for Paulette's lobster lunch, a cash infusion would be a good thing. But I was aware of Dave's financial situation and, although he had a larger discretionary fund than I did, it wasn't huge. I suspected that what he'd offer wouldn't come close to compensating me for the pain I'd suffer in the process of telling Allison. Besides, although I'll admit to having a moral code that sometimes bent or flexed, I didn't want to appear to be the kind of person who could be bought— or at least not bought too easily or cheaply. "Not happening."

He slumped into the cushions and slapped the ice pack over his eyes again. "How long do I have to enjoy life as I know it before I tell her?"

I checked the kitchen clock and did the math out loud. "Graduation's really early. Let's estimate you'll need 30 minutes with Allison. Fifteen seconds to tell her and the rest to explain

131

your reasons and hopefully get her to listen to reason and come down from the ledge. Then you'll need to change your clothes and I'll have to freshen up a little. It will take about 20 minutes to drive out there and probably 10 to park and 10 more to walk to the amphitheater and a few minutes more to find a seat. So, that gives you approximately . . ."

I paused, making him sweat.

"Approximately what?"

"One minute before you tell her."

"Crap."

"Right. And—double crap." I thumped the back of my head against the sofa. "I just thought of something. Given the state Allison was in, do you think we should we leave her home alone and fuming?"

Dave's lips moved as if framing an answer. No words emerged.

"She told me she was over thinking about hurting herself," I said, "and maybe she meant it. But that was yesterday. This could send her into a tailspin."

"Arrggghhhh." Dave gripped the ice pack and cocked his arm.

"Throwing that won't solve anything," I cautioned. "Although if it would, I'd be okay with you knocking that gnome for a loop."

"Sometimes I hate being a responsible adult." He stood and carried the ice pack to the sink. "In fact, *most* of the time I—" He turned, a sly grin on his face. "The obvious solution is that I stay home with Allison while you go to graduation."

"That's one obvious solution." I swiped at my phone. "The other is to see if Jim is available."

"But if I don't go to graduation, it solves two problems." Dave's voice rose with excitement and conviction, and he did

132

what looked a whole lot like an end zone victory dance. "First, Allison doesn't get mad at me. And second, she's not alone."

"And third?" I prompted.

"Third? There is no third."

"There's a huge third. If you stay home, Allison transfers all the anger we would have shared onto my head. And maybe, before she calms down, she tries to get you to pick sides, or tries to turn you against me because, after all, she's your daughter and she'll always be your daughter while I'm—"

"I get it." He slouched to the sofa and sat beside me. "We're stuck, so I guess we might as well be stuck together."

Not the most romantic or relationship-building statement I'd ever heard, but it was a start.

He turned and nuzzled my neck. "Fortunately, there's no one I'd rather be stuck with."

That was more like it.

I kissed his forehead and the side of his face Harvey hadn't punched. He kissed my lips and nibbled his way down my neck. I felt my muscles turn to jelly and—

"Let's put this on hold." I wiggled from his grasp. "I've got to find cards and call Jim."

"Right." Dave moved a few inches away. "Rain check?"

"Definitely." I crossed to my rolling deskette to dig through the selection of cards I keep on hand. Anniversary? No. Thank you? No. Birthday? No. Puppies on the front and nothing written inside? They'd have to do.

I tossed them on the coffee table, tapped the icon for Jim on my cellphone, and froze.

"Crap."

"Again?"

"Don't get up. I just remembered Jim is helping Big Chill with her graduation duties out at the amphitheater."

133

Dave made no attempt to hide his relief and delight. "So we'll go with my plan?"

"With some tweaking."

"What kind of tweaking?"

"You tell Allison you insisted I go to the ceremony to support Luke. You don't let her manipulate you in any way. You don't pay her off to get her to stop whining about it. And you don't tell her—ever—that we gave Josh a check."

"Done. I'll write it now. On my account."

I handed Dave the cards. "Sign these while I get ready."

"Sure." He peeled himself from the sofa. "I'll write a check for Luke on my account too. To make up for you taking the hit."

As I showered, I realized we were, in a weird way, back to me accepting a bribe to go to the ceremony without him. Granted, I wasn't the one who would profit. In fact, I stood to be the big loser. No matter what Dave told Allison, and no matter how hard he sold his involvement in the decision-making, I expected she'd still be furious at me for not taking her side and refusing to attend.

Chapter 14

Hoping to make my escape before Allison returned from the pool, I slapped on makeup, brushed my teeth at record speed, and pulled on a pair of white slacks and a dressy top sporting a sequined hummingbird—a gift from Mrs. B. I texted Lana Dylan, Luke's mother, and asked her to save me a seat, hunted up a pair of sandals, and collected the cards from Dave as I zoomed to the door.

Allison was closing the pool gate as I approached the stop sign at the end of the parking lot. She was focused on her phone but, doing my part to keep up the relationship, I gave a cheery smile and a wave in case she looked up.

I was running late, but making a rolling stop was out of the question. Not because Reckless River police officers staked out the area, but because Bernina Burke regularly accessed security camera video and kept a list of offenders. Bernina didn't have the power to write tickets or impose fines, but she was fond of reading names and numbers of offenses at condo board meetings. When it came to shaming others, Bernina had no shame.

Laying rubber was also out of the question. For one thing, there were amusement park bumper cars with more ability to accelerate than my junker vehicle. For another, my tires didn't possess rubber to spare.

135

Graduation was all Dave had claimed it would be, but I got a thrill seeing so many kids I knew march in, some confident, some embarrassed, and most nervous. The speeches were many, but brief. The cookies Lana brought sustained us.

"I'm glad I made a special batch with dark chocolate chips and double the amount called for," she told me as I munched on my third. "Sounds like you've had a hard time with Allison."

"It's a roller coaster," I agreed. "A hormone-powered, high-speed roller coaster."

"Well, hopefully she'll do some growing up and that roller coaster won't go off the rails." She tucked hair—once more gray than blond but now the color of honey and cut in a feathery style—behind her ears and gestured to the front of the seating area where her son waited with other graduates to receive their diplomas. "I wake up every morning singing since Luke passed through his rebellious stage and his lack-of-thinking stage and his I-couldn't-care-less phase and became a human being. And every night I thank my lucky stars that you took on that hateful woman who accused him of stealing her cat and showed her for what she was and got him out of jail. And I thank the power that keeps the earth turning that Mrs. Ballantine bought that horrible burger place and started the sandwich shop and gave me a wonderful job managing it, and—"

I shushed her with a finger to my lips. "Old news."

"But I never feel I say it enough."

"Trust me, you do. And if you don't stop you'll miss Luke's name when they call it."

Lana laughed and hugged me. And she said a few more words. Magic words. "I have a sack of cookies in the car for you to take home."

When I got home hours later, however, I found out there would be no time for savoring those cookies. To be accurate, I discovered that fact when I was several blocks from 90 Columbia Lane and spotted Dave and Lola. She had her nose down and was moving at a trot and tugging at her leash while Dave jogged to stay with her and on his feet.

I screeched to a halt, fishtailing on balding tires.

"Did you see Allison?" Dave pointed back the way I'd come.

"No."

"She ran away. I fell asleep and she took off. Left a note saying she was never coming back."

"Crap."

I made the sloppiest broken U-turn on record, caught up with him and drove alongside.

"I took the blame," he panted. "Just like you told me to. And now she hates us both."

I scraped the recesses of my mind for something to say and came up with nothing that wasn't meaningless or a cliché or both. I abandoned talk and went for action. "I'll drive ahead and scan the side streets. Maybe she's headed for the bus stop."

Even as I said it, I knew it was a reach. As much as Allison loathed riding the school bus, it was a safe bet she'd loathe public transportation to a greater degree. More likely she was headed for a friend's house. The possibilities were many. I knew a few of her gal pals, but mostly by their first names. And I also knew how loyal teens were to each other. I didn't doubt some of her friends would take her side and claim she wasn't with them if I called.

I came to an intersection and peered into the twilight gloom along one street and then the other. No Allison.

I was about to drive on when I heard a faint shout and glanced in the rearview mirror. Lola was crossing the street

137

with Dave in tow. As I watched, she reached the sidewalk and, nose still to the ground, turned toward home.

Wrenching the wheel, I did a 180 in the intersection, breaking a variety of traffic rules including the one about signaling your intentions.

(For the record, I have no idea if there's a correct way to signal an illegal turn in an intersection. But the longer I drive, and the longer I observe other drivers, the more I become convinced that we need additional signal options beyond the standard right and left turns and brake lights to indicate slowing and/or coming to a stop. And we need vehicles that can read minds and activate a signal if the driver forgets or is too busy breaking laws by phoning or texting to manage that simple task. And we could use signals to signal that signals aren't working.

For example, I'd like a signal that conveyed the intention to go straight. How many times have you faced a driver across a busy intersection and wondered what that driver will do when there's a break in the cross traffic? Neither turn light is blinking, but is that because the one that should be blinking is broken, because there's a short in the wiring, because the driver forgot to hit the signal, or because he's actually planning to go straight? You won't know until he pulls out. So, if you're cautious, you stay put and try to ignore the drivers behind you leaning on their horns.

For another example, say you're behind a car going up a hill on a foggy night and, because the driver takes his foot off the gas but doesn't hit the brakes, you find yourself almost in his trunk. For situations like this, we could use a whole catalog of signals to let other drivers know you're slowing to search for an address, hunting for someone to provide directions, running out of gas, or wondering if that was a wallet in the road. But enough of this. Back to the story.)

I'd barely completed the turn when I spotted a vehicle coming toward me. Actually, the challenge would have been in *not* spotting the vehicle. It was large, moving fast, and taking its half of the road out of the middle.

And it was very familiar.

So was the driver.

Allison leaned so far forward her chin nearly touched the steering wheel she gripped with both hands.

Even from a distance I could see her eyes were wild and her mouth was set in a grim line.

This was no time to contemplate a game of chicken.

The street was narrow and lined with cars on either side. The only safe space was half a space, but this was no time to worry about legalities, whether my bumper was high enough, or whether my alignment would suffer. I yanked the wheel and squeezed in at a right angle, bouncing the front wheels on the sidewalk with a tooth-snapping, neck-cracking THWOMP.

I heard the learn-to-drive mobile thunder past.

I heard Dave shouting and Lola barking.

I heard my heart pounding in my chest and wondered if it could thump my lungs so hard they'd collapse.

But that wasn't really a problem because I wasn't using my lungs. I was holding my breath.

"Are you hurt?" Dave called.

I let out a rush of air, wheezing like a defective organ. I gulped, swallowed air like water, got some to my lungs, and wheezed it out again.

"You okay?" Dave attempted to squeeze into the narrow space between the driver's door and the rear bumper of the car beside me. When he couldn't make it, he flopped across its trunk so his face was on the same level as mine.

"I'm fine," I said in the kind of tone you might use after treading water in the middle of the ocean for, say, half a day.

"Your tires didn't blow. You were lucky. Now you have to back up," he said in the calm and rational voice a rescuer would use to instruct the exhausted swimmer to keep going a little longer. "I'd get in and do it for you, but the doors won't open more than a few inches."

I tipped my head and saw that he was right.

"That was a smart move," he said in that same calm voice. It was an impressive performance from a man who must be frantic about his daughter and screaming on the inside. "Good reflexes. Good driving."

I gave myself a virtual pat on the back. Up until that moment, no one had ever said I was a good driver. Mostly I imagined them wanting to make statements that were a variation on the theme of "To my surprise and delight, we got here without loss of life, major trauma, or damage to property." Often I was convinced they would like to add "There's a bus stop nearby, and I've been thinking I should make more use of public transportation, so I'll get home that way."

"Now," Dave said, "Lola and I will get out of the way and you take a few deep breaths. When your hands stop shaking, all you have to do is back up. Keep the wheels straight. Slide out exactly the way you went in."

Easy for him to say.

And why the heck did he bring up the shaking hands thing? I hadn't noticed, but now they seemed to be the size of fans and trembled like leaves in a stiff breeze. In a few seconds my knees got into the act, knocking together and causing my foot to slide on the brake pedal.

"Slowly," Dave cautioned.

I tried to answer, but my tongue seemed frozen. My teeth, meanwhile, chattered like castanets.

Dave reached through the open window and stroked my hair. "You're okay. You can do this. Think of it like subbing for a class filled with 50 of the most difficult kids any substitute teacher has ever come up against."

"Challenging," I managed to mutter. "We call them challenging."

"If I had your job, I bet I'd call them something a lot worse."

I forced a smile.

"We'll make a list later, okay?"

"And have a drink?"

"Definitely. But now you have a job to do."

I told myself if he could be kind and patient with all the pressure he was under, I could get my car out of this spot. And, so what if I scraped a bumper or two? That's what bumpers were for, right? And I had insurance. Plus, I had a car already sporting a vast collection of dings and scratches. A few more hardly mattered. Besides, now that I'd seen Allison in action, I knew I wasn't the worst driver on the roads.

When Dave and Lola were clear, I checked both ways for traffic, focused straight ahead through the windshield, put the car in reverse, and wished once again I could afford a newer car with a back-up camera. Then I anchored both hands on the wheel and gave the gas pedal a sharp tap.

(For the record, I know that isn't the approved method. But when I look over my shoulder, I tend to steer in the direction my head is turned.)

The car thudded off the curb and slid into the street.

"Turn the wheel," Dave called.

141

Thankfully he didn't say whether I should turn it left or right because that would have involved making a decision. More thankfully, my hands took over for my brain and turned the wheel so the car faced the direction in which Allison had gone.

Dave opened the rear door behind me and helped Lola climb in. "I hope she isn't using that car as a suicide vehicle," he said in a voice so low it was almost a whisper.

My hope was the same, but I reassured him with what passed for logic. "If that was her intention, she could have driven into the river by the condo, or smashed into a tree or a building. I think she's running away."

He slid in beside me. "Going where?"

Good question. With Mrs. B and the gang out of town and Josh out of the picture, Allison's options had dwindled. "I don't know. To a girlfriend's house? Or maybe she doesn't know where she's going. Maybe she's just getting away from us."

"I hope she doesn't get on the freeway. I hope she doesn't try to cross the bridge."

Allison knew how to get downtown and could find her way to Captain Meriwether High School, but I doubted she knew which streets fed into ramps to the freeway. As a passenger, she focused on her phone and seldom noticed scenery, signs, or landmarks. What I said was, "She may go somewhere familiar."

"The mall? The sandwich shop? The high school?"

"Maybe the high school." I speeded up. "Seniors load onto the buses there for the all-night party."

Dave didn't say anything, but I could almost hear him imagining Allison roaring up to confront Josh.

"Watch for scrapes and scratches on parked cars along the way," I advised. "Those could tell us we're on the right trail."

142

"First time I ever hoped to see damaged cars," Dave muttered as he swiveled his head left and right. "She knows how to use the brakes, doesn't she?"

I let that ride without responding. Her instructors would all have major injuries and we would have had to replace the air bags and front bumper several times if she didn't. Instead, I tossed in a reassuring fact I'd just remembered. "The tank was almost empty when she drove with Mrs. B on Tuesday. And she doesn't seem to know how to fill it." And probably didn't want to learn because a princess didn't dirty her hands with mundane chores.

While I considered pitting Allison and Cheese Puff against each other in a competition to see who felt more entitled, the school loomed ahead. I slowed, threaded my way through packs of parents heading for their vehicles, and cruised around the parking lot. A few straggling seniors were climbing aboard the fifth and final bus in line.

Dave sighed. "I don't see her. Or that urban assault vehicle."

I headed for the auxiliary lot behind the building. "Let's check around here to be sure. Then we'll strafe the lots around the mall. It will be closing soon."

Dave pounded the dash, making Lola whine. "Sometimes I'd like to lock her in her room until she's an adult."

This was no time to launch a discussion of what determined whether you were an adult, so I simply nodded. And then I had an idea. "How about locking her up until court is in session on Monday? Or threatening to? She's driving without a license. And recklessly. In a vehicle she took without permission. Aren't those grounds for arrest?"

Chapter 15

"You want me to arrest her?"

His voice was high and squeaky and fearful. I guessed he was imagining the trajectory of their relationship after he slapped cuffs on his daughter and delivered her to the juvenile jail.

"No. But I want you to let her know an officer might stop her for speeding or driving erratically. I want you to tell her she could be in major trouble if she doesn't get off the road and wait for you to come to her. And I want you to make it clear you won't be able to get her off the legal hook if she's picked up."

He mulled that as I navigated the streets to the mall. "She won't answer her phone if she sees it's me. Or you."

"But she'll check a message you leave."

I was sure of that. She'd want to know she scored against him, want to hear pain and frustration and anxiety in his voice.

He pulled his phone from his pocket. "What do I say?"

I had a dozen suggestions, but I figured it didn't much matter what he told her. Given the mood Allison was in, she'd take it the wrong way—even if she had to twist and mangle the message to find a wrong way to take it. As I circled the mall parking lot I went with, "Your daughter. Your decision."

"Thanks a heap."

Dave thought for a moment then tapped the icon for Allison's phone, waited a bit, and spoke. "I know you're hurt and angry, but when you got behind that wheel you broke the law. If you get stopped by a patrol officer, your emotional state could work against you. You could be arrested and taken to the juvenile facility. I'm your father and I love you, but I've pledged to enforce the laws. I can't—and I won't—ask for favors and special treatment." He sighed and went on, his voice cracking. "I expect that will make you even more angry, but I hope when you get some distance on the situation you'll see things in a different light. I hope you're off the road and not driving when you're listening to this, and I hope you'll call so I know you're safe."

He tapped to disconnect and groaned. "That will go down in history as the all-time worst—"

"It was fine." I scanned the last of the lots around the mall. "You said everything you needed to. Now it's up to her to reason it out."

"The part about reason is not encouraging."

I agreed, but said only, "Let's head downtown."

Dave checked his watch. "Won't everything be closed? Except the taverns?"

"The pizza parlor stays open late."

"And if she's not there?"

"Then . . . then I drop you off at home in case she comes back, and you call all the friends you can think of and anyone else she might know. Call your buddies at the cop shop and ask them to keep an eye out. I'll fill up the tank and drive until I'm so tired I can't see the road."

And I did.

But, to be honest, I reached the can't-see-the-road point pretty fast.

My biological clock is set to early rising and early retiring. So by 1:00 AM I was toast—tired toast doing no good for anyone and longing for a soft spot and a pillow. Dave, on the other hand, was full of energy—manic energy I assumed was fueled by a nearly empty pot of coffee and the sack of Lana's cookies, reduced to a few small crumbs and one lonely chocolate chip.

To put it out of its misery, I swallowed it as I glanced through the pages of the notepad on the dining room table. The first few pages listed people Dave had called—a list that included Detective Charles Atwell, Dario, Jake, my sister, and, of all people, Bernina Burke. Later pages contained notes on return calls and jottings about where they'd searched and who they'd called. Dario and Jake had crossed the bridge to search in Portland. Atwell had headed east up the river. Bernina hadn't called back.

Dave's phone rang. His eyes got a hopeful gleam as he tapped it on and clapped it against his ear. In a few seconds his eyes dimmed and he shook his head. The whole time, he continued to pace back and forth across the living room at a carpet-scorching speed.

I didn't ask if he'd heard from Allison, and he didn't ask if I'd seen her.

I also didn't say she must be okay or we would have heard something.

In fact, I didn't say anything.

I plucked Cheese Puff from the crevice of his favorite chair, stretched out on the sofa, and held him close. He grunted, but didn't try to escape. In fact, after opening his mouth wide to display his bling, he licked my nose and snuggled against my neck. Even though I was beyond the valley of worried and into the canyon of fear, I didn't kid myself that I could stay awake with Dave. I didn't make a pretense about remaining vigilant. I set my glasses on the coffee table and gave him an honest appraisal of my physical and mental state.

"I'm fried. I need to rest for a while. But if you think of something you want me to do, wake me up and I'll swill down a cola and get on it."

He gave me a wintry smile. "Thanks. Right now I can't think of a thing we haven't done except track her phone." He punched air. "I should have insisted on a monitoring app."

"Couldn't you have someone at the cop shop trace it?"

"Maybe. Probably. But . . ."

I waited a few seconds before filling in the blank. That would be professionally embarrassing and require calling in favors and taking a ribbing if it turned out Allison was with a friend who had lied for her.

On the other hand, what was a little embarrassment or a few favors compared to his daughter's safety?

I never got to argue the point, however, because sleep took me down like an undertow.

Three things woke me up. One was Lola barking. The second was Cheese Puff scrambling across my face to get down and join her at the door. The third was Dave calling, "Who's there?"

I sat up, rubbed my eyes, fumbled for my glasses, and noted it was nearly 6:00 AM. Lola barked again, Cheese Puff yipped, and Dave asked, "Where have you been?"

"I'm sorry, Dad," Allison said. Her voice was a low and plaintive croak. "Please don't be mad." She didn't whine or command as usual. "I mean, I know you are really angry, and I know it's my fault, and I know I scared you and Barbara, but please don't yell. Okay?"

"I'll yell if I want—"

147

"—to wake the neighbors." I finished the sentence as I hustled down the hallway.

Dave held the door wide, glaring at his daughter who stood on the threshold. Lola and Cheese Puff sniffed at her bare toes and knees, taking in the scents of her adventure. Or perhaps I should call it a misadventure. Her feet and legs were spotted with dried mud and blood, her shorts and tank top were snagged and torn, her arms were scratched, her face was puffy, her eyes were streaked with red, and her short brown hair was tangled with twigs and leaves.

I stopped a few feet away and silently opened my arms.

Sobbing, Allison ducked under Dave's arm and leaped for me.

I patted her back and combed her hair with my fingers, feeling each shuddering breath she took, feeling her tears, hot and wet on my shoulder. Dave closed the door and stood beside us, clenching and unclenching his fists, opening and closing his mouth, alternately scowling and wiping tears on the sleeve of his T-shirt.

"Hungry?" I asked Allison.

"Yes," she whispered.

"I'll make breakfast." I grasped her shoulders, turned her toward Dave, and gave her a shove. "You tell your father all about it."

For a second, Allison stood in limbo between us, head hanging. Then Dave reached out and drew her against him for a brief hug.

While I made cocoa, pancakes, and eggs, Dave sat silently with a stern expression on his face, sending a series of texts to those who'd helped search. Allison gulped orange juice, blotted tears, blew her nose, and blurted out bits of her story. I confess to missing the first few segments because every time she

148

repeated "It was all my fault" or "I'm so sorry" or "I'll never do anything this stupid again" my inner voice cheered so loud I couldn't hear anything else. Still, I got the meat of the tale.

"And then there was a road and another road and they kind of twisted around and I didn't know where I was. And the road got real narrow and there were no more houses and I couldn't turn around and the road went into the trees and up a hill."

Apparently the tank had more gas in it than I thought. And she hadn't stuck with familiar routes. Somehow, she'd gotten out of the heart of Reckless River and into the hills.

She poured another glass of juice. "And then the car kind of chugged and stopped. I tried to start it again and I don't know what I did wrong but it fell in a ditch."

"Fell?" Dave echoed. It was the first word he'd spoken since she came inside and his tone was sharp and demanding.

Allison recoiled, pressing herself against the back of her chair. "Yes. It fell over on its side in a ditch."

I set a loaded plate in front of her. "Were you hurt?" I asked in a tone I hoped was sympathetic—but not *too* sympathetic.

"I had my seatbelt on," she said with a note of pride.

That may not seem like something to be proud of, or even something worth reporting, but Allison had fought the buckle-up law with a vengeance. Her reason? Belts were ugly and left wrinkles in her shirt.

"I had the window down so I climbed out and tried to jump to the road but I slipped in the mud and went in the ditch. It was a really deep ditch. And there were frogs and maybe snakes." She stuffed a slice of pancake in her mouth and mumbled around it as she held out her arms to display dozens of scratches. "And stickers everywhere."

149

"After you shower we'll get some ointment on those so they don't get infected," I advised. "And let me know right away if you get a rash or if a spot doesn't stop itching."

"Thank you." She forked up a bit of egg. "And thank you so much for making breakfast."

Two expressions of thanks within a few seconds? That was newsworthy. We were seriously breaking new ground. I bit my tongue so I wouldn't yell, "Alert the media."

I set a plate in front of Dave and then stood by the stove with my own, wondering where I should sit so I wouldn't appear to be taking sides. I settled on dragging a chair around to the end of the table so we formed a triangle. "What did you do next?"

Avoiding eye contact, she mashed egg yolk with her fork. "I was gonna call Jim or Dario or somebody, but I couldn't get a signal. So I walked and walked and walked. And my flip-flops broke and the road was all full of rocks and my feet hurt and I kept trying my phone and there was nothing. And then it died."

She said that last bit as if the phone was a friend struck down by a sudden illness and gone from her life forever. I couldn't say I felt her pain because I didn't have the same intimate relationship with my phone that Allison—and many teenagers—did. I, after all, remembered life before cellphones became ubiquitous and so relatively inexpensive that even I could afford one.

"And I remembered a story we read in middle school and essays we had to do after on what to do if you got lost. And I thought about going back to the car and staying there but it was a long way so I kept going downhill and it got really dark and I heard all kinds of weird noises in the woods and coyotes howling and . . ." She raised her head and looked at her father.

"I was real scared, but I remembered how half of me comes from you. And you wouldn't be scared even a little bit."

Dave's stern expression softened about 10 degrees, but he said nothing. I also kept quiet although I was impressed that her knowledge of genetics indicated she might have paid occasional attention in biology class.

"So I kept walking, feeling with my feet so I'd stay on the road. And then the moon came out and I could see a little and the road got better, but I didn't see any lights or houses or even hear any cars. And 'cause I played your message I started hoping maybe a police car would come along and I could give myself up and go to jail where I could get a drink of water and where there wouldn't be any snakes or bugs."

Having spent time subbing at the juvenile jail, I almost laughed at her take on incarceration. I controlled it by stuffing my mouth with a slice of pancake.

"And then there was another road and a bridge and my feet hurt and my legs hurt so I stopped and sat down. And I hoped you were looking for me." She raised her head and met Dave's gaze. "But I decided I wouldn't be mad if you weren't because you probably get really tired of me doing stupid stuff."

"We looked for you," I told her. "Lots of people looked. How did you get home?"

"A woman came in a van filled with wind chimes. She makes them out of spoons and forks and little pots and stuff. She sells them, but I forget where." Allison dug in the pocket of her shorts, produced a crumpled bit of stiff paper, and smoothed it beside her plate. "She wanted to give me one but I told her I'd rather save up and buy one—a really big one—to thank her for bringing me home."

"I'll buy one too."

Dave scowled.

151

I scowled right back. The purchase wasn't about Allison as much as helping the woman who rescued her buy gas and craft materials. Maybe, because of our contribution, down some other road on some other day, she'd pick up someone else in need of help. So it was a paying-it-forward kind of thing.

Allison stopped smoothing the card and used her fork to draw patterns in the gloss of egg yolk and syrup on her plate. Dave watched her the way a hawk might watch a mouse, but said nothing. I felt his silence like a weight pressing on my shoulders, and got up to clear the table, trying to appear relaxed and nonchalant and wondering if I should bolt up the stairs and let them settle this. Then I told myself we were a family. I'd also been affected by what happened, and would be affected by what came next. Whatever that might be.

I'd cleared the last dish, loaded the dishwasher, and was starting to scrub the frying pan when Allison spoke. "What happens now? I mean, I know I get punished. And I won't complain because I know I deserve it. But what happens after that?"

"What do you mean?" Dave asked. "Are you asking how many privileges you lose and for how long?"

"No. I know I'll lose a bunch and for a long time. I mean, do you still love me? Will you ever trust me again?"

My eyes prickled with tears, but I kept scrubbing, although in a slow and quiet way so I could hear Dave's answer.

"Of course I still love you," he said in a grave voice. "And I'm glad you weren't hurt. But you scared the heck out of me. I need time before . . . before we all talk about where we go from here."

He shifted his gaze to me and I nodded my support. We all needed a timeout. And we all needed long naps. And, later,

152

pizza and ice cream. And, for me and Dave, an adult beverage—
or two.

Chapter 16

And so it came to pass that, while Dave got the word out to the sheriff's department about his desire to locate the learn-to-drive mobile, Allison made a long list of potential punishments and Dave pared it down to no wardrobe acquisitions for three months, keeping her room neat, taking on additional household chores, sticking to her curfew, adding a locator app to her phone, and either getting a job to pay for damage to the learn-to-drive mobile or putting in an equivalent number of volunteer hours. Then she made a list of ways to rebuild trust. We looked them over together and went with going nowhere without asking permission, returning home on time, having conversations without texting at the same time, cleaning up after herself without being told, walking the dogs, and learning to drive without drama. Allison made two lists and posted them on the refrigerator door, studied them for a moment, then added "It's not about me" to the bottom of each list. After that she added "I need to grow up." And, after a moment, she penned in "Find my own road and follow it."

"You told me that once," she said to Dave.

From his puzzled expression, I assumed he didn't recall, so I jumped in. "Great advice."

"As long as the road doesn't always lead to the mall," Dave said with a grim smile, "or back to the high school the year after you're supposed to graduate."

Allison clenched her fists and sucked in a breath, but in a moment she forced a smile and wrote along the side of the trust list "Take the SAT. Graduate on time."

(For the record, I have illusions about a lot of things—losing that extra ten pounds, for example—but I had no illusions about whether Allison would stick to the lists without backsliding. Sure, I was encouraged by her demeanor after a life-altering experience, but she was still a teenager. So, while I wasn't a card-carrying optimist, I hoped I'd be pleasantly surprised and she'd become a new and improved version of herself.)

Dave was wrapping up a call about having the learn-to-drive mobile towed to a repair shop, and I was wrapping leftover pizza slices from our evening meal and wondering if 7:00 PM was too early to go to bed, when the phone rang. As I reached for it, the display spelled out my sister's name.

I recoiled. "Arrrggh."

"Iz?" Dave and Allison asked as a chorus.

"None other."

"You talked to her this morning," Dave said. "Can't you institute a once-a-day rule and let the machine pick it up?"

"If I do that she'll call my cell. And if I don't answer that, she might come over."

Allison groaned, but then took the high road. "She's your sister. She worries about you."

Dave laughed. "She worries you'll grow more of a spine and draw a few lines in the sand."

And most of the time I'd like to. But even if I didn't owe her, she wasn't the kind of person to respect boundaries or lines—especially those drawn in sand.

155

So, gritting my teeth, I picked up the phone. "Hi, Iz. What's up?"

"You are. Tonight."

"Huh?"

"Penelope and I are going to see the old guy with the ghosts. She thinks I may be right about faulty wiring and wants to check it out. Could be what makes him think he's seeing spirits."

"And it could be a fire hazard," Penelope called.

Penelope was a licensed electrician. She'd know exactly how to determine if a problem existed and exactly what to do about it. That led to the obvious question. "Why do you need me?"

"To keep that little mutt of yours focused on the job."

I glanced at Cheese Puff, burrowed between the seat cushion and the arm of his favorite chair. "What job?"

"Ghost detecting."

I slapped my free hand over my mouth to contain my amusement—amusement on many levels. First because Iz thought I could keep Cheese Puff focused. He was smart, he was clever, and he was sneaky. On top of that, he had a stubborn streak that would make a mule turn green with envy. I had about as much power over him as I had over the weather or the stock market or companies that stopped making a product about seven minutes after it became my favorite. Second because although Cheese Puff had mastered a number of complicated dance steps for his Las Vegas performance with Mrs. B, and although he'd also mastered the art of being annoying and entitled, ghost detecting wasn't something I'd ever imagined he had a knack for. In fact, the thought had never crossed my mind. Or even made it to the starting line to get in position to cross my mind.

156

"Cats are good at it," Iz said.

"At ghost detecting?"

"Haven't you ever noticed how they stare up at the ceiling and hiss?"

"No."

(For the record, I haven't spent a lot of time with cats. Don't get me wrong, I like them. Apricot, the young cat next door to Mrs. B, had won my heart when she took on the rogue duck assaulting Cheese Puff last year. But I'd never had a feline decide to own me. And now that a parrot had taken up residence in Apricot's condo, the kitty was too busy trying to open the cage to spend much time visiting with neighbors. And, lest you're worried about the parrot, Mrs. B had assured me the cage was substantial, the door was padlocked, and the bird had a lethal beak and pointy talons and would clean Apricot's clock.)

"Well, cats do the staring thing a lot," Iz said. "So they must see something. They're predators. They hunt. They wouldn't waste their time checking out something that didn't exist."

I wasn't sure I bought that theory. I mean, sure, cats are predatory animals, but would a house cat, a cat that didn't have to hunt and kill in order to eat, make a distinction about what to check out and what to ignore. Maybe the average house cat was bored enough with its routine to stare at dust particles as a way to pass the time. Or maybe that staring cat was messing with the minds of the humans who served it.

I knew better than to bring up any of those issues and thus launch a verbal sparring match I couldn't win. So I agreed with that point, but made a conversational U-turn. "I'm sure you're right. Cats are smart. But Cheese Puff isn't a cat."

"He acts like one."

True, he hated to get wet, had food snubbing down to an art form, and demanded to be petted at inconvenient times. "Just because he has some feline attributes doesn't mean he can search for ghosts. If you need a cat, why don't I see if we can borrow Apricot?"

"Already checked. They're not home."

Drat.

"Don't you know anyone else who has a cat?"

"Only people I'm not speaking to."

Or, more likely, people who weren't speaking to her. Have I mentioned my sister can be as abrasive as pumice?

"What about hiring a ghost hunter? There are a couple of guys in town who check out possible manifestations. Jake interviewed them a few weeks ago."

(For the record, he'd made a mess of the interview in his usual slipshod and unprepared manner. He'd gotten their names wrong, asked how to do a séance, and said paranoidal instead of paranormal. Three times.)

"They're up in Centralia checking out some old buildings," Iz said. "Won't be back until Wednesday."

"Well, maybe you could wait un—"

"Bring the dog," she ordered. "Meet us at 11:00."

"You're kidding. That's . . . that's an hour before midnight."

"Amazing. You've mastered subtraction."

"I'd like to subtract you from this town," I muttered.

"What?"

"If you make spiritual contact you'll be renowned."

"Why don't I trust you?" Iz rattled off an address. "We're going over earlier so Penelope has daylight to check the wiring outside. Then she'll make sure it's all good inside and after that we'll wait for the ghost."

"How do you know the ghost will show? I mean, it's Sunday. Maybe he took the weekend off."

"Don't try to weasel out of this," Iz warned. "And don't be late."

Notice that I hadn't dug in my heels and refused to participate in what could be dubbed Mission: Incorporeal. Only about 15% of my lack of refusal was due to fear of my sister's wrath. The rest was due to curiosity—about the haunting and about the possibility of seeing . . . well, something. Iz and I didn't have a whole lot in common, but we shared a resistance to letting go of anything that puzzled or intrigued us.

"Wait. What if Cheese Puff doesn't show an interest in, um, things we can't see?"

"Oh, he will." She paused and then added, "He better."

The way she said those final words made me a little weak in the knees. My sister had no use for my dog—partly because he was male, partly because he got more attention than she did, and partly because the feeling was mutual. If Cheese Puff did possess the ability to see spirits, I had little doubt he'd dial it back, or turn it off, the second he understood that Iz wanted him to use his skill. If Iz suspected he wasn't cooperating, she'd be angry. She wouldn't hit or kick Cheese Puff, but she'd raise her voice to a level that could cause days of temporary hearing loss.

And, if by some remote chance ghosts exist, Perry Walker's house was haunted, and Cheese Puff possessed the ability to see spirits, how would he let us know? I imagined myself coaching him. "Bark once if it's ectoplasm. Bark twice if it's an apparition in human form. Bark three times if it's a poltergeist. Run as fast as your stubby legs can carry you if it's malevolent."

159

I slipped the phone into its cradle and noticed Dave and Allison staring at me. "I heard only your side of the conversation," Dave said, "but it was—"

"Weird," Allison said. "Cats and ghosts. What was that about?"

I filled her in on Perry Walker's situation and his belief that the ghost of his son visited many nights. "Penelope plans to check the wiring to see if that's causing the lights to dim and brighten and make weird shadows he believes are ghosts. Iz thinks Cheese Puff can see the ghost if it's there."

Cheese Puff lifted his head and twitched his nose as if considering a) whether he was capable of that, b) whether the gig was worth getting up for, and c) whether he wanted to reveal his hidden power to a pack of mere mortals and, more especially, to my sister.

"I want to come." Allison popped up from a sprawl on the sofa. "Can I? Please."

Seniors were finished at Captain Meriwether High School, but tomorrow was a school day for everyone else. I pointed to the calendar and the lists on the refrigerator. "I think you can answer that question yourself."

Allison chewed her lower lip. "It would be way past my curfew. And I have to finish the book about all those rich people and Gatsby and Daisy."

Dave nodded his approval. "If Cheese Puff turns out to be a ghost hunter, he'll have other offers and we'll go along on one of them."

"Congratulations on saying that with a straight face," I told him.

"Hey, anything's possible. The little guy may have hidden talents."

160

"Right," Allison agreed. "He blew them away at the competition in Las Vegas. And then there was the time he pooped in the drug dealer's car and made him lose his cool, and the time he let Dad know where you were in the river, and the time he untied Lola and saved her from the drug dealers."

Cheese Puff sat up, raised a paw, and licked it as if to say it was all in a day's work for a dog of his caliber. His gold tooth flashed as he licked.

Dave yawned. "You better take a nap. The last time you were up past 10:00 it was . . . well, it was last night."

A nap was a grand idea. Three hours of sleep would make me feel like . . . well, frankly, it would make me feel like I needed three more. But I'd signed up for this adventure, so I'd make do with what I could get.

But first, I made myself unavailable for a subbing job on Monday, and then I put in a call to Mrs. B to check up on Sybil and the gang.

"I was just about to call and say I believe you're a genius, dear," she gushed. "Harvey has been such a help. He watched Sybil all night so the rest of us could sleep. What a relief!"

"It's a relief for Dave to have him out of the way. How long will he stay with you?"

She laughed. "Considering how much he's enjoying ordering room service, I expect he could linger for months."

"Good thing you're made of money."

"Isn't it just. But to give you a more specific answer, I believe we'll return in a few days. Verna's getting all fired up about a tax issue the city council is planning to take up that may affect the sandwich shop, Ardie needs to get her summer program going, and I miss Dario. And the little prince, of course."

"The little prince is about to launch a career as a ghost hunter."

"Really?"

"Really. Although it may be an extremely short and unsuccessful career."

I told her about what Iz had in store for him and she made appropriate sounds of surprise and disbelief and wound up with, "I have no doubt he'll amaze you, dear."

Recalling the evening he ran amok in a casino, I ladled on a dollop of sarcasm. "He usually does."

My nap was shorter than I hoped since it was interrupted by a whirring, chattering sound broken now and then by grunts and curses. I trudged to the bedroom window and looked out over the deck, but spotted nothing except a few joggers. The sound persisted, my nap-addled brain cleared, and I realized it was coming from the parking lot side of the complex, the side overlooked by Allison's bedroom window. Normally, my policy is that I don't enter her room unless I'm concerned because she's late for school, disturbed by the noxious quality of an odor, or invited to enter. Quite honestly, given the usual state of it, I'm happy to stick to the policy. So I hesitated on the landing. But then the sound came again, my curiosity soared, and my policy went out the window.

Allison had a day of grace before putting her improvement/punishment plan into action, so her room resembled a minefield after a series of detonations. I tiptoed on a serpentine path to the window and peered out into the summer evening. Below, hedge trimmer cocked like a baseball bat in the hands of a batter anticipating a pitch low and outside, was Bernina Burke. As I watched, she brought the trimmer around, driving it into the heart of the low hedge instead of using it to clip new growth along the top and sides.

Entranced, I watched her take another swing, wondering if I should intervene. I wasn't a member of any landscaping police force and therefore not authorized to order Bernina to step away from the shrubbery. And the hedge in question, while located between the tiny lawns and short walkways leading to my unit and that of Mrs. B, was owned by the association as a whole.

I gazed up and down the complex. All the other hedges were scruffy, but intact. Not one was surrounded by a rash of clippings. Apparently Bernina had decided to trim mine first— either as part of the learning process or to irritate me. Or perhaps for both reasons.

But why was Bernina doing this grunt work? Granted, thanks to nitpicking, micro-managing, and paying late, she'd run off half a dozen landscaping services. But the economy wasn't all that great. There must be someone, somewhere, willing to work at 90 Columbia Lane.

Unless this was a cost-cutting effort. Or unless the condo association bank balance was closer to the red than she'd reported at the beginning of the month.

By now there was no chance I could return to the arms of Morpheus. Or return to the fingers or even the toes of Morpheus.

(For the record, I know exactly who Morpheus was. Or maybe *is*, depending on your beliefs. The Morpheus I'm referring to doesn't appear in *The Matrix* films. He's listed as the Greek god of dreams and had the power to appear to mortals while they slept and deliver messages from the gods. And, in case the first part of his name looks familiar, it's where we get the word "morphine" from.)

163

But, moving right along, I dressed in something a little more appropriate for wearing in public—something that included a bra and pants—and went forth. "Bernina's trimming the hedge," I told Dave as I passed his office.

He didn't shift his gaze from the ballgame on his big-screen TV. "It's the bottom of the ninth," he said in a tone indicating that was a valid response.

"The hedge is losing. Bernina's at bat."

"Keep score. I'll be out at the next commercial break."

Chapter 17

I opened the door and surveyed the field of one-sided battle. The hedge, I decided, would survive, but it would need major watering and fertilizing. Bernina, meanwhile, needed a major infusion of something you'd find in the kind of dart that can drop a charging rhino and send it into serious slumber. Her hair was matted with sweat, her face was the color of borscht, and the safety goggles she'd donned made her look like a giant poisonous frog. To further mix images, the way she panted and puffed made me think of an old engine working up a head of steam to pull a train through the Rockies.

I thought of a dozen snide comments while I watched her wrestle the trimmer free of a tangle of branches too thick to cut. Those comments were all world-class observations of her lack of style and skill. They were stinging and sarcastic. Several even compared her efforts to those of my ex-husband Jake during his brief tenure as a handyman. (In case you've forgotten, that tenure ended when he nearly electrocuted himself using a pressure washer and then drilled a hole through a pipe creating an indoor geyser.)

You'll have to trust me on the quality of those comments, however, because I didn't use a single one from my sterling collection.

I didn't have to.

165

Bernina glanced my way, aimed a forefinger, narrowed her eyes, and uttered a threat. "One word and I'll go to work on your hair when I get this loose."

It didn't appear that would happen any time soon, but I held my silence. I did, however, raise both brows and offer a smirk.

Bernina responded with a string of curses worthy of a seasoned sailor. She turned her head and aimed the verbal assault at the trimmer, but I suspected it was meant for me as well. Proud of my mime-like emoting, I gaped, took a step back, and traded the smirk and raised brows for wide-eyed innocence.

"I wasn't talking to you," Bernina shouted. "You can't prove I was, so you can't complain to the board."

"I wouldn't dream of it." And then, of course, I did just that—dream, that is. I imagined the reaction from two of the more staid board members if I repeated even a single word plucked at random from Bernina's extensive off-color vocabulary.

"Yes you would." She grasped the trimmer with both hands and gave it a wrench that tore small branches from the hedge and sent leaves and twigs flying. Thrown off balance, she flailed her arms, spun about, tangled her feet in orange electrical cord, flung the trimmer aside, and fell across the hedge.

If I'd been a judge at the Olympics, I would have awarded her points for enthusiasm and strength, but deducted for lack of fluidity during the dismount. The math would have been a snap. According to my esteemed sister, I was a master of subtraction.

"Need a hand?" I offered.

"Not yours," Bernina replied.

(For the record, her reply wasn't that succinct and contained a few expletives. Since I'm trying to keep this story family-friendly, I'll leave them out. If your family isn't the friendly sort, feel free to insert a few of your favorite words here and there to spice things up.)

"And stop watching me."

I vowed to try.

But I couldn't.

Bernina had slimmed down considerably thanks to the efforts of Gabe Hendricks, a physical therapist who had taken her on as a project. But she was still bulky, and not the least bit graceful. Watching her free herself was like watching a walrus try to ride a bicycle. Not that I've ever seen a walrus attempt such a feat, but you get the drift.

I wandered to the parking lot and retrieved the hedge trimmer. Several teeth were bent and the front end curved to the left. I doubted it would ever trim shrubbery in this town again.

Humming a funeral march, I returned with it to Bernina who had triumphed in her struggle and was yanking twigs from her hair. She'd pulled off her goggles and sported red rings around her eyes where they'd dug into her skin. "This is what I get for working my butt off saving you people money on maintenance costs."

That sounded like code for "condo finances are still a mess so I'm trying to make you think I'm working hard." I almost asked if she'd made a win-back-trust list like Allison. And I also came close to mentioning that she still had plenty of butt to work off. But I said not a word as I handed over the mangled trimmer.

While Bernina made an attempt to bend it into shape by standing on it, Dave emerged from the condo, surveyed the

167

situation, and grinned. "Wow. Looks like there was quite a scuffle. Is the hedge filing assault charges?"

Bernina's only response was to stomp on the hedge trimmer, release another string of curses while hopping on one foot, and stalk off into the gathering twilight.

"Did you get video?" Dave asked.

"Shoot. I didn't think of it."

"Too bad. It would have gone viral by now."

"If I got it uploaded before she caught me and trashed my phone."

"Babe, if you can't outrun Bernina, you better get a personal trainer. But NOT Gabe."

I smirked. "Because you think he's way hotter than you?"

"No. At least not *way* hotter. Sure, he's younger, and in slightly better condition, but I have more experience." He struck a body-building-competition pose. "And I exude an aura of take-charge manliness."

I waved a hand beneath my nose. "Is that aura the same as the odor of a man who was up all night worrying and has yet to shower?"

"There are certain similarities." He pulled me close and nibbled my earlobe. "Allison went to bed. Perhaps we should go upstairs and shower and discuss this further."

I shivered. "How much further did you have in mind?"

"As further as we can until the moment you have to leave to go ghost hunting."

An hour later, tired but glowing, I popped Cheese Puff into his harness and drove to the address Iz had provided. The house was in an older neighborhood where tall trees surrounded streetlights. Leaves cast flitting shadows as a gusting breeze combed through the branches. Although

Halloween was more than four months away, I found myself watching for kids clutching bags of sugary loot and zigzagging across the street without checking for traffic.

A porch light flicked on and off.

My sister trotted across the lawn of a large two-level house and intercepted me before I could pull in the driveway. "Go up another block and park around the corner," she ordered.

"Why?" I glanced at the driveway and saw room for at least six cars. "You invited more ghost hunters?"

"No. Why does everything with you have to be an argument?"

Seriously?

"Asking a simple question is an argument?"

"Maybe not in itself, but it's the way you usually start one."

Me?

I started the arguments?

As if reading my mind, Cheese Puff snarled.

I seized my opportunity and laid the foundation for an excuse to be used later if needed. "You're upsetting him. He won't be able to detect anything if he's not calm."

Iz snorted in disgust. "Have it your way."

"You mean I *can* park here?"

"No. I mean I won't hold up my end of the argument."

"I wasn't arguing."

"You are now!"

Allowing as how she had a point, I pulled away from the curb.

"Park in a shadow," she called.

Rolling my eyes, I tooled up the street and tucked my car into a pool of darkness created by the arching branches of two enormous maples. When I opened the door, chilly air swirled in, making it clear that while summer was nearly upon us, it

169

wasn't here yet. I'd thought to toss in a sweater, but hadn't brought socks or sneakers. My toes would have to suffer for my negligence.

With Cheese Puff showing all the enthusiasm he displays on a visit to the vet, I made my way to Perry Walker's house along a sidewalk buckled by thick roots. The cracks bristled with clumps of determined weeds.

"Do what you have to do here and now," I urged my entitled dog as I thrust my arms in the sleeves of the sweater and buttoned it all the way to the top. "These are nice houses, so no lifting your leg on anything inside."

He paused to sniff at a slug and I tugged at his leash. "And no eating anything you'll throw up inside, because I guarantee my sister will threaten to stuff it back where it came from."

Cheese Puff yipped as if to say he'd gnaw her fingers to nubs so she'd never stuff anything anywhere again.

"Shhhhh." Iz seized my arm and hustled me to the house and into a pine-paneled entranceway with a tile floor. Once she snapped off the porch light and closed the door, the only illumination came from a tiny nightlight in a socket far to my right and the glow of urban light pollution filtering through gauzy curtains drawn across tall windows in a living room the size of the entire first floor of my condo. Here and there faint light gleamed off the glass in a picture frame, or the curve of a crystal candlestick, or the face of one of the many clocks hung on the wall. More clocks, some under glass domes, crowded a fleet of tables along with wraith-like porcelain figurines, all squatting on doilies and embroidered bits of cloth. Their tiny faces all seemed to be turned my way.

In a word, it was creepy. In three words, it was dark and creepy.

Iz snapped a lock and dragged me forward.

"What is up with you?" I broke from her grip and rubbed my arm, then picked up Cheese Puff who had practically tattooed himself to my ankle. "And why are we in the dark? Did Penelope find problems with the wiring?"

"Not a single issue," Penelope answered. "It's all upgraded and all to code."

I peered into the dusky dimness and spotted a female-shaped shadow in a doorway at the far side of the room.

"So now the ghost theory holds more water," Iz announced.

I didn't ask how much more water. In my opinion it wasn't much. Somewhere in the vicinity of a few drops. Maybe as much as a quarter of a cup. But nowhere near a gallon.

"I thought we'd improve the chances of the ghost showing up if we didn't make ourselves too obvious."

I swallowed a snort. The day my sister was anything less than obvious would be the day seals lost their appetite for fish.

"And I locked all the doors and windows. So we'll know whatever or whoever appears to collect a coin didn't get in like a normal human."

"Although there are still other possibilities," Penelope said in a quiet voice. It was barely audible over the ticking that seemed to clot the air and make it difficult to breathe.

A little part of me wondered if she was going with a Santa Claus theory for gaining entry. Then I gave myself a virtual smack. This was Penelope, the most serious one of the group.

"There may be other reasons for what Mr. Walker experiences," she said. "He's not . . . well, you'll see."

"He's in the library." Iz took my arm again and steered me across the living room. "Come on. Stay with me and watch out for all the knickknack shelves and cabinets. The place is full of them."

171

As we navigated the room, my feet seeming to sink to the ankles in the carpeting, I remembered she'd said Perry Walker had collections. I wondered if anyone came in to dust and polish. Buffing up this room alone would take at least an hour. Fortunately, during the rainy season in the Northwest, dust didn't get much of an opportunity to float in through windows and doors and settle on surfaces. But summer was drought season, time to give rags and dusters a workout. If, that is, you were the kind of person who went after that layer of dust before it grew thick enough to write your grocery list in it.

We passed along a hallway, made a turn, and arrived at a high-ceilinged room filled with shelves and free-standing bookcases that in turn were stuffed with books of all sizes. A single lamp was switched on. It revealed a sofa and two puffy reclining chairs hunkering in the center of the room and covered with what appeared to be maroon velvet. The lamp also revealed Perry Walker, asleep in one of the chairs. His feet, stuffed into a pair of fleece-lined leather slippers, were elevated on the footrest.

"A year or so ago he stopped going upstairs and moved to what used to be the maid's quarters off the kitchen. But he starts the night sleeping in here," Iz said in her normal voice. "Says the ghost told him to."

"It's actually fairly comfortable." Penelope sat in the chair opposite and rocked back. "It reclines, there's plenty of padding, and he's got a pillow. Besides, he says he doesn't sleep much."

"Shouldn't you be whispering?"

"He's hard of hearing," Iz told me. "Takes his hearing aids out at night. Doesn't have any idea we're holding a conference right in front of him."

172

Since that claim came from the mouth of my sister, I didn't trust it to be true, but as I studied our sleeping host I found myself agreeing. Perry Walker's head was tilted on the slender stalk of his neck. His mouth hung open, and a trickle of saliva ran from one corner and across a jaw with only a trace of stubble. He wore a dark blue cotton bathrobe over a pair of tan pajamas. His bony hands, the nails neatly trimmed, lay on the arms of the chair, the fingers curled slightly toward his palms, a silver dollar in each.

"Put the dog down," Iz ordered.

"Where?"

"Anywhere."

"How about by that display case?" Penelope pointed to a long wood and glass stand in front of a set of maroon drapes. "If you look inside, you can see the depressions where coins used to be."

"Coins he gave to the ghost," Iz said. "For the ferry."

"I have a theory about that."

"You have a theory about everything," Iz snarked. "Take the dog over there and stop jabbering."

Sheesh.

I shrugged, carried Cheese Puff to the case, and held him above it. "Smell anything?"

Cheese Puff turned his head and raised one side of his upper lip, displaying his bling.

"I'll take that for a negative."

"How can you tell?" Iz asked. "It looked to me like he was snarling."

And maybe he had been, but I wasn't about to suggest my sister might be right. Reminding myself that she had little interest in pets and therefore wouldn't know if I was making things up, I decided to display all the confidence I didn't feel. "He was taking in more air."

I'd conducted a few moments of Internet research before I left the condo but, for what I went with next, I drew on my prime source of knowledge about the supernatural and detecting manifestations—*Ghostbusters*. Since it had been several years since I last watched the movie, my memory wasn't clear or complete. I played fast and loose with the bits I dredged from my mental file cabinets. "By taking in more air he can screen more effectively for lingering odors left by, um, traces of, uh, spectral slime."

Iz grunted.

"Because the odors are faint, they dissipate quickly," I said in my most authoritative substitute teacher voice. "Let's see what he can pick up from the carpet. It's possible that bits of ectoplasm drifted to the floor."

Iz grunted again and I congratulated myself on plumbing her well of knowledge with that statement and finding it about as deep as the plastic buckets toddlers take to the beach. See, what I'd learned from my limited research on the Internet—a place where truth doesn't always reside—was that ectoplasm exudes from mediums. So, unless Perry Walker happened to be a medium and was channeling his son, or one of us happened to have that ability and wasn't aware of it, or what I'd read was baloney, there shouldn't be any ectoplasm around. And if there was ectoplasm around, perhaps it was of a variety that drifted up, down, or even sideways.

But who knew?

Maybe I had this ectoplasm stuff backwards. Or mixed up. Or wrong.

I vowed to do more research in the morning, unhooked the leash, and set Cheese Puff on the carpet. He proceeded to flop and roll.

"What's he doing?"

Odds were that he was scratching an itch, but I went with more BS. "He's, uh, charging up with static electricity."

"Will it make him more receptive to emanations if his hair stands on end?" Penelope asked.

I didn't know Penelope well enough to know whether she asked because she thought it was a possibility, or whether she was poking fun at the whole idea of Cheese Puff as a ghost-detecting dog. Penelope was far more serious than I was, but I knew she had to have a lighter side. In my opinion it wouldn't be possible to live with my sister and keep at least a few shreds of sanity unless you could mine a little humor from most situations.

"Possibly," I answered in a noncommittal tone.

"Interesting," she said in a tone that implied it actually was.

"What's he doing now?" Iz asked.

Cheese Puff had stopped rolling and was sniffing along a bottom shelf loaded with tall and wide books. He halted at a gap in the row and stuck his head in.

I suspected he was sniffing the trail of a mouse or perhaps had caught the scent of a bit of cookie or potato chip, but while I was thinking up a ghost-related reply, he moved on to another gap, and then another. I scanned the room and, even in the dim light, spotted at least two dozen gaps. Some, on upper shelves, were wide enough to have contained three or four books. "Has Mr. Walker's ghost been taking books as well as coins?"

"Don't know," Iz said.

I scanned the shelves again. Every remaining book possessed a pristine dust jacket. First editions? But how would we know a book wasn't there if . . . well, if it wasn't there? "Have you seen any kind of catalog or list of the books he has?"

"No," Iz said.

"But we haven't looked," Penelope added. "Want me to?"

"Later." Iz pointed. "The dog's going to the door."

And he was.

In a moment he was trotting along the hallway.

Iz shoved ahead through the doorway and we took off in hot pursuit.

Chapter 18

Given that Cheese Puff's night vision was significantly better than my day vision—even with my glasses on and the lenses cleaned—he was soon several yards ahead.

"Kitchen's that way," Iz said.

And no doubt that's where he was bound. Since Perry Walker had no pets, Cheese Puff wasn't likely to find a forgotten dog biscuit beneath the stove. But the average kitchen—and by that I mean one that's used as often and thoroughly cleaned as seldom as mine—has crumbs and drips and smears.

Sure enough, we found him licking the floor in front of the refrigerator.

I rushed to scoop him up. "Turn on the light so I can see what he got."

"No lights except in the library," Iz said. "Don't want to scare off the ghost. That's butterscotch sauce. I made Perry a sundae. He loves ice cream. Says he has a big bowl every night."

"It's nice to see you mastered the art of gourmet cooking," I teased, leaving Cheese Puff to his treat.

Penelope giggled.

"We don't have to cook gourmet stuff," Iz grumped. "Just heat up frozen meals and make sandwiches and soup and salad and stuff like that."

"And the cleaning?" I needled as I nodded toward Cheese Puff who was licking a widening circle on the floor, getting up every bit of the sticky sauce.

"He's got a cleaning service, so that's not much work, either," she admitted. "Nothing like spring cleaning in our old neighborhood in Nebraska."

I shook my head in an involuntary spasm of awe and wonder, with a tinge of fear. Spring cleaning back there and back then was almost a competitive sport and anyone who wandered into the arena would be sucked in and set to work. Cleaning went on from first light until nightfall. I recalled women beating rugs slung over clotheslines, the sound of vacuum cleaners and floor polishers, the odors of ammonia, bleach, lye soap, furniture wax, and moth balls for packing away winter sweaters, socks, and jackets. I once made off with a dozen and tried using them as marbles.

(For the record, they were too light and usually didn't roll in a straight line. Further for the record, I was sent to my room for what seemed to be weeks for the high crime of scaring my mother who feared I'd eaten them.)

"What I have to do is mostly little stuff," Iz went on. "At least at this place. But every client has different needs."

"Besides the cleaning service, Mr. Walker has someone to shop and cook for him," Penelope said.

"Sharlene mostly stands by while he showers and shaves. She trims his nails and massages his feet and gets his pills in the right slots. And she makes the bed and washes his robes and pajamas and underwear."

All tasks Iz could handle—if she determined they weren't beneath her.

I glanced at the clock on the stove. 11:48. "Do you want Cheese Puff to check out the upstairs?"

178

"Might as well," Iz said. "But so far he's been as worthless as an expired credit card."

Although I was mildly interested in how she'd deny responsibility and reinterpret recent history to place blame elsewhere—probably on me—I didn't remind her that this little adventure had been her idea. Instead, I picked up Cheese Puff and gave him a pep talk. "Your integrity as a ghost hunter is being questioned, dude. So I want you to go on upstairs and give it all you've got."

Cheese Puff closed his eyes, perhaps indicating he had nothing to give, was bored, or wished I'd stop talking.

"He's concentrating all his energy in his third eye," I told Iz.

"I had a friend do that before she read my aura," Penelope said. "She said she pulled all her energy up from her toes and centered it in her forehead so she could use it to see."

Iz snorted.

Honestly, the woman needed to expand her repertoire and come up with some new ways to register disgust.

Penelope ignored my sister, something I bet she had a lot of practice doing by now. "My aura is blue. Or at least it was when she looked at it. We should have her read yours, Barbara."

I almost quipped that mine would, obviously, be the color of cheesy snacks, but instead I chose a response that would cause my sister to snort again. "Great idea. We should get up a group. Wouldn't that be fun, Iz?"

She snorted as expected. "Fun. Right. Maybe afterward we could go to the supermarket and guess the weight of the cantaloupes, or see how many balloons we can blow up in an hour."

179

Snickering, I snapped the leash on Cheese Puff's harness and lowered him to the floor. Then, led by the tiny penlight Penelope aimed ahead of us, I towed him along the hallway, past a dining room large enough for a dozen guests to chow down in comfort, past a bathroom, past the library, and finally to a staircase outlined by strips of tiny lights. He mounted the first step, and sat.

"Does he sense something?" Penelope asked.

"He senses he wants to be carried," I told her.

"Spoiled little hairball," Iz muttered.

"Shhhhh." Penelope put a finger to her lips. "Don't criticize him. I think he's really trying."

"Yeah, he's trying my patience."

Even though I felt the same, I didn't let on. Telling my sister I agreed with her was like admitting to a grizzly bear that I couldn't outrun him, especially uphill. I'd be mauled—verbally in this case—in no time.

I ordered Cheese Puff to get moving, but of course he didn't, so I picked him up in a less-than-pampering manner, slung him over my shoulder, and climbed. Or, as the case was, slogged. The same thick carpet and spongy pad had been used on the stairs, and it seemed like I was walking in an inch of sticky mud. When we reached the top, a wide but fairly short hallway led to our right while a longer one ran straight ahead. A nightlight halfway along showed us the way, but little more.

"Six bedrooms," Iz informed me. "And four baths."

Cheese Puff made a sound that could have been a groan but might also have been a yawn. I showed him no sympathy and lowered him to the floor. "Let's get moving."

And so we did, following Cheese Puff and, with the help of the faint beam of the penlight, checking out the few places where he paused to sniff. We discovered an old dog bed in a closet, a bird cage on a window seat, a place where a mouse had gnawed the baseboard, and a mummified something about three inches long that I hope I never see again. Not once did Cheese Puff stop and stare at a corner of the ceiling or a wall.

"Total waste," Iz growled as we descended the staircase.

Penelope patted her shoulder. "You gave it a shot."

"But that sorry excuse for a dog didn't."

"We don't know that," I said, compelled to launch a defense of my entitled little mutt if only to avoid siding with my sister. "Maybe there was a ghost bird in that cage or a ghost dog in that old bed. Maybe—"

"Sssshhh." Penelope clutched my shoulder. "Did you hear that?"

"Hear what?" Iz asked.

"I don't know. A click, maybe. Hold still and listen."

We did.

Well, all of us except Cheese Puff. He pawed at my ankle signifying he wanted up. At the same time, I felt an eddy of cool air. "Feel that?" I whispered.

"Yes," Penelope said.

"Feel what?" Iz asked.

"Cool air."

We stood in silence for what I guessed was a full minute, but heard and felt nothing more. "Must have been the cooling system kicking on," Iz announced.

Penelope squeezed my shoulder and I turned to see her shake her head. Of the three of us, she had the most experience in that area. The little worry meter in my gut kicked up a notch.

Cheese Puff whined. Maybe because he sensed my growing anxiety. Maybe because I hadn't responded to his pawing.

"Or maybe Perry got out of his chair and opened a window," Iz said.

Penelope shook her head again.

My worry meter jumped two more notches.

"Or you imagined it." Iz descended the final few steps and marched toward the library.

I gathered up Cheese Puff and followed, pausing along the way to watch Penelope play the beam of her penlight across the thermostat. "Off," she whispered.

My worry meter fluttered, but then settled back. Maybe Iz was right about Perry opening a window.

But when we reached the library the curtains were still pulled. And Perry was still asleep in his chair.

Iz stood in front of him, pointing with a trembling finger, at his right hand.

The coin he'd held was gone.

I leaned to one side and peered around my sister.

So was the one in his left hand.

I laid Cheese Puff across my left shoulder and pressed him against my neck, fighting a chill that wasn't caused by cool air. Shuffling about, I got my back against Penelope's and felt her press against me. She made a low humming noise—it sounded a lot like "I Whistle a Happy Tune" but maybe that was my imagination.

"Coins probably fell," Iz said. "Give me the light."

Penelope passed it over and Iz dropped to her knees and studied the carpet around Perry's chair. She felt beneath it, then flopped and peered under the sofa and the other chair.

Meanwhile, I scanned the room for . . . well, I didn't know what I expected to see. All I knew was that I didn't want to see anything that wasn't familiar and real and not scary. And, because my brain was tossing up images—mostly frightening and, again, drawn from *Ghostbusters*—I missed them the first time. And the second. But the third time my gaze swept the

room I spotted a gap between books that seemed wider. Then I saw another gap where a book leaned in to an empty space.

"I'm turning on more lights," Penelope said in a shaky whisper. "Come with me."

I didn't have to be asked twice.

And I gripped right back when she took my free hand.

We shuffled to the door and she clicked the three switches beside it. Two more floor lamps came on, bulbs lit up in sconces over a mantel I hadn't noticed, and lights glowed along the top of the bookcases.

The additional illumination didn't disturb Perry Walker's sleep.

"That's better." Penelope's voice was less shaky, but she didn't release my hand.

Fine with me.

I gave her a sickly smile of encouragement and she did the same back at me. She never wore much makeup, but she favored pale pink lipstick and I noticed she'd chewed every bit of it off her lower lip. With her free hand, she buttoned the light khaki jacket she wore over pressed jeans and a blue-and-tan checked blouse. "Is it cold in here, or is it me?"

I didn't know how to answer that. I also felt a chill, but thought it had more to do with fainthearted anxiety than air temperature. Someone had been in this room while we were upstairs.

I definitely didn't want to consider whether that someone was human or ghostly, so I started humming a tune of my own. I favored "Walking on Sunshine" but fear kind of closed down my humming muscles, so I hit only a few of the notes.

Cheese Puff growled, more of a vibration than a sound.

I held him tighter.

"No sign of the coins." Iz lumbered to her feet.

183

"I think at least two books are missing," I said.

"And *I* think the click we heard was the front door closing," Penelope added. "That would also explain the cold air we felt around our legs right afterward."

"The door was locked." Iz patted a pocket of her cargo pants. "I have the spare keys that were under the planter. The one for the knob and the one for the bolt."

"There may be another spare set," I suggested. "Or the person who was in here made a copy of his own so he could come and go whenever he wanted."

"And carry off stuff," Penelope added. "Maybe a lot of stuff. Did you notice how all the surfaces upstairs were relatively bare compared to down here? I saw only half a dozen figurines. And hardly any clocks."

Iz thought about that for a few seconds. "You're saying somebody's looting the place? Taking more than coins?"

I shrugged.

Penelope did likewise.

"You're saying there's definitely no ghost?" Iz asked.

"I won't say 'definitely' until we have more evidence," Penelope said. "Maybe a ghost can pass through walls or float out through the ceiling, but could a ghost carry books and coins with it?"

Great question.

We all stared at each other.

Even Iz didn't try to bluster out an answer.

I made a vow to check the Internet when I got home. Right or wrong, there was bound to be some kind of theory about whether ghosts could pass solid objects through walls. Heck there might even be a video. Maybe it would be set to music.

While I was trying to come up with an appropriate tune, a creaky voice said, "I must have been asleep when he came."

184

We all turned to see Perry Walker staring at his empty hands.

"Did you see him when he took the money? Did he talk to you?"

Iz bent over him, wiped drool from his cheek with a tissue, then leaned him forward, and fluffed the pillow supporting his head and shoulders. She did it with a gentle skill that surprised me. "We were upstairs."

"We must have just missed him." Penelope released me, sat on the sofa arm, and took one of his hands. "You didn't feel anything when he took the coins?"

"Not a thing. But these hands don't feel much these days, except aches and pains."

"Would you like to go to bed?" Iz asked. "Would you be more comfortable there now that . . . now that you gave your son money for the ferry?"

Perry Walker nodded and Iz helped him from the chair and along the hallway to the kitchen, turning on lights as they went. I put Cheese Puff down and followed with Penelope, checking out rooms along the way.

"Do you think he—or it—knew we were here?" she asked. "We whispered. We didn't turn on any lights. And the rooms upstairs are all carpeted so he couldn't have heard our footsteps."

"Floors creak," I reminded her. "Especially in old houses."

"I was trying to forget that fact." She gripped my left wrist with both hands. "It's creepy to think he—I'm going to call him that because calling him 'it' makes it even creepier—was just a few feet from us."

"Maybe he was creeped out too." I pointed to the ceiling. "Maybe he thought we were real ghosts clanking around up there."

185

"Or maybe he knew exactly who we were. Maybe he was watching the house and saw us arrive."

I thought about that for a moment—at the same time wondering how long it would take for my fingers to fall off thanks to lack of blood flow if she didn't loosen her hold. "I kind of doubt that. From what we know, it seems he's been coming almost every night for several weeks. He probably watched and listened the first few nights, but I bet now he's got a feel for the neighborhood and Perry's schedule, so it's all routine. He's probably not careless, but I doubt he's as careful as he was at first. Maybe he just scans the block for people out walking or vehicles he hasn't seen before. Then he gets in and out. Maybe he wasn't in the house long enough to hear us."

It was all just speculation, but Penelope seemed to find enough comfort in it to release my arm. I tucked my hand behind my back and shook it, easing the throbbing in my fingers. I didn't mention what had just occurred to me—that if the intruder heard us, he might stake out the area to see who emerged from the house.

And me without a disguise.

"Do you think the ghost, or the man pretending to be a ghost, is referring to Charon?" Penelope asked after a moment.

"That would be my guess."

"But not everyone's." She poked her chin in the direction my sister had gone. "I'm always surprised by what she takes literally. And by what she knows and what she doesn't."

"Her education was spotty," I said, recalling how I'd covered for her when she was booted out of college. "Plus she focused on the women in mythology and ignored the men."

"Still . . . Do you think you could bring up the mythological angle? Otherwise she's likely to descend on the people who run

186

that little ferry across the Columbia up at Cathlamet and demand the gold back."

I almost laughed at the image of my sister storming aboard and perhaps being tossed overboard. Or arrested on the assumption she was high on a controlled substance or just off her rocker.

What stopped me from emitting even a faint chuckle was the thought of how she'd react to being presented with something we knew and she didn't. "So, I shouldn't mention that you also think it's a reference to mythology. You don't imagine she'll surmise that you, a woman named after the wife of Odysseus, would have recognized that?"

"Oh, I expect she will. Eventually."

"And you'll say what?"

Penelope thought for a few seconds and then grinned, her blue eyes sparkling. "I'll blame my father. I'll say he was so deep in Greek history and mythology and heroes that he never talked about anything else and it bored me to tears so I tuned him out."

It was a great excuse and I had no doubt my sister would accept it. First because the blame was placed on a man, and second because Penelope had demonstrated her power as a woman by not listening. "Wow. You're good at this."

She grinned again. "And getting better all the time. Once you know where someone's blind spot is, it's easy."

"Or, to use a term from mythology, once you spot the Achilles heel."

Penelope giggled.

I snickered.

She chortled.

I chuckled.

Cheese Puff yipped.

187

We both laughed.

"What's so funny?" Iz strode along the hallway toward us.

"Nothing much," Penelope said. "We're just tired."

"And I get silly when I'm tired."

"I know. And it's annoying. I've been telling you that for years." Iz tossed that last bit over her shoulder as she headed for the front door. "Let's get out of here."

"Shall we meet someplace and talk about—"

"No," Iz practically shouted in a brittle voice. "Not tonight."

Penelope and I exchanged a shrug and I scooped up Cheese Puff and followed her to the door.

There she paused, staring at the bolt. "It's not locked."

Chapter 19

It wasn't. The button that locked the knob was pushed in, but the oval handle on the bolt wasn't as Iz had set it.

"I saw you lock it," I assured her.

"So the ghost man unlocked it," Penelope whispered. "And left it that way. Why would he do that?"

"Maybe it's usually not locked," I said. "And he was in a hurry and forgot it was when he came in."

What I didn't say was that maybe he'd been sending a message, letting us know he was aware of us.

"Enough talk." Iz opened the door and ushered us out. I watched her push the button for the knob lock, turn the key for the dead bolt, and tip the planter.

"Are you leaving the keys where you found them?"

"Why wouldn't I?"

Because if the looter knew the game was up, he might tell a friend—perhaps a friend prone to violence. That friend might clean the place out. He might harm Perry Walker in the process.

But, because my sister almost always took the opposite view, I didn't say any of that. "Just curious."

"Does Sharlene have a set?" Penelope asked.

"She uses these." Iz tossed them beneath the planter while I wondered how many people Sharlene had told about the keys.

189

Then, as we made our way down the walkway, I wondered how many people could guess there would be keys somewhere close to the door because many people stashed spares outside. Especially people Perry Walker's age, people who remembered when Reckless River was a small town and neighbors came and went, dropping off canning jars and homemade jam, and returning umbrellas and casserole dishes.

"Are you going to tell Sharlene about tonight?" I asked.

Iz pressed her lips together before she said, "No. Technically I don't think I should have been here without her—either time."

"But you were here as an interested person," Penelope said. "Like a friend checking on another friend."

"Yeah, but Sharlene might not see it that way. She'd go to the program director as fast as her skinny legs could carry her."

And Iz would be bounced from the program.

"Penelope's truck is past your car," Iz told me. "We'll all walk together."

It was an order I was happy to obey.

Okay, not *completely* happy because the order came from my sister. But I was happy enough to comply that I didn't drag my feet.

The shadows were darker and wider than when I'd arrived. One streetlamp now seemed to cast a more yellowish light, while another was on the gray scale. A third flickered. Far up the street, a raccoon with a hump-backed gait raced from the shelter of one tree to another.

Cheese Puff growled and struggled to get down.

"Forget it," Penelope whispered. "He'd tear your face off if you caught him."

Cheese Puff growled again as if to say he was a match for any raccoon in the county.

190

"Shut that dog up," Iz ordered.

Her voice was edgy and—this wasn't my imagination—a little shaky. I halted and peered around. Then, afraid I might see something peering back at me from the shadows, I scooted ahead, opened the car door with trembling fingers, and tossed Cheese Puff inside.

Call me a coward if you will, but it occurred to me once again that perhaps the midnight visitor had stayed behind to see who had been inside the house. The tone of my sister's voice told me she might have come to the same conclusion.

"We should talk about this," I whispered. "Soon. We should talk about what happened and what we should do next."

"We should," Penelope agreed. "We should tell Dave what went on. I'm sure he can find a way to do something to stop the looting and help poor Mr. Walker, and maybe others, without involving you, Iz. And you trust him. Deep down, you know you do."

My sister's sour expression made it clear that trust was so deep down she couldn't feel it. What I sensed was she felt Dave was more trustworthy than other men, but not by much. In a moment she huffed out a breath. "Might as well," she said with the kind of enthusiasm reserved for someone accepting a bet to, say, swallow a live scorpion because the alternative was to swallow a cobra.

To tell the truth, after Penelope mentioned Dave, I felt kind of the same way. When it appeared I was off on a wild ghost chase, he'd been amused. But, as they say, the case had altered. Once I told him about the missing coins and books and the click of the lock, he'd be concerned.

And, I admitted to myself, he'd have good reason. I doubted there was any one thing of tremendous value in the house, but add the values of everything together and, even

191

discounting a bundle for fencing or pawning or whatever, the total could set someone up for life. And that meant the person doing the looting might be willing to take other lives in order to finance his future.

"Tomorrow evening," I said before I could think this through again and come to a different decision. "Around 7:00?"

"We'll be there," Penelope said in a firm voice.

I drove home pondering several questions.

Heck, "several" didn't cover it. The list was longer than that.

Should I tell Dave, in vague terms, about the intruder in advance of the meeting with Iz and Penelope?

If I did, would that cushion the full report?

If I didn't, would he accuse me of hiding things?

Was Sharlene in any way connected to the man/ghost?

If so, was she a pawn in the game, or was she running the operation?

Was the man/ghost the "John" who visited Mavis Dupree?

And what about Sharlene's other clients, past and present?

Had they all been taken to the cleaners in one way or another after she was hired to help them?

And, regarding my sister, did her general distrust of men go back to the death of my brother? Was it rooted in an unrecognized sense of abandonment?

I wasn't—given my sister's ability to stonewall—likely to get an answer to the last two questions. But the others were worthy of pursuit. And once I caught up on my sleep, I intended to do just that.

The quest for sleep didn't go well. To paraphrase from *Macbeth*, I couldn't knit together the torn and unraveled sleeve of care. In other words, I was awake for hours doing a mental

192

review of events. Then, long before my subconscious had spliced the loose ends of thoughts and ideas, there came a knocking at the door.

Okay, so it was more of a thudding and thumping in the kitchen than a knocking at the door. Still, it was enough—coupled with a few whines from Lola and a yip or two from Cheese Puff and a glance at the clock to ascertain that neither Dave nor Allison would be home from work and school yet—to make me rise and descend the staircase.

I found the whole intervention crew milling around Mrs. B who was unloading the contents of several paper bags onto the kitchen counter. No one seemed to find it strange that, with her condo right next door, they'd descended on my place. And, with the aromas of ginger, shrimp, onions, fried rice, and sweet and sour sauce wafting toward me, I didn't raise the issue.

Mrs. B's sapphire eyes widened when she saw me. "You didn't sub today?"

"Are you sick?" Verna asked.

Ardie rushed over and clamped a hand to my forehead. "No fever."

"I'm fine. Just tired."

"Everyone here is tired," Sybil announced. "Except me. Isn't that odd?"

The response to that question was a group eye roll. But not even Harvey Goodspeed pointed out they were tired because they'd been watching her. Of course, that could have been because Harvey was already loading up a plate with rice and beef and shrimp, carefully moving vegetables aside as he did.

"Well, my intention was that we have an early lunch and leave what was left—along with a couple of cartons just for you—in your refrigerator for your dinner," Mrs. B said. "But now . . . Will you join us?"

"Try to stop me." I glanced toward Sybil. "How did it go?"

"Very well, once we got past the initial glitches."

"Muriel means it went well once I stopped being a brat." Sybil popped a shrimp in her mouth, dribbling sweet and sour sauce on her chin and on the front of a frilly pink blouse. "After Harvey showed up and took charge."

That earned another eye roll, but Sybil didn't notice since she was scooping fried rice onto her plate. She took the chair beside Harvey who had eyes only for the contents of his plate. That plate, by the way, seemed in danger of snapping in two given the weight of the food mounded on it.

"Took charge?" I whispered to Mrs. B. "Harvey took charge?"

She sighed. "I won't argue with that interpretation of events since it appears the intervention is working."

"Even if it seems to be working for a darn peculiar reason," Verna added. "Sybil appears to be smitten with him."

Chuckling, Ardie braced her hands on my shoulder blades. "I'm here to break your fall if that announcement rocks you back on your heels."

"Thanks. Is the feeling about Harvey mutual?"

"I doubt it," Verna said. "At least not at this stage. Harvey seems to be infatuated with himself and with taking in as many calories each day as a bear about a week from hibernation. I wouldn't be surprised if the room service waiter has to be treated for back spasms from all the lifting and carrying the poor man had to do."

I watched as Sybil transferred a bit of chicken to Harvey's plate and urged him to try it.

"Is she using baby talk?"

"Oh, yeah," Ardie said. "Makes me want to puke."

194

"Makes me want to smack her," Verna grumped. "She's acting like a teenager. And at her age, that's ridiculous, pathetic, embar—"

"Now, Verna." Mrs. B patted her friend's arm. "Let her enjoy herself. She's not hurting anyone."

"She's hurting her dignity," Verna sniffed.

Personally, I'd never considered Sybil to be someone in possession of a whole lot of dignity. In fact, I thought she had the kind of dignity that could only be damaged by something along the lines of posing in the updraft from an air vent like Marilyn Monroe and then realizing she'd forgotten to put on underwear.

"And he's . . . he's . . ."

It was my turn to pat Verna's arm. "I suffer the same inability to find words to describe him."

(For the record, that was a white lie. I found plenty of words to describe Harvey, but they weren't words I can use on these pages without making readers blush, toss this book in the trash, or delete the file from their e-reader.)

"Well, let's eat now and page through a thesaurus later," Mrs. B said. "And let's not be too critical of Sybil. If a little crush—even a crush on Harvey Goodspeed—helps divert her from gambling, I'm in favor of it."

Verna sighed. "I can't grasp what she sees in him."

"She sees someone who is interested in her," Ardie said.

"Because Muriel pays him to be," Verna retorted. "And . . . and she's so much older than he is."

"When you've logged six decades on this earth," Mrs. B asked, "what does that matter?"

"Six decades, my Aunt Tilda," Verna hissed. "Try seven."

Mrs. B waved that aside. "Well, the state of his health adds a few years to his age."

Harvey shoveled in more fried rice. I increased her estimate. "Make that a dozen years. At least."

"You can't fight the heart," Mrs. B said. "Why don't we take our meals out on the deck?"

"Yes." Verna rubbed her stomach. "Sitting at the table with that man would give me indigestion."

"You'd think he's trying to eat himself to death," Ardie observed. "I hope he doesn't do a belly flop into a coffin before we get the summer project off the ground."

"I want to hear about this project. But after we eat." I grabbed a plate, filled it with vegetables and fried rice, and headed to the deck where I moved several chairs and small tables as far from the door to the condo as possible.

My faithful dog companion hung back, waiting to see if something dropped from the buffet on the counter, and then waiting to see where Mrs. B would perch so he could worship at her feet. I'd long ago abandoned any illusions about his loyalty to me, the woman who found him whimpering beneath a shrub on a cold and rainy night and shared her meager resources with him. Once he met Muriel Ballantine and realized how much money and attention she was prepared to lavish upon him, he snubbed me into second place. A distant second place. And, lest I seem to be a melodramatic whiner, I was okay with that. Mostly. There were, I admit, a few times when I wanted to smack his entitled little bottom or wring his scrawny neck—but only enough to get his attention.

"The project is still in the planning stages," Ardie said after she'd chased the last grain of rice around her plate twice and finally wedged it between the tines of her fork. The woman could be a poster child for a waste-not-want-not campaign.

"I beg to differ," Mrs. B argued. "We have all the pieces of the puzzle. We haven't fitted them together yet."

196

I couldn't help but notice the use of the pronoun "we" in that sentence. It meant Mrs. B had assigned herself a role, a large role, in Ardie's project. Glancing at Ardie I saw no sign of resentment. But Ardie worked with challenging kids occasionally prone to swearing at her, throwing books, and displaying the kind of attitude expected from a cornered mountain lion.

"Especially that extra piece." Verna nodded toward the condo. "The really large extra piece. Until we can trust Sybil not to gamble again, they're a package deal. And I can't see that man knitting or painting pictures on bits of wood or giving cooking lessons or leading a field trip to identify trees in the downtown park."

Apparently the others couldn't either, because no one argued.

After the silence had stretched for almost a minute, Mrs. B said, "I thought hiring him to watch her was a good idea at the time."

"No one's saying it wasn't," Verna assured her. "But the next phase will require more thought." She turned to me. "You know him better than the rest of us. What does he like to do?"

"Besides talk and eat and belittle people and alienate—?"

Mrs. B raised a hand, palm out. "That's all true, dear, but at the moment we're searching for positive attributes."

"Better bring a microscope for that search," I muttered before lapsing into silence with the others and trying to put aside my history with Harvey. "He's persistent," I said after a bit. "He wants answers. He took his job seriously. But sticking him in a room with a bunch of kids might not be the greatest idea since the invention of the wheel."

Ardie nodded. "If he expects respect and obedience, he's in for a rude awakening. Most of the kids we'll serve don't get

197

lessons on etiquette at home. And most don't see the benefits of good manners. Some think it's a sign of weakness to be respectful and polite."

"It will be like dealing with a hundred versions of Allison," I added. "On steroids. Having a bad hair day."

"Now, dear," Mrs. B said, "you know you're prone to embellishment."

A nice way of saying I tended to exaggerate.

"She's not embellishing by much," Ardie said. "At least not about some of the kids that may turn up. The thing is, if they didn't turn up, they'd probably be home alone, and maybe without anything nourishing to eat. Or they might be hanging with older kids with attitudes that are even worse. They might end up in gangs or in jail."

Mrs. B's sapphire eyes clouded. "Then we have our work cut out for us. Perhaps, unless we arrive at a better use for his talents, Mr. Goodspeed can function as a deterrent to bad behavior and as a force for good."

"Like security guards in the schools?" Ardie asked.

"If you will. And perhaps, as time goes on, the experience will change his behavior as well as that of the children."

Personally, I thought that was about as optimistic as hoping the rate of pay for substitute teachers would double for the next school year, but I kept my lips zipped. Verna, a realist with a capital R, did the same. But Ardie said, "We won't know unless we try."

Chapter 20

Coincidentally, that was the same approach I used on my sister when she balked at telling Dave about our experiences. "We'll give it to him a little at a time. If you decide he's not taking us seriously, we'll clam up."

Iz finally agreed and then, to my surprise and trepidation, told me I was in charge of laying out the story. "You have more experience with men than I do."

Just as I was taking that as a compliment, she added, "Most of it bad."

I wanted to argue but, as you know, she had a point. All she'd have to do was come out swinging with reference to my lying, cheating, embezzling ex-husband Jake, and I'd slink to my corner and forfeit the bout. On the other hand, my bad experiences contributed to my overall knowledge of the male sex. So, when we sat down on the deck with Dave that evening, I took the lead with a hypothetical question.

"Suppose someone came across evidence of a crime while that person was someplace he or she shouldn't necessarily be and—?"

"Was this on the ghost-hunting expedition or somewhere else? What happened? What did you see?" He set his beer bottle on the deck with a clunk and his voice ranged higher. "Is

199

someone liable to try to kill you to keep you quiet about what you witnessed? Are you going to have to be rescued like usual?"

Like usual?

Seriously?

Okay, I admit that Booth Abernathy-Chambers and Kymberli Weador wanted to silence me permanently. And, yeah, I've occasionally needed a little help in the rescue department. But it wasn't like that happened every week. A couple of times a year didn't add up to "like usual" in my book.

I longed to jump in and say just that, but sometimes silence is best. So I crossed my arms and, careful not to disturb my entitled mutt, leaned back on my edge of the lounge chair he'd commandeered.

Dave turned his attention to Iz and Penelope. "Were you two with her? Did you encourage her to do something dangerous?"

Stone faced, Iz glared at him. But Penelope launched an Academy-Award-worthy performance of offended innocence. "Why would you think that? Any of that?" She pasted on an expression of first-degree amazement and shook her head. "I know that your training as an officer of the law and your experience in the field make you skeptical of everyone's actions and motives, but don't you think you're carrying suspicions and mistrust too far?"

Dave didn't give the question even a second of consideration. "No. Not when it comes to Barbara and her ability to sniff out trouble and take a running jump in the middle of it."

"But—"

"And when she told me she'd made strawberry shortcake and invited her sister over for dessert on the deck, I smelled a rat. Several rats. A whole herd or a flock or a raft of rats. More rats than—"

"We get the point," I said. "There's a regular rodent reunion going on and only you can smell it."

"Right. Something is rotten. And not in Denmark."

"An allusion to *Hamlet* doesn't make your case stronger," Penelope said.

I turned a thumb up and flashed Penelope a grin. Way to smack down Dave's attempt to use Shakespeare against us.

"If we're being accused of a crime," Iz said, "we have a right to see the evidence."

Spoken like someone who would know. During her rabble-rousing years, Iz spent many hours refuting—or attempting to refute—charges related to events that took place when gatherings or marches or protests got out of hand.

Dave scowled, crossed his arms, and rocked back in the canvas sling chair he favored.

And there we all sat, at an impasse.

I was about to offer seconds on shortcake with extra whipped cream when Dave grumbled, "All right. Tell me about it. Hypothetically."

He said that last word with a sneer.

"For all you know it *is* hypothetical," I challenged.

"Right. Maybe you're asking for a friend." He leaned forward. "A friend who isn't here with us right now."

"Possibly."

Another long silence passed and then he sighed. "Go ahead. You pretend it's hypothetical. I'll pretend I'm not a police officer."

"Technically you're in the sheriff's de—"

"Enough." He rocked forward, the legs of his chair thumping the deck. "Spit it out before I reach retirement age."

201

"I will. But only if you don't jump to conclusions before I'm finished."

He crimped his lips, considering. "I can't guarantee that."

"Can you at least guarantee you won't interrupt to lecture or interrogate me?"

"I'll try."

I turned to Iz. "What do you think?"

"I think he's gotten wise to you," she said with a smirk.

"Is that a compliment in disguise?" Dave asked.

"If that's how you want to take it."

"My advice is to take it," Penelope said with a rueful smile. "Months could pass before you get another one. Years might—"

"I give you compliments," Iz insisted. "This morning I—"

"Enough." I made a timeout sign. "Do I ask him about the, uh, hypothetical situation or not?"

"Oh, go ahead," Iz said with a backward flip of her hand. "Tell him whatever you want. I'll probably wash out of the program anyway."

She seemed resigned and I wondered again if giving up her former life to stay in Reckless River with Penelope was the best thing for her. I mean, Iz had never been an optimist, but she hadn't required a positive outlook because she had a massive ego and the confidence to go with it. She'd also pretty much always played by her own rules, mostly making them up as she went along. But now she no longer had a national stage and faced a whole raft of rules made by others.

Dave studied her for a few seconds. "What happened on the ghost hunt could jeopardize your training?"

"Maybe. But not because what we did was illegal," I said. "It wasn't."

"But it also wasn't strictly within the program rules," Penelope added. "Although I think the welfare of an elderly client—"

"Get on with it," Iz said. "Tell him what happened."

So I did, painting Iz as a candidate for some kind of humanitarian award for her concern for a frail and confused elderly man who was being victimized by someone playing on his love for his dead son. When I finished, Dave grilled us like racks of ribs on a barbecue.

"He didn't invite you in, but you didn't break in? You didn't see anyone? You're certain the door was locked when you went upstairs? Both locks? You have no idea how many books or coins or figurines are missing?"

And on and on.

I refilled our drinks and got Iz seconds on shortcake. I woke up Cheese Puff and took him to the tiny rose garden to do his thing. I watched a sailboat zigzag along the river toward its moorage. Finally I interrupted the interrogation. "What can you do to help Mr. Walker?"

He scratched his head. "I can tell you what I'd like to do. I'd like to hide over there and catch this ghost pretender in the act."

"But . . . ?"

"But there are holes and gaps and issues and considerations here that call for a cautious approach. And don't forget that I'm the new guy on the block in the sheriff's department. I'm still getting my feet on the ground. I think I better run this past a few of the honchos and see how they want to handle it."

"You're kidding!" Iz and I chorused.

"How long will that take?" Penelope asked in a calm and reasonable tone.

Dave spread his hands. "Maybe a few days."

"And meanwhile the looter keeps looting?" Iz asked.

"Or maybe he decides he's had enough of the piecemeal approach," I raged. "Maybe he cleans out the whole place. Maybe tonight."

Penelope grasped my sister's arm. "What if he ties up poor Mr. Walker? Or knocks him out? Or worse?"

"I don't think he'll go that far," Dave said in his most rational voice. "He appears to have left the house because he heard you. That could indicate he doesn't want things to escalate."

"*Could* indicate? That's crap." Iz stood, kicking over her water glass as she did and sending ice cubes sliding along the deck. "If the law can't do anything, then it's up to civilians. It's up to us."

She patted the pockets of her cargo pants.

Once again I wondered what she carried in the way of weapons.

"Right." Penelope got to her feet, retrieving my sister's glass and her own. "And if we have to break the law to stop this crime, that's exactly what we'll do."

"Yeah." I stood and added my voice. "That's what we'll do."

"No." Dave grabbed my wrist. "That's *not* what you'll do."

I pulled loose and glared at him. The setting sun gave everything a wash of red, so I couldn't tell how angry he was, but if I had to guess, on a scale that ran to 10, I'd peg him at 9.935.

I'd peg myself at 9.938.

But before either of us said the kinds of things we'd look back on later with pride or sorrow or regret or even more anger than we felt at this moment, Penelope spoke. "Iz and I've got tonight, Barbara. You need your rest. You had a lot of stress with Allison and you might have a subbing job tomorrow. Besides, the ghost man might not show. Mr. Walker says he doesn't come every night. He still has the coins in the morning."

But Perry Walker was hard of hearing and a sound sleeper. The ghost guy might pop by to claim other items.

I was about to argue those points when I realized I *was* exhausted. "Okay. You take tonight. But promise me you won't do anything stupid."

"Stupid is your department," Iz said.

That tore it. With a choice between a long night of sniping from my sister or a lecture from Dave that would be over in a few minutes, I opted for the lecture. "Fine. But call me if anything happens. And call 911 if there's even a hint of—"

"Don't worry." Penelope flashed her phone. "I'm on it. But we'll call only if something happens. Otherwise we won't disturb you."

"What she sees in your sister I'll never know," Dave said when the door to the condo closed behind them.

"You know that Iz says the same thing about us, don't you?"

Dave took a step back and feigned delight. "Are you saying that she wonders what I see in you?"

"No, she wonders— Oh never mind. Just give me the lecture and let me get some sleep."

"No lecture. I admit I wasn't concerned when I thought it was about creaking floorboards and faulty wiring, but now . . ." He pulled me against him and kissed the top of my head. "I love you, but I don't own you. If you want to camp out in a haunted house, I can't stop you unless I handcuff you to the refrigerator. And, as determined as you are, I bet you'd find a way to pick the

205

lock with the pop top from a soda can or a crispy Chinese noodle or a dried-out string bean."

And, given that things had a way of migrating to the rear of the refrigerator and becoming mummified, there might be several lock-picking implements readily available. I congratulated myself on not blurting out an apology for my failure to maintain a higher level of cleanliness. After all, three of us—not counting my sister and other visitors—used the refrigerator. Housekeeping chores shouldn't all be dumped on me.

"For all you know, I might have anticipated you'd cuff me," I teased. "I might carry lock picks in my pocket at all times."

"Nah. But your sister might. Who knows what she keeps in those pockets."

"I dare you to ask."

"Not me. Sometimes not knowing is the best option. And, should something from one of her pockets be used in the commission of a crime, it gives me deniability."

He kissed me again and steered me toward the door. "Let's get some sleep. You might be hearing from Big Chill early tomorrow."

"Or my sister," I reminded him.

"Or Iz," he agreed. His tone implied he'd rather hear from a federal tax auditor.

Iz didn't call.

And, when the phone rang before dawn broke, it wasn't the Chillster.

It was Dario O'Brien.

"I need a favor," he said before I offered a greeting. "A huge favor. I know how you feel about working with Jake—"

"The same way I feel about dancing the tango with an alligator. So if that's what the favor involves, you can forget it."

Dave flopped onto his side and raised himself on one elbow. I tipped the phone so he could hear.

"I'll owe you," Dario pleaded. "Muriel will owe you. You can name your price. We'll pay by check or cash. Just please produce the show this morning. It's an emergency."

That last word piqued my interest. "What happened? Where's Deming?"

Deming Featherstone, an eager kid with a flock of freckles and an English accent, had joined the radio station team as Jake's producer at the end of March. He'd hit the ground running and done a great job of reining in my ex-husband while developing fresh ideas for his talk show and attracting more callers every week. In addition to screening calls, he did an opening back-and-forth with Jake to introduce the issue of the day and review some of the history and present differing views.

"Deming's here," Dario said. "But he's not . . . here."

Chapter 21

"There but not there?" A veritable trove of information. "What does that mean? Is he in a trance? Did an alien life form suck out his brain? Did he fall down the stairs and knock himself out? Did he eat something he's allergic to?"

"You're close on that last guess," Dario said when I ran out of breath. "He's over caffeinated. He drank too much coffee."

"Coffee? I thought he drank tea."

"He did. Earl Grey. English Breakfast. Twinings of London. Got a shipment from his mother every month. But last week he discovered the new coffee shop downtown."

"What's to discover? Except for the name it's no different from any other coffee place in town."

Dave joined the conversation. "The blond barista is different."

I narrowed my eyes. "How different?"

"Just, uh, young. And, um, perky. But I, uh, I hardly noticed her because she's, um, barely out of her teens." He kissed the corner of my mouth. "I'm all about mature women. Did I mention that she's too young for me?"

"She's not too young for Deming," Dario groused. "The boy was there all yesterday afternoon and evening. And then he took her out for coffee. Like he needed more of that! He's bouncing around like this is a gravity-free zone."

I checked the clock on the nightstand. "Jake's show doesn't start until 6:00. Maybe Deming will come off the high by then."

"Doubt it. Poor guy's sweating, too. Panting. Shaking. Having heart palpitations and dizzy spells. Jake had him drink a bunch of water to flush his system, but he threw it up."

"On Jake?" I asked hopefully.

"Almost."

Drat.

"He says he felt better after that, but I don't believe him because he's started quacking like a duck at the end of every sentence. And sometimes in the middle. It's like some kind of weird verbal punctuation."

I chuckled at the thought of Deming quacking. He'd been named for the New Mexico city where his mother had lived for a year as an exchange student, a city famous for its duck races.

"Laugh if you want, but we have a serious topic today—the summer fire season. If he's quacking, callers will think we don't care if forests turn to charcoal."

And Jake would probably think that would benefit anyone planning a barbecue. My ex, as you know by now, is not a deep thinker—when he bothers to think at all. "I hope Deming wrote Jake's intro material before he overdid the wakey juice."

"Researched and wrote it yesterday. It's great. Comprehensive. But I can't trust him to deliver his part without quacking. How fast can you get here?"

"Twenty minutes. Call a cab and get Deming to a doctor to make sure he's okay. Better yet, take him yourself. See what they can do to get him back on earth. When you take off, leave the back door unlocked and put a copy of the script on the console for me."

"Done."

"Great. And have coffee ready. Good coffee."

209

"There will be."

"And I want a clean mug."

"I'll wash one."

"With soap."

"Lots of soap. Anything else?"

"I want a doughnut. No, make that a breakfast burrito."

"I'll order it now. They'll deliver to the back door and you can pick it up at a commercial break. Is that your final demand?"

I was on a roll and enjoying having my wishes granted, so I went for the brass ring. "No. One more thing. Promise you'll never ask me to work with Jake again."

"Never. I promise."

"Good, because no matter how far I am in debt to Muriel and how many favors I owe you both, I will do this once and only once."

"Message received. Now hurry."

And I did, sliding into underwear, jeans, T-shirt, and sandals. I didn't bother to wash my face or comb my hair, and skipped a fresh application of deodorant because I wouldn't want Jake to think I'd gone any trouble. For good measure, I didn't brush my teeth.

"Whoa, Barbie." Jake clutched his chest when I entered the studio. "You look like five miles of bad road."

Dang.

I'd been aiming for nine miles, at least.

"Funny you should say that." I tossed my purse on the floor, set my coffee mug on a low stand, plopped myself in the chair on the opposite side of a narrow table, and swung the boom microphone to within a few inches of my lips. "That's exactly the look I was going for."

"I get it that you didn't have time to wash your hair," he groused, "but it takes only a minute to comb it."

"Not worth the effort. Didn't brush my teeth, either." I grinned as wide as I could and blew out air with each word.

Big mistake. One of my molars sent out tendrils of pain. I checked the calendar. Six days until my first dental appointment.

Telling myself the pain would subside once I was no longer in the same room as Jake, I spun my chair to face the bushy-haired board op in the tiny room on the other side of a thick window. He'd worked at the radio station back when I produced for Rick Rivers and, although he'd hung on longer after the last recession hit, he'd also been downsized. Dario had lured him back with the promise of a boost in salary that wouldn't all be sucked up buying gas for the commute to Portland or paying Oregon income tax. The deal-clincher was a work environment no longer polluted by Rick Rivers. "Did you get a level?"

He made an okay sign with his thumb and forefinger.

"You don't have to ditch good hygiene to make yourself unattractive," Jake said. "I'm not interested. I've moved on since we split up."

"From what I've heard, you've moved on several times. At least once because she came to her senses and changed the locks."

"All a misunderstanding," Jake said in the tone of an attorney mounting a defense. "I accidentally accessed her bank account instead of my own."

"Right. That kind of thing happens a lot. Why I bet I did it three or four times last month. Once to a complete stranger."

Jake nodded. ""See? It's easy to do. But she stayed mad even after I paid her back in only three installments."

211

He said that last bit with a genuine tone of wonder. The man never failed to amaze me.

"You know, Jake, with your experience in this arena, you should suggest a program on bank security and how it could be improved."

The board op laughed, pounded the edge of his console, and flashed me a victory sign.

"Great idea." Jake beamed one of his smarmy smiles.

I deflected it with a snide comment. "Your first piece of advice to your listeners should be a no-brainer. Warn any females who might be susceptible to your charms to squander their funds on shoes and jewelry before they meet you. Why should *they* pay for fresh highlights for your hair?"

Reflexively, Jake patted his hair.

"That's not glitter among the strands, is it?"

He blushed. "Just a little."

The board op pounded the console so hard I felt the floor shake.

"See," Jake said, "I met this girl, uh woman, and—"

I raised my hand, palm out. "Don't want to hear about it until she's old enough to vote."

"Okay. That would be in three months. No, five. No . . ." Jake began counting on his fingers.

The board op pounded the console harder and wiped his eyes on the sleeve of his T-shirt. He reached for a switch and flipped it, opening the channel to a speaker high on the wall. "Two minutes," he called.

I skimmed the script. Along with a short intro about fires already burning in the Pacific Northwest and fears about what was projected to be a long, hot summer, it included plenty of additional, in-depth information. A chart showed the number of square miles in farmland, in both public and private forests, in pasture, and in cities and developed areas. Deming had also tucked in graphs showing rainfall and temperature patterns and summarized burning policies going back a century. After that, he'd detailed the number of fires caused by lightning and human carelessness, the yearly cost of fighting wildfires, benefits of controlled burns, and so on.

"Impressive," I said.

"My hair?" Jake asked.

The board op and I exchanged an eye roll.

"Deming's research." I waved the script.

"Oh. That." Jake moved his mug from his copy. The first page was a smear of ink and coffee.

"That's going to be tough to read. Want to copy mine?"

"No time. I'll just wing it."

The board op mimed strangling himself.

I nodded. Jake on the wing could mean talking about fire season creating more opportunities for smoking meat or roasting marshmallows. Or he might speculate about what female firefighters wore under their official gear. And it wasn't beyond him to wonder if firefighters should hydrate with beer and thus add more enjoyment to the experience.

According to the clock, we had less than 30 seconds before disaster struck.

I waved my script. "This is pretty dry stuff. Facts and figures. Necessary for the topic, but dull, lifeless. If I read it, your listeners won't think you're, well, becoming a dork, a dweeb, a nerd."

Using those words was like presenting a vampire with a crucifix, a string of garlic, and a handful of holy soil.

Jake recoiled, a look of horror on his face.

Honestly, this was way too easy.

213

"But I open the show?" Jake jabbed a finger at me. "Right? Because it's my show."

"Definitely your show." And I'd rather be having the skin sanded off the bottoms of my feet right now than be here taking part in it. "All I'll do is the stale, stodgy, and stuffy, uh, stuff."

He narrowed his eyes. "You sure? You won't jump in and start talking before I'm finished? Like you did all the time when we were married?"

"Definitely not." Although I'd be tempted. Sorely tempted. And, given Jake's ability to bypass the topic and pass off fiction as fact, I'd be frequently tempted.

Any way you sliced this, I was in for a nail-biting, tongue-chewing, remark-swallowing morning.

"On the air in five," the board op called.

I took a deep breath and a long swallow of coffee. The opening music played. It wasn't actually Sinatra's "My Way," but it sounded a heck of a lot like it. Appropriate for Jake.

I skimmed the script again and tried not to gag while Jake blathered on about what a beautiful day it was and how happy he was to be spending the morning with his thousands of fans and how much he was looking forward to what they had to say about the day's really hot topic, a topic so hot it was burning up. After what seemed like a century, he introduced me as a special guest for the day, a woman he knew well. "Really, really, really well, if you get my drift."

By imagining Jake drifting in the middle of the Pacific on a 20-quart cooler surrounded by sharks, I managed to stay in my seat and not rip his face off. Dario didn't know it, but this was the favor that would wipe out all other favors. After this morning, the slate was clean—except for the financial debt I owed Mrs. B.

The board op pointed at me, signaling that my mike was hot. Good manners called for me to thank Jake and say something about being delighted to be on his show. But we all know I manage to tell enough lies as it is, so I saw no need to add another. Instead, I plunged in, reading Deming's script, tossing in a lot of his facts and figures, and generally hogging the air.

After two minutes, Jake circled his forefinger, the signal for me to wrap it up.

I ignored him and plunged on.

Another minute passed and Jake drew his finger across his throat, the signal for me to stop.

I didn't. I still had plenty of information to spew.

Jake scowled and made the sign to the board op.

The op, head down, didn't respond. He appeared to be checking something on the console and therefore wasn't in a position to see the sign. But I would have bet the contents of my wallet ($5.47 and a coupon for 20% off a single purchase at the local hardware store) that nothing needed checking and he was acting.

Jake made the sign to me again.

I nodded, but went on, slowing my delivery as I neared the bottom of the final page of the script. Then, as Jake stood and went to the window to get the board op's attention, I wrapped up fast. "And that's an overview of the situation. Back to you, Jake."

Jake scurried to his seat, shot me a scowl that could curdle cream, and invited callers to share their views. Much as I hated to admit it, he was good at talking with listeners and drawing out their opinions without being smarmy or sarcastic and occasionally even without expressing his own views.

215

Dario and Deming burst in as the last notes of the theme music played. "Great show," Dario boomed. "Terrific job, Barbara."

"Very professional." Deming mopped his brow with a tissue clutched in a shaky hand. He wasn't back to normal, but at least he wasn't quacking his punctuation.

"She hogged the mike," Jake groused. "I told you not to call her in. I told you I couldn't trust her not to make me look like a fool. And she lied to me. She promised she wouldn't interrupt."

"And I didn't." I scooped up my purse and the mug. "You tossed it to me and I set the scene for questions. That's all."

"Took you forever," he muttered.

"It's a huge issue." Deming mopped his face once more and slurped water from a bottle the size of a mailbox. "Lots of ground to cover."

"I could have cov—"

"I'm outta here." I brushed past the whiner, bound for the kitchen to drop off my mug and toss my burrito wrapper in a trash can.

"Thanks again." Deming thrust a paper at Jake. "Promos. For tomorrow's show on the recycling crisis. We'll record them in ten minutes."

"Recycling." Jake groaned. "That's, like, garbage."

"Right. Recycling becomes garbage if people don't pay attention to what can go in the barrel and what can't. And that costs us all a lot of money."

Jake seemed to be considering that for an entire second or maybe even two. Then he said, "Speaking of money, can I borrow $40 for lunch?"

Deming paled. More sweat popped out on his brow.

"I'll answer that for you, Deming," I said. "No, Jake, the answer is negative. Because I'm confident you haven't paid him back the last loans. And note, I said loans. Plural."

"You're always exaggerating, Barbie. It's just two loans, not a whole plural. Whatever that is."

"Three loans," Deming said in a faint voice.

"Three?" Jake managed an expression of stunned surprise. "Well, okay. How about you make it four? I'll pay you back on Friday. You can trust—"

"You can trust him to ask you to make it five." I patted Jake's gelled and glittered hair. "As always, spending time with you made me appreciate almost everyone else on the planet. But now I've got to run."

After I hit the kitchen, Dario followed me to the door. "You're the greatest. Let me know what we owe you and I'll have a check cut."

"You don't owe me a thing . . . except to stick to your promise that I won't have to work with Jake again."

"Right. And I will. But . . . Look, I know you said you never wanted to work in radio again after your experience with Rick Rivers, but would you consider working with someone you like? Producing a show once a week? Just for the summer?"

I paused with my hand on the doorknob. "I can't consider until you tell me who that someone else is."

Chapter 22

"It's Muriel," Dario said.

"Mrs. B? Mrs. B's getting a radio show?"

"Yeah." He drew in a breath. "At least I hope so. She doesn't know yet."

I released the knob and turned to face him. "She doesn't know? But if it's a summer show, it must start—"

"This coming weekend. If you sign on." Dario scuffed the toe of his shoe on the carpet. "She needs something to do, something besides shopping and planning dinners, something that's all hers."

"Something where she doesn't run the risk of stepping on other people's toes and meddling in their projects?"

He raised his hands in protest. "I didn't say that."

"And I didn't hear you say it. But you're right. Her part in the intervention is over and she's made some good suggestions about Ardie's summer program. It might be a good time to step back. Without stepping into another random hobby."

"Right. Or stepping in at the sandwich shop."

Or, worse, jumping in to plan the wedding Dave and I had yet to set a date for. "What did you have in mind?"

"It's Deming's idea. Came up with it while we were waiting to see the doctor and Muriel was on the phone trying to convince me she should drive down and badger the doctor to make sure the kid got the best treatment. It's one of those on-air garage sales."

"A swap show?"

"Right. You know how much she loves flea markets and garage sales, and how much she knows about antiques and collectibles, and how much she loves a bargain."

"Even though she needs a bargain like a kangaroo needs a belly pack."

Dario laughed. "Yeah. But I guess even if you're rolling in dough it's nice to think you're getting a deal. So, are you in?"

"Sure. It sounds like fun. Want me to do some research on how they do it, how it's working out in other markets? And I can write promos if Deming is too jammed up."

"Sure. Good idea. But maybe you better talk with Deming. Only wait until he stops sweating."

We shared a laugh.

"I'll send him an e-mail," I said. "When are you planning to break this to Mrs. B?"

He checked his watch. "In a few hours. At lunch. Think she'll agree?"

I considered for a moment. "Yes. But first she'll hesitate. It's something she's never done before. She'll need a little coaxing."

"That's what this is for." He drew a slender box from the pocket of his suit jacket and opened it to reveal a necklace with a perfect blue pearl dangling inside a silver quarter moon.

I smiled. Dario was taking a page from Mrs. B's book and using pearl power to influence her. "It's gorgeous. I don't think she has anything like it."

"Hope not." He tucked the box in his pocket. "It's not easy buying for a woman who has everything."

"Especially pearls."

219

When I hit the parking lot, I found Stan Stewart leaning against the driver's door of my car. Despite the increasing heat, he wore sagging corduroy slacks and a tweed jacket with one dog-eared pocket and permanent wrinkles around his elbows. The *Reckless River Roundup* didn't pay huge salaries and didn't provide clothing allowances. Even if it did, I had a feeling Stewart would dress the same way. I doubted he subscribed to the clothes-make-the-man theory. I also believed his clothing choices—and his unkempt hair and beard—were at least partly in the way of costume. In other words, he dressed as he thought an investigative reporter would. Or should.

Beyond that, he didn't have time for serious shopping. He spent half his waking time trying to find something worth investigating in Reckless River. He devoted the other half to revising his resume and sending it out to editors at larger newspapers in larger cities. He was fortunate that most resumes could be submitted with a click of his computer mouse. Otherwise, even with the additional bucks he made providing short news inserts for Jake's show, he'd have to live in his car to finance postage and mailing envelopes.

"Heard you on the air," he said. "Nice job."

"Thanks. Did you drive over here to tell me that, or are you meeting with Dario and Deming?"

Notice I didn't include Jake in that question. By now you're painfully aware of Jake's lack of awareness when it came to news, current events, the environment, and the state of the world in general. So, a meeting to discuss upcoming programs and Stewart's ideas for expanding a topic, or generating a news story to tie it to, wouldn't involve my less-than-esteemed ex.

"Nope. Met yesterday. How come you were filling in? Did Deming quit?"

"No."

"Is that the truth or the corporate line? Because I had today in the office pool on when he'd pull the plug, so if he handed in his resignation after mid—"

"You don't win. He didn't quit. He has no intention of quitting."

"You sure? Because, at 50 cents a day since the end of March, there's enough in the pool for a decent dinner."

"I'm positive he didn't quit. He's inside right now. He went to the doctor this morning because he was feeling shaky. He had an allergic reaction. A minor reaction. Nothing life-threatening."

I thought my delivery was convincing, but Stewart—he preferred to be called by his last name, claiming he was more a Stewart than a Stanley or even a Stan—got that eager, reporter-sniffing-out-a-story expression. He jumped on my statement like a cat pouncing on a laser dot. "A reaction to Jake?"

"No."

"Jake's cologne?"

"No."

"Jake's political views?"

"No."

"Jake's hair gel?"

"No."

"Jake's skin cream?"

"Enough."

"If Deming quit, would you take the job?"

"Yes. But on two conditions."

Stewart narrowed his eyes. "What conditions?"

"They discover a library system on Mars, and Jake undergoes a personality transplant."

He considered for a moment. "So, probably not."

221

"Definitely not. But Deming isn't leaving. At least not soon. Say what you want about Jake, but working with him provides Deming with lots of experience."

"Mostly bad experience. Jake's an ego-powered demolition derby. He's a demolition derby on the freeway. In the snow. During rush hour."

"He's all that." I laughed. "But preventing collisions—and doing damage control on the ones he can't—presents Deming with opportunities for creative management he wouldn't get—"

"—anywhere else." Stewart finished my sentence. "Way to paint a rosy picture of a black hole. Now, let's talk news. What have you got for me?"

Thoughts of Perry Walker and the looting ghost made me pause for a few seconds before I said, "Nothing."

"Ha! You hesitated. You have something."

"I don't."

"You do." He straightened from his usual slouch. "Give it up. You owe me for holding back on the real story of what happened with Booth Abernathy-Chambers. I know he didn't rescue you. But unless I uncover a witness, I can't prove it."

Thankfully.

If Stewart revealed the truth about why Booth tried to drown me and what my sister did to rescue me, his powerful widow would turn my life into something that would make hell seem like a tropical resort.

"Come on," he said in a tone that was half wheedling and half threatening. "Give it up. I need a story I can get my teeth in. I need a story with legs."

Now there was a bizarre juxtaposition of images.

I made a mental note to wash my mind out with soap later.

"You may have decided you like being stuck in Reckless River, but I want out." He held a thumb and forefinger a

222

centimeter apart. "I've been close. This close to a job in Detroit. This close to a job in Miami. This close to a job in San Diego."

As he ticked off the cities, I ticked off my reaction to them. Too cold in the winter. Too hot in the summer. Pleasant, but expensive.

"Help me," he pleaded. "I know you've got something. I can see it in your eyes. Is it another cold case? Drug dealing? Government corruption?"

I waved him aside so I could open the door. "It's none of the above."

He didn't move. "It's something."

I sighed. "Okay, it may be something. But not yet."

"When? Tomorrow? Next week?"

He reminded me of a puppy—a really large and annoying puppy—piddling on my feet. I was about to give up on talk and shove him aside when Mavis Dupree popped into my head. Naturally I couldn't tell him what I'd learned from my sister about her male visitors, but Mavis might be featured in a story about the erosion of the ridge. Roll in a few of her neighbors also facing possible loss of property and it could appear Mavis was just one of the crowd.

And, if Mavis was as chatty as she'd been with Iz, Stewart would sniff out a story. The man had more curiosity than a dozen cats. But if he didn't tumble to the fact that she might be the victim of a man pretending to be a client at her long-closed house of ill repute, I could always drop hints by way of an anonymous letter.

Okay, I admit this wasn't my greatest plan ever. But I was tired. And the sun was in my eyes.

Literally.

I moved a few steps to my left. "I don't know how big a story this is . . ."

223

"Cough it up. I'll decide."

I coughed, cloaking the facts in a veil of fiction about driving by the scene of the cat crisis on a trip down memory lane and thinking about the problems some residents of Portland's hills had with the ground sliding and wondering if the same thing could happen in Reckless River if there were heavy rains this winter. "Some houses on that ridge are huge," I finished up. "And a lot of them have pools and tennis courts and extra garages in the back. That's more weight on the slope. And the runoff from all those roofs and driveways probably gets concentrated. That could cause more erosion."

Gee. I sounded almost like I knew what I was talking about.

"There was one—I think it was brick, but it definitely had pink shutters—where it looks like part of the back yard is falling away. I could see trees leaning over like they'd been in a hurricane."

How's that for fabrication?

"Hmmm." Stewart pulled a notebook and stubby pencil from one drooping pocket. "Sounds pretty dull, but if there's a slow news day, I'll check it out."

Spoken like today *wasn't* a slow news day.

Spoken like he hadn't come here to beg me to toss him a crumb.

Or a sliver of a crumb.

Have I mentioned the man had "desperate" written all over him?

I played along. "Sorry. That's all I've got."

"I don't buy that." He shuffled aside. "But if you come up with anything else, call me. Call me before anyone else."

I opened the car door. "Even before 911?"

While he was considering his answer, I drove off.

My intention was to go home, dive between the sheets, and snag a nap, but Big Chill had other plans. When her number lit up my cellphone, I pulled over. "Get in here," she commanded. "Stat."

"Now you're running a hospital?" I teased.

"I'm running you off the list of substitutes if you don't move it. This is an emergency."

Chapter 23

She disconnected before I could ask for her definition of an emergency or tell her I was dressed more for failure than for success.

I made a sharp turn on the first street heading toward Captain Meriwether High School and hit the gas.

There were two reasons for speed. First, the school year was nearly over, but Big Chill could hold a grudge until September. Second, reporter Stan Stewart wasn't the only one in town with rampant curiosity. I wanted to know the nature of this emergency.

And of course I wanted to do all I could to help out.

At least that's what I told myself.

And then I steamed into Big Chill's office and found the emergency involved Brenda Waring and the culinary arts.

I don't mean art on the level of the greatest chefs of all time, chefs like James Beard or Anthony Bourdain. What I mean is art on the level of a toddler trying to pass off mud pies as Cornish pasties or presenting a handful of grass as pesto.

"I need you to cover her classes. Tremaine took her to an emergency clinic to have her stomach pumped." Big Chill waved her hands. "Or whatever they do when you eat something toxic."

"What did she eat?"

"Some kind of tart. She made three different kinds last night and brought in a carload. Said she wanted to spice up the senior breakfast."

"What was in them?"

"Berries, goat cheese, wild onions and mushrooms, rhubarb, dandelion leaves." Big Chill shrugged. "Plenty of other stuff, and who knows what kind of seasoning. Tremaine took samples along so a lab can check them out. She ate one of each trying to convince the kids they were healthier than what was on the tables."

The senior breakfast was a buffet laid out for graduates to snack on while they dropped off textbooks, picked up their diplomas, exchanged yearbooks for signing, and said their farewells to the teachers who kicked them through the goalposts and out into the world. It was an informal event with juice, muffins, fruit, and bagels, and kids liked it that way. It needed spicing up about as much as a porpoise needed a life jacket.

I combed my hair with my fingers. "How many kids got sick?"

"None. By the time they're seniors, they're smart enough to steer clear of her concoctions."

"And critics say kids don't learn anything in high school," I scoffed.

"Be sure to tell your legislator that." She pointed to a stack of papers. "Finals for her classes. We're on testing schedule today. And we're out an hour early."

Testing schedule meant classes would be double the usual time. But early release trimmed that by 20 minutes.

"When's lunch?"

"For you, right now." She checked her watch. "You've got nine minutes."

Nine minutes wasn't much, but I had a lot of hard days of subbing under my belt and in eight minutes I was unlocking the door to Brenda's classroom while balancing the stack of tests, a bottle of water, a pack of gum I'd filched from the Chillster, and a cardboard boat filled with salad. The salad itself looked fine, but I wasn't so sure about the dressing I'd pumped into one corner of the boat. It was the color of the coral lipstick popular with friends back in junior high, and I suspected it might taste about the same. That was probably a benefit since the calorie count per tablespoon would run to three digits. What I didn't eat wouldn't end up on my hips.

Brenda's room was twice the size of a regular classroom. It had tables, chairs, a teacher's desk and a whiteboard at one end, and six cooking stations at the other. As I offloaded the tests on the desk, I breathed in stale air and the scents of vanilla, cinnamon, fried onions, scorched toast, and fish long out of water or refrigeration.

I've never been a huge fan of air freshening sprays, but I zoomed to the kitchen and opened cabinets in search of one. I found only a half-full box of baking soda. It was doing its best to absorb the odor in a refrigerator and failing in the attempt. I also found the source of the fish stink—wadded plastic wrapping wedged beside another refrigerator. Plucking it loose with the tips of two fingers, I wrapped it in paper towels and stuffed it in a freezer compartment in an attempt to contain the smell.

When I turned to the classroom area I was greeted with a round of applause from a half dozen kids. "Way to go, Ms. Reed," a girl with pink and green hair called out.

I took a bow. "Hope that helps."

"Can we open the windows?" a boy in a hoodie asked.

"Sure."

"Miss Waring doesn't let us," the girl informed me. "She says outside air will 'dissipate the potpourri of aromas' in here. She says aromas are vital because they inspire creativity in a cook."

And, in Brenda's case, inspire diners to take up fasting as a hobby.

"I think I already took care of the potpourri of aromas by ditching the fish wrapper," I said, "so open away. And don't worry about culinary creativity. It's the end of the school year. No one will be expressing themselves in this room until September."

"The windows are right above the trash and recycling containers," the boy pointed out. "Those don't smell all that great."

"They smell better than it does in here," the girl argued.

He thought that over for only a second or two before opening a window as far as it would go. The girl found a fan behind a stack of textbooks and got the air moving. The smell joining us on warm air coursing through the open windows was robust and heady, but far easier on the nostrils than what it replaced.

Even Tremaine Scott noticed when he came by to thank me for coming in to cover for Brenda. "First time this room didn't smell like something that died on the beach last week."

He'd attempted to whisper, but his voice had a tendency to boom. Even kids at the far tables heard and snickered.

I plucked the sleeve of his pale blue shirt and led him to the kitchen area. "I don't mean to tell you how to do your job, but these kids want an update on Brenda's situation. And they'll know you're lying if you try to sugarcoat food poisoning and call it an upset stomach or the flu. They trust you to tell them the truth and quash the rumors."

"Rumors?' He winced. "There's more than one?"

"Three that I know about. They all heard that the tarts were accidentally toxic because she combined weird ingredients or used mushrooms she picked herself. Then there's the rumor that she was out to get some of the seniors she didn't like but mixed up the tarts and ate the ones she'd doused. And then there's the rumor that she had a feud going with the cafeteria cooks and intended to make herself sick and blame it on them."

He groaned and this time managed something closer to a true whisper. "How do you know all this? You haven't been in the building more than half an hour."

"I'm a substitute teacher. Kids pay about as much attention to me as they do to the pattern in the carpet or the classroom rules posted on the bulletin boards. Some of the things I've heard would make you blush for a week."

Tremaine grinned, his teeth brilliant white against his dark skin. He raised one brow.

"Okay, maybe you wouldn't blush. But I bet I'd find you at the computer looking up urban slang with your eyes bugging out and sweat beading on your forehead."

His grin faded. "Every time I nail down what they're saying, they change the language."

"They're teenagers. Their mission is to confound us. But you need to be straight with them. Blame it on contaminated ingredients or a combination that produced a toxic substance, or a faulty oven or refrigerator—just don't try to make it seem like her illness has nothing to do with the food." I paused for a minute and added, "I mean, play it that way if that's what you think is best."

He snorted and shook his head. "Sometimes I wonder why we keep you on the sub roster. And sometimes I wonder how we'd get along without you."

While I was mulling whether to ask which frame of mind he was in at the moment, he straightened his tie, strode to the front of the room, and rapped on the desk for attention. Without cracking a smile, he explained that Brenda Waring, one of the most creative cooks on the continent, hadn't foreseen the chemical reaction that would occur with a daring mixture of ingredients and was being treated for a digestive upset but would be back in the morning.

Then, like a politician under fire from unhappy constituents, he ignored the questions they called out, wished them luck on their finals, and left with the kind of speed he once exhibited on the gridiron.

"Was that bogus?" the girl with pink and green hair asked. "That chemistry stuff?"

"No," I said firmly. "Every bit of it was true."

As far as it went.

Between classes I sent a text to Allison to let her know I was at school and would give her a ride home.

"Going with Josh," she texted back.

Huh?

What?

I read the text again. Then I told myself I shouldn't be surprised. After all, it wasn't like I hadn't broken up and made up with boyfriends at that age. When a relationship has history, it can be tough to let it go. Unless the history was mostly bad. And even then . . .

I drove home wondering how the making up came to pass. Had the new-and-improved version of Allison reached out? Had Josh? Had a friend arranged for them to meet on we-were-both-to-blame middle ground?

231

I told myself it was none of my concern and ordered the curiosity cells in my brain to take some time off.

As you might have guessed, they ignored me.

But when I got to the condo complex, I found something to take the focus off Allison's love life.

To be exact, I found two somethings.

My sister.

And Stan Stewart.

They were leaning against his car in the visitors' parking lot and chattering away like people who meet by chance in the beer line at a concert and discover they went to the same high school 20 years earlier. Neither seemed to notice me as I drove past, but I noticed my sister nodding in agreement as he spoke.

I blinked.

Yes, she was definitely nodding. And not scowling. Or frowning. Or glowering.

I glanced up at the sky.

Only one sun.

And right where it should be this time of day.

And the sky was blue, the trees were green, and the numerous signs Bernina Burke had posted about speeding and staying off the grass were all in place.

So I probably wasn't on an alien planet.

Still, it was possible aliens were somehow involved. Perhaps they'd performed a brain transplant on Iz to make her agree with what a male of the species had to say.

I blinked again.

She stopped nodding and started talking.

Stewart took his turn at nodding.

My curiosity cells were working so hard I checked the mirror to see if smoke was pouring from my ears.

It wasn't.

Yet.

What I wanted to do was run—or at least walk at a fast clip—over there and see what was up. But if I appeared too eager, Iz would hold back and make me beg.

I hated that.

So I got out of the car, stretched, pretended to notice them, sketched a little wave, and then strolled their way.

"This story will be my ticket out of here," Stewart enthused as I joined them. "Your sister is a genius."

Iz blew on her fingernails and polished them on an extra-large man's dress shirt that must once have belonged to Dario. The color of ripe eggplant, and sporting bright yellow buttons and stitching, it did nothing positive for her complexion. What it did do was bring to mind a real oldie of a song, Sheb Wooley's "Purple People Eater."

(For the record, I'm soooo not old enough to remember when that came out. But I've heard it played on oldies radio stations along with other tunes from the same era like the one about the itsy bitsy bikini, the one about the witch doctor, and the one about short shorts. I'm sure you could add a few to the list without half trying. They don't make lyrics like they used to, do they?)

Before I could conjure up an image of my sister taking to the air like the creature in the song, Stewart jabbered. "This story has it all. Villains and victims, scammers and scammees, a madam from Reckless River's seamy past, and even a ghost." He gave me a light punch on the shoulder. "Get this—the house with the sliding back yard used to be a red-light district all to itself and the woman who lives there ran the place."

While I debated whether to feign surprise, Stewart rushed on. "Back in the day, she had dirt on the movers and shakers of

233

this not-so-fair city. And, believe it or not, your sister knows her and knows about the guys named John who visit her."

Stewart paused and caught his breath.

Iz did the fingernails thing again.

I reminded myself she outweighed me and was inclined to fight dirty. An attempt to strangle her wouldn't end well for me.

"I spent an hour there this morning. What a house. What a history. What a scam. Convincing a former madam she's still in business so you can get into her house and steal her blind." His fingers twitched on an air keyboard. "Once I get the other part, this will practically write itself."

"Stan's coming with us to Perry Walker's tonight," Iz said. "That's the other part."

"A meeting with a ghost." Stewart rubbed his hands together. "I hope."

"If he shows, it will be the last haunting of his life." Iz pulled a pair of handcuffs from a pocket of her cargo pants. "I'll make a citizen's arrest."

Yikes!

My sister, taking the law into her own hands. There were at least a dozen ways this could go south. "What if he resists?"

"I'll kick his phantom fanny."

"What if he has a gun?"

She patted another pocket of her cargo pants. "I'll handle it."

Double yikes.

As Stewart charged on, rhapsodizing about beating the competition to the story and beating law enforcement in the pursuit of justice, I made another mental note to ask what she carried in those pockets.

Later.

When I was less tired, less stressed, and less likely to say something that might start an argument about Constitutional rights.

"After we take him down," Stewart said, "and after he answers all my questions, we'll call the authorities."

"You're not worried about, um, having the case thrown out because the arrest was, uh, irregular? I mean, what about reading him his rights? Would the arrest stick if you didn't?"

Stewart and Iz exchanged glances.

He pulled his phone from the dog-eared pocket. "I'll do some research."

"We won't call it an arrest," Iz said. "We'll say we witnessed a crime and acted to keep him from escaping."

Stewart nodded. "Good idea."

Two people who had almost no use for each other since the day they met were now as thick as thieves.

And they'd hatched a plan that was half-baked, reckless, and dangerous.

So naturally I said, "I'm coming with you."

"Great," Stewart said. "If you're along the story will get better. You're always tripping over bodies or annoying killers or drug dealers."

"I am not *always* doing stuff like that."

"But it happens a lot," he insisted.

"Not always. It happens once in—"

"What about Dave?" Iz interrupted with a sly smile. "You plan to tell him you're part of the posse?"

"Probably," I hedged.

I did a mental review of my conversation with him last night but found details were fuzzy. I was pretty sure I hadn't promised not to go to Perry Walker's house. I was also pretty sure he'd indicated he wouldn't try to stop me. Or maybe he'd said he might try but not succeed. I remembered something about handcuffs and a refrigerator but couldn't remember how that connected to Perry Walker's ghost. And, frankly, it sounded more than a little kinky, and that sent my train of thought off the tracks.

Iz traded the smile for a full-blown smirk. "You're not going to tell him, are you?"

Chapter 24

Have I mentioned how much I hate it when my sister is right? Have I mentioned that my knee-jerk reaction is to deny the truth? Have you noticed that my self-control isn't robust, or even just a few centimeters on the positive side of wimpy?

"You're wrong." I put my fists on my hips. "I'll tell Dave. Of course I'll tell him."

Only, maybe not until after the fact.

After some discussion, we arranged to meet at 10:00 PM on the street behind Perry Walker's house. "I scoped it out this morning when I was there with Sharlene," Iz said. "The place behind his with the platoons of garden gnomes doesn't have a fence in back. Neither does Perry's. We can walk right up to his back door."

"Trespassing through gnome man's land." Stewart whipped out his notebook. "The suspense builds."

Iz scowled.

"If we're going through the back so we won't be seen, how will we get in?" I asked. "The spare keys are by the front door."

"More spares." Iz pulled two shiny keys from one of her many pockets. "Borrowed the set for the back door from the hook in the kitchen last night, had a friend of Penelope's cut copies, and had the originals on the hook again before dawn.

237

And I loosened the bulbs so the security lighting won't come on when we approach the house."

Stewart made another note.

"That's not going in your story," Iz said. "If I see any of that in print or hear you spouting it on the radio, I'll break your face."

"Not for the paper." Stewart tucked the notebook in his pocket with one hand and shielded his face with the other. "I'm thinking a book."

"A book?" My sister's scowl faded as she echoed the word.

"Sure. Maybe with a few details left out if an editor believes people will make a stink about breaking a few little laws to stop a crime wave. Wouldn't want to get arrested or sued. Although that might add to the hype."

"A book," Iz mused.

Her tone told me she saw herself as the intrepid heroine, righting wrongs, shoving the rusty wheels of justice along. A snarky little part of my brain created images of her in camouflage cargo pants and an oversized green T-shirt with some kind of logo. But what? A couple of X chromosomes with their fists raised?

"Or a movie?" Stewart said.

Iz stood up straight and threw back her head. I just knew she was imagining how she'd play the part of herself, win awards, and salute her adoring fans as she tromped up the red carpet. I didn't envy the casting director or assistant producer in charge of telling her to forget it. I didn't envy the actress cast to take on the role. Iz would find fault with every word and every gesture.

I glanced at Stewart and saw he seemed to be entering the same land of fame and fantasy.

As for me, I had not a single illusion. What I had was hope that if this landed on the big screen I'd be played by someone thinner, someone with longer legs and better hair. No way did I want to play myself in a movie. Heck, sometimes I wished I didn't have to play myself in real life.

"A movie would be terrific," I said in a rush. "But it could be years away. I mean, it could take months to write a book, find a publisher, and get it in print. And then there's the screenplay. Sometimes they're rewritten and changed and tweaked over and over."

They both glared at me. "Don't you get tired of being a soggy little cloud raining on everyone's parades?" Iz asked.

"I'll write the screenplay first," Stewart announced. "Then the book."

He and Iz exchanged a high five.

Whatever happened to mutual dislike and distrust? Whatever happened to life as I once knew it? I felt like the earth had tipped on its axis and spun out of orbit.

"Well, gotta work my city hall beat," Stewart said with all the enthusiasm of a man frightened of reptiles heading off to milk venom from snakes. "See you tonight."

As he drove off, Iz gave him a wave—a cheery little sorority-girl wave. I almost felt the earth tilt a few more degrees beneath my sandals.

"Don't be late," she warned me. "If you're not at the house behind Perry Walker's at 10:00 on the dot, we'll go in without you."

"I'll be there," I promised in a voice as cheery as her wave. "Gnome doubt about it."

Hoping to snag a brief nap or, preferably, a not-so-brief nap, I hustled to my condo and hustled Cheese Puff out to the

239

rose garden. On a rainy day, that would have been a quick trip, but when the sun shone, the breeze blew, and the ground was warm and dry, minutes crawled at the pace of slugs harnessed to tiny sleds made of concrete. Finally he condescended to leave his mark. Then he scooted up the stairs and across the deck and into the arms of Mrs. B.

Now, you know I love and adore my neighbor. But, hopefully, you also know there are degrees of love and adoration and you're aware that emotions ebb and flow depending on so many things like, right now, my need for sleep. Still, I'd had practice doing cheery, so I mustered a smile without straining too many muscles.

Her smile was the real thing. "I'm thrilled to death you agreed to produce my show, dear. We'll have such fun!"

Spoken like someone who'd never experienced the panicky feeling brought on by watching the second hand creep around the dial while listening to the non-sound of dead air. Spoken like someone who didn't doubt we'd have hundreds of listeners and dozens of items they wanted to swap. In other words, spoken like someone who had no idea there were a hundred ways for the show to crash and burn.

She hugged Cheese Puff close and kissed his knobby orange head. "And of course the little prince will join us. I'm sure there's something he can do to assist. Perhaps draw names for prizes."

"Prizes?"

"Of course, dear. We *must* have prizes. At least until we develop a following."

Maybe she wasn't as naïve about this venture as I'd thought.

"Gift certificates," she said. "For the businesses that advertise with us. That will encourage more advertising."

Maybe she wasn't naïve at all.

"Would you like to have our first official meeting this evening?"

"I'd love to," I fabricated, "but I got called to school right after I talked with Dario and haven't had time to research shows in other markets." I paused for a yawn not entirely fabricated. "Plus, I'm really tired."

"Then you go rest, dear. I'll take the little prince to my place for the afternoon and later he can come along to the movies with Dario and Verna and Sybil and Harvey."

Now there was a diverse group, a group with tastes all over the map. A big map. A map of, say, the known universe. "Which movie are you going to?"

"A classic. *The Sting.* It has something for everyone—costumes, music, money, gambling, gunfire, the quest for justice." She nuzzled Cheese Puff again. "And two of the most handsome men I've ever laid eyes on. Except for my Marco."

Her voice cracked a little at the mention of her late husband and I gave her a one-arm hug. "He was a gem."

"Not that Dario isn't a fine man," she said with a sniffle.

"But he's a little rougher around the edges than Marco." I recalled her favorite picture of the man who had showed her the world—literally. "I can't imagine Dario looking quite as dapper in an opera cloak."

"Or jodhpurs." She twinkled a smile and kissed my cheek. "You run along now. I'll keep Cheese Puff overnight so I don't disturb you after the movie. Tomorrow I'll fill you in on Sybil's progress."

"You know how curious I am. Fill me in now."

"All right. But I'll make it short. Sybil's not backsliding. Some of that is likely due to Harvey's vigilance. He's a stickler, but she seems to need someone to hold her accountable—at least for the moment. She's getting so involved in Ardie's summer project we're hoping she'll soon find she doesn't feel the need to gamble."

"So you'll be able to trim Harvey from the payroll."

"Oh, he already trimmed himself, dear. With his pension and tax situation, he says he can't make too much outside money." She paused, a tiny frown creasing her brow. "Of course, he did ask me to provide him with certificates for free meals at a few restaurants of his choice."

"How many meals?"

The frown lines deepened. "We didn't settle on an actual amount. He suggested I establish lines of credit. Open-ended."

"Those lines of credit will be as long as the distance around the equator if you don't set limits. *And* his favorite places serve a lot of the foods he shouldn't have—in quantity."

The frown lines deepened and then smoothed out. "That's an excellent point, dear. I don't begrudge him the meals, and you know I can well afford it, but perhaps I should restrict him to restaurants that offer healthier choices." She tapped her chin with her forefinger, rings flashing in the sunlight. "And perhaps I'll see if Sybil might take on the task of watching him while he's watching her."

"Sly move," I noted. "Amazingly sly considering that you're wearing only one pearl today."

She tapped the pendant I'd last seen in Dario's hands. "Isn't it lovely? I think there's as much pearl power in this as in any five strings in the necklaces I purchased for myself. At least I hope so, because in a few minutes Verna and I are meeting with Bernina Burke."

"On purpose?"

242

"It was Verna's idea. We've waited long enough to begin repairing the flood damage. And we've waited *too long* for Bernina to get the financial records in order."

"So Verna's taking that on? It could be stressful—not just the numbers, but dealing with Bernina. Do you think she's recovered enough?"

"She says she has. And, you know, I think she's happiest when she's crunching numbers and organizing systems, tasks she can do without taxing herself physically." Mrs. B's lips pressed together for a second. "As for dealing with Bernina, well, that's my department."

And it was a familiar department. Mrs. B had taken Bernina in hand before, once even taking her shopping and arranging a hair and makeup makeover. The result had been a kinder, gentler condo manager. At least for a few days.

"Are you planning to use the carrot or the stick?"

"I've offered quite enough carrots to Bernina in the past, so I believe I'll simply allude to them. As for the stick, I hope not to use it, but the more I review her duties and her performance, the more I realize we're foolhardy to trust her to follow through in an appropriate manner, and the more I become convinced that we should try another approach when her contract expires."

"Such as?"

She shrugged, drawing a grunt from Cheese Puff who had dozed off in her arms and resented even a slight movement if it interrupted his snoozing. "Perhaps a small group of residents— three or four—willing to take turns being on call to supervise maintenance and resolve issues. We have a number of retirees with many years of experience who might appreciate a bit of additional income. Verna and I will sound them out in the coming weeks."

Was it possible? Could my nemesis Bernina Burke be on the way out?

Part of me turned virtual cartwheels of joy. Another part felt a weird emptiness. In a crazy kind of way, I'd come to depend on Bernina Burke to make everyone else—with the possible exceptions of my sister and Harvey Goodspeed—look better than they might otherwise. Even me. At least one morning a week I stumbled from bed for a subbing assignment, peered into the bathroom mirror and told myself my complexion resembled a bucket of cold grits and my hair resembled a nest made by a particularly sloppy rat, but at least it wasn't Bernina's reflection I saw.

Did I want to admit that to Mrs. B? Did I want to admit to a woman I admired that I was so childish? So petty?

Not unless my life depended on it.

"I'm confident you'll do what's right for all the residents," I told Mrs. B. And then, to show myself I could be a more highly evolved person, I added, "And I'm confident great opportunities will open up for Bernina if she loses her position here."

Not.

What I was confident about was that word was out about Bernina in Reckless River. She'd have trouble getting a job managing a storage business with more than two lockers.

"That's very kind of you," Mrs. B said in a way that made me wonder yet again if she could read my mind. "Now go get some sleep. Tomorrow we'll talk about my show."

And with that she did a little shuffle and tap and was gone.

Since actually running along would raise my pulse rate and blood pressure and make it more difficult to fall asleep, I didn't so much as break into a jog on the way to my bedroom. But I did proceed at a steady pace. And I managed to sock away nearly three hours of shuteye before the sounds of Dave scavenging provisions for dinner awakened me.

I huddled beneath the sheet, telling myself to work out how—or whether—to discuss my plans for the night with him. But the aroma of toasting bread reminded me that lunch had been long ago and hardly substantial. In fact, since I'd lost my appetite while dealing with the fish wrapper in Brenda's classroom, lunch had been hardly . . . well, it had been hardly. Period.

I hurtled from bed, showered, and dressed for the night's adventure. Deciding that dressing completely in black would telegraph my intentions to the trained law officer downstairs, I went with dark gray running shoes, jeans, and a deep purple T-shirt.

Dave turned from the stove as I entered the kitchen. "Grilled cheese sandwich with tomato. Want one?"

"Like a stockbroker wants a risk-prone client with a mattress full of cash."

"Sit." He thrust his chin toward the table he'd set with the essentials for fine dining—a bottle of beer, a bag of barbecue potato chips, and a strip of paper towel. "White or rye?"

"Rye, please."

He buttered a slice, slapped it on the griddle beside a sandwich oozing pale white cheese, and cut thick slices from a brick of sharp cheddar before attacking a beefy tomato. My stomach rumbled approval and I tossed it a couple of chips by way of an appetizer.

"How are things at the sheriff's office?"

"Better than they were—if that's what you're really asking." He flashed me a grin. "But if you want to know whether I talked with anyone up the food chain about the ghost situation, the answer is negative."

245

"Tomorrow?"

"Maybe. It's all about when they're available." He flipped his sandwich. "I take it, since your sister hasn't called to say she told me so, the ghost didn't put in an appearance last night."

"Right." I ate another chip, one that was folded over on itself twice and wore a thick coat of orange-brown barbecue-flavored powder. In short, it was a gourmet treat. "No ghost."

"She going back tonight?"

I shrugged and peered into the chip bag to avoid eye contact. "Probably."

He laid slices of tomato and more cheese on my bread and topped it with another slice of rye. "What about you?"

He asked in a casual tone, but I knew it was anything but a throwaway question. I knew it was bait. I knew he was trying to get me to drop my guard, trying to lure me closer so he could spring the trap and drop a net of guilt over me.

And I didn't blame him. I'd probably do the same if I was worried about a course of action he was about to undertake. So I had a lot of mixed feelings—not about taking part in tonight's adventure, but about whether I should be honest with Dave, acknowledge his feelings, somehow scissor my way out of the guilt net, and then head to Perry Walker's house.

This relationship stuff was like looking in those funhouse mirrors where everything is smaller or larger or wavy or distorted. It was like pulling taffy and trying not to get it in your hair or on your nose when you scratched an itch. And that guilt net was clingy. I might slice my way free, but strings could stick to my shoes and clothing.

I munched a chip before I responded. "Huh?"

"Are you going with your sister?"

I widened my eyes. "Me? Going with Iz?"

246

Dave laughed and slid his sandwich onto a plate. "You could strain your optic nerves pasting on a look of innocence like that."

I did the hand-over-the-heart thing. "I have no idea what you're talking about."

"Okay. I give up. Have it your way." Frowning, he sliced his sandwich and carried it to the table. "You'll do what you'll do and I'll see you at the hospital later."

Chapter 25

Honestly, Dave was taking a page from Stan Stewart's book. I didn't *always* end up in the hospital, just like I didn't *always* stumble across a body.

But I didn't say that. In fact, I said, "Something's burning."

Dave rushed to flip my sandwich. "Just a little cheese."

And from then on our conversation steered clear of my intentions for the evening. We talked about Allison now at a movie with Josh, about Brenda Waring's toxic tarts, Deming's caffeine crash and Mrs. B's radio show, about Sybil and Harvey Goodspeed, and about Verna and Mrs. B bearding Bernina in her den. When we ran out of topics that didn't touch on ghosts or thefts from the elderly or my sister, we watched a sitcom. I can't remember the title. What I do recall is that it was more sit than com.

And then, at 9:00, Dave stood, stretched, and headed for the stairs. "I'm going to bed."

Notice that he didn't ask if I planned to come along.

"I had a long nap this afternoon." I scooped up the remote. "Think I'll surf the news channels and see if I can pick up ideas for Jake's show."

Dave gave me a look that questioned my sanity.

"Deming's still getting adjusted to the Northwest and regional issues."

He nodded and climbed out of sight. "If you say so."

Another way of saying he thought I was full of a substance I won't mention here.

I flipped to a 24/7 news channel and clocked the latest. War, war, war, impending war, drought, starvation, political corruption, threats of war, weapon stockpiles, failed negotiations, and war. Unfortunately, all that added up to normal for this day and age.

I clicked off, twisted my engagement ring, and wondered what others might do in my situation. My sister, of course, would charge ahead without considering Dave's concerns about whether the ghost/man might return and whether he might resort to violence if he discovered the jig was up. Paulette, whose airline pilot husband was often away from home and not available for consultation, would likely do the same after weighing concerns about Perry Walker and deciding that should take precedence over all else. Ardie, who could move like a shadow and hide among them, would go for it, but try to gather evidence without confronting the crook. Mrs. B wouldn't hesitate about signing on, but would bring Dario for protection. I supposed I could do the same, but if Dario came, Mrs. B would tag along. More people staking out the house added up to more chance of someone being spotted.

Besides, we had no guarantee the ghost guy would even show. Maybe he'd decided the risk was too great. Maybe he'd decided to take a few weeks off and wait for us to lose interest. Maybe he had other victims to milk. Maybe he'd already milked so much from Perry Walker that he was willing let the rest go.

But did a thief ever get so fat and happy he retired from a life of crime and no longer answered to the siren song of pitting his smarts and skill against others? Did a thief ever give up on the heart-pounding thrill of facing possible peril and walking away unscathed and significantly richer?

249

While I was pondering all that and paying no attention to the passage of time, the hands on the kitchen clock crept around to 9:40. It was too late for me to have an adult conversation with Dave and make it to the meeting place by 10:00.

As quietly as I could, I dug a mini flashlight from the junk drawer in the kitchen and stuck it in my pocket along with Dave's smaller jackknife—the one that he always swore he put away in his office. In case of further emergencies, I added a book of matches and a chewy granola bar. I would have preferred cheesy snacks, but it wouldn't do to give myself away by munching a crunchy snack.

Snatching my keys in a tight grip to prevent jangling, I crept to the front door and slipped out into the night. As sometimes happens in June, the wind had died to an anemic breeze and humid air lay over Reckless River. It trapped and magnified odors of decay and rot from the riverbank, the smells of car exhaust from the interstate bridge, and the sharp scent of a paper mill up the river. The resulting mix of stinks reminded me of things I'd rather not think about. I didn't linger on my way to the car.

It started on the second attempt, and I took that for a good omen. I rolled to the stop sign at the far end of the parking lot before turning on my lights. Not that Dave would see them— unless he peered out of Allison's window overlooking the parking lot. And, if he woke up and noticed she hadn't made her school-night curfew, he might just do that. But by the time he got downstairs, I'd be long gone. And—bonus—he didn't know where Perry Walker lived.

Of course, he could find out with an Internet search or a single phone call to someone on duty at the sheriff's office. And with another phone call he could abort our mission by claiming he had information about a break-in involving people meeting the descriptions of Iz, Penelope, and yours truly.

I put that thought aside, tucked my purse under the seat, and stepped on the gas.

With five minutes to spare, I pulled up at the house behind Perry Walker's. Iz hadn't exaggerated about the garden gnome population. A nearby streetlamp didn't throw much light, and overgrown shrubs cast dense shadows, but I spotted enough of the little guys and gals to tip an election for city council if they found a way to register to vote. Most were about a foot tall and wore pointed caps and what I thought of as traditional gnome gear. They carried tiny spades and rakes and baskets of flowers. But some wore camouflage and carried what appeared to be grenade launchers and assault weapons. One gnome, standing by a plant he appeared to be watering, wore nothing at all.

(For the record, since I'm busy blocking the image from my mind, I'll leave it to you to figure out what the gnome was using to water that plant. Here's a hint: it wasn't a watering can.)

Iz stepped from a shadow a little farther up the street and motioned me forward to a spot at the edge of the property, behind Penelope's truck. As I got out of the car, Stan Stewart pulled his clunker in behind mine. "I went by Mavis Dupree's house on the way," he said in a low voice. "She was dressed for entertaining circa 1978. Did you know she has a disco ball in the living room?"

"Later," Iz growled. "Follow me. And stay between the stars."

I was about to ask what she meant when I noticed two trails of tiny glowing stars on the grass. Obviously someone had thought ahead, bought some glow-in-the-dark stars, and placed them beneath a lamp to power them up. Even more obviously, that thinking-ahead someone was probably Penelope. Sure enough, when we were deep in the back yard I spotted her laying down a moon and a comet by a gap in a hedge.

"Mavis called me John," Stewart whispered. "Totally forgot my name and that I'd been there earlier. Said it would be a while before I could go upstairs but I should put the money in the box on the coffee table, have a drink, and make myself comfortable. While I was checking out the labels on her Scotch selection, I heard someone on the stairs."

"Shhhh," Iz hissed. "Stop talking and hurry up."

Stewart obeyed, but I was used to disregarding my sister's imperious commands. "Did you see him?" I whispered over my shoulder.

"Just his back."

"Darn."

"But I'll know him if I see him again. Unless he dyes the patch of gray hair behind his left ear."

"Shhhh." Iz hissed again. "How many times do I have to tell you to do something before you do it?"

(For the record, I was tempted to respond with an exact number. Perhaps one in the 200 to 500 range. But Iz would take my response seriously and, after our adventure was over, deliver the mother of all lectures. Or maybe even a whole series of lectures. Since I was already facing a lecture from Dave—or the kind of non-lecture that would make me feel even worse—I decided to skip the smart remark and go with a meditative silence. What I meditated on was whether my decision demonstrated maturity or simply a desire not to have to listen to Iz pontificate. I decided to go with maturity—even if that wasn't the choice a true adult would make.)

Stewart and I hushed and caught up to my sister at the hedge. As you know, horticulture isn't my strong suit, so I was maxing out to recognize it as some kind of evergreen and possibly related to gorse. I'm not sure I'd recognize gorse if I sat on it, but I knew you didn't want to toss firecrackers into a clump of gorse in a dry season. Gorse burns hot and fast. If you don't believe me, read up on the gorse inferno that torched Bandon, Oregon, in 1936.

I took a step forward and felt a chill.

Odd.

I'd been thinking about fire, and the night air was warm.

The chill grew chillier.

I jerked about and peered over my shoulder.

"What?" Stewart asked.

"I don't know. Do you see anything? Hear anything?"

"Nothing but gnomes. They're not noted for being great conversationalists."

"Will you two zip it? Or do I have tape your lips closed?"

Not a threat I wanted to put to the test. For all I knew, one of my sister's capacious pockets contained half a mile of duct tape. And for all I knew, she'd attempt to tape my nose closed as well.

We squeezed through the gap in the hedge, breaking twigs and dislodging a shower of needles and dust. I held my nose to contain a series of sneezes, feeling my eyes bulge and my ears pop with each one.

Penelope, sensibly, had tucked her hair under a black ball cap that matched the rest of her wardrobe. Like Stewart's, my sister's hair was too short to pick up more than a few needles. But mine, down to my shoulders, had swept up enough bark and bits to start a campfire. I paused to untangle a few, but Iz yanked the sleeve of my T-shirt. "Come on."

I trotted along behind her across the lawn. It felt thick and lush beneath my feet and even in the dim city-glow light, I could tell the grass was clipped and cared for like the greens on

253

an upscale private golf course. We jogged left and right, passing neatly edged flowerbeds with plants spaced out like ships on bark mulch lakes. Perry Walker obviously didn't skimp on his landscaping service.

In two minutes our little troop was up three steps and across a narrow porch. In another few seconds Iz had the door open and we crowded into the kitchen. In the faint green glow cast by digital readouts on the stove and microwave, I saw all was much as it had been the last time I visited, down to the shiny dribbles of butterscotch sauce on the floor in front of the refrigerator. "Looks like Perry had his ice cream."

"The man sticks to a schedule." Iz tore a paper towel from a roll near the sink, wet it, and wiped up the dribbles. "And he always makes the same mess in the same place."

"At least you know where the mess will be and when it will occur," Penelope said in a voice that held a note of consolation and another of what sounded like resignation. The light was so dim I couldn't scope out her expression, but I was willing to bet a day's subbing pay she was thinking of messes my sister left in her wake. Once again, I wondered what Penelope saw in Iz, and once again I concluded that a) it takes all kinds, b) even if I knew, it might not make sense, and c) I was glad she saw something because—speaking selfishly—the relationship mellowed my sister.

Iz tossed the paper towel in a trash can that opened when she waved her hand across the top. "We'll check on Perry and then get to our stations."

"Where?" Stewart asked.

"I'll show you." Iz headed for the hall. "But not until *after* we check on Perry."

Typical Iz.

"She's all about being in charge, so save your argument energy until you really need it," I advised him. "Don't wear yourself out on the small stuff."

He grunted and followed me to the library where Perry reclined in his usual chair, eyelids drooping. As before, he held coins, this time half dollars, three in each hand.

"These are all I have left for the ferryman," he said in a mournful voice. "All the gold is gone. And all the silver dollars."

"What you have is plenty," Iz assured him.

"It's just the right amount," Penelope agreed.

Stewart tapped my shoulder and whispered, "Who's the ferryman? What ferry is he talking about?"

"The one in Greek mythology."

"Huh?"

Sheesh. Had his education skipped over myths and legends? Or had he always intended to be a journalist and confined his reading to political history and current events?

"Look it up," I hissed.

He sighed and yanked his phone from his jacket pocket. If a few more frayed stitches gave way, it would soon be nothing more than a flap.

"Put that away," Iz ordered. "No phones or lights from now on."

Stewart opened his mouth.

"Not yet," I cautioned. "Save it."

He snapped his teeth together and trailed behind me as we followed my sister to the living room.

It was also, from what I could make out, as cluttered as before. The ticking of the many clocks created an overlay of sound at once soothing and maddening. Iz pointed to a sofa not far from the door. "I'll be behind that. I'll jump out and tackle him when he tries to escape."

255

That was fine with me. No way did I want to do the tackling and—let's face it—my sister was built for the job.

"I'll be against the wall just inside the kitchen." Penelope displayed a pink tube. "If he tries to get out that way, I'll douse him with pepper spray."

Iz pointed at me. "You'll be upstairs. First door along the hall that leads straight ahead."

"Upstairs," I whisper-squawked.

"Right. In the linen closet."

Chapter 26

Forget the whisper. This time I squawked like a chicken that just laid an egg the size of a ripe grapefruit. "The linen closet?"

"It's a big closet," Iz said. "There's a step stool you can sit on. And it's the safest place for you."

"Have you been talking with Dave? Or are you saying I mess things up? Or do you just want me out of the way?"

"She hasn't been talking to Dave," Penelope said. "But we both feel you're a danger magnet. We worry about you."

I questioned the "we" part of that last statement. Penelope might be concerned for my well-being. She was other-directed and cared about living things in general. But my sister? Not so much. "So why let me come along at all? Just so you could enjoy yourself by sticking me in a closet?"

"You have a job. You'll listen to him moving around upstairs so we know which rooms he goes into," Iz said. "I took photographs in every room, so we'll know what's missing."

"And you'll have to rely on the photographs if you don't tackle him and he escapes with the loot."

"He won't escape." She leveled a forefinger at my nose. "When you get in that closet, you'll be as quiet as a mouse—a mummified mouse."

"What about me?" Stewart asked.

"In the library. Behind one of the display cases. So you can watch him take the money. So you'll hear if he says anything."

"Got it." Stewart dug a small recorder and a camera from the pocket that wasn't in danger of becoming a flap.

"No photographs." Iz shook her head. "Not unless he's already been upstairs."

"How do we know he'll go upstairs?" I asked. "From what we saw the other day, there isn't much up there worth looting. Maybe there never was."

"There was plenty," my sister said in the smug tone of a candidate who has the Electoral College sewed up. "I found a woman on the cleaning team. She told me she was glad Perry was decluttering because she used to dread this place and all the knickknacks she had to dust once a month, even the ones upstairs where no one went anymore."

"Nice work," Stewart said. "I'll need her name."

"Tomorrow. Now, back on task. There are still a few things upstairs, but if he skips them, he'll take something from in here or the dining room." Iz pointed at Stewart. "If he's got a load of loot when he comes for the coins, *then* you grab your shot."

The word "shot" caused me to channel Dave. "What if he has a gun?"

"He won't," Iz said. "That would up the penalty if he's caught."

That sounded logical. But I'd come to realize that logic and criminal activities didn't always go together. "But what if you're—"

"Maybe you should go home," Iz suggested. "Then you can worry all you want without annoying us."

I zipped my lips, but Stewart said, "Maybe this guy didn't get the memo. Maybe he isn't up on the law. Maybe he always carries a gun. Maybe—"

"Maybe he's a space alien," Iz jeered. "Maybe he's Bigfoot. Maybe he's D.B. Cooper."

She paused, glaring at Stewart and me—mostly at me. "We don't have time for this crapola."

"If he has a gun," Penelope said in a peace-making voice, "he'll probably have it where we can see it. If we see it, we'll stay hidden."

"There," Iz announced. "Fake problem solved. Discussion closed. Silence your phones and get to your stations."

Stewart grunted in a way that told me he also had doubts about whether this plan would stay on the rails, but he headed for the library.

A less-than-happy camper, I trudged up the stairs and turned the knob on the linen closet. It clicked softly and the door swished open on hinges that gave out not the faintest squeal or squeak. It closed the same way and settled with another soft click. Switching on my flashlight, I saw the room bore little resemblance to the linen closet in the condo, or to closets in houses I'd owned or rented. First, it was at least 10 times larger. Second, it had its own heat vent in the floor, an exhaust fan, louvers at the top and bottom of the door, a fold-down ironing board, and shelves of all widths. It was stocked with enough blankets, comforters, sheets, pillowcases, towels, washcloths, soap, and toilet paper to outfit a boutique hotel. There were also stacks of tablecloths and snowy napkins, and a dozen boxes marked to indicate the number of napkin rings they contained and whether they were plain, engraved, silver, gold, or for a specific holiday. It appeared Perry Walker's place must once have been crawling with friends and relatives gathering around the table, staying the night, and perhaps lingering for weeks.

259

Drawing in a series of breaths, I isolated the scents of bleach and starch, lilacs and sunshine, rain and roses. I ran my hand across a stack of pillowcases, enjoying a sensation that was at once cool and crisp and buttery. Maybe they'd been ironed. Probably they were of a far higher quality than the ones I had at home.

I fingered a stack of towels. Thick and soft and fluffy and a gorgeous blue that reminded me of photographs of Caribbean lagoons. One appeared to be large enough to use as a blanket on a twin bed. Perhaps the next time Mrs. B insisted she take me shopping, I'd steer her away from clothing and toward the bed and bath aisles.

Reminding myself why I was here, I folded the step stool open, planted it close to the door, and perched on the second step. It wasn't on a par with an easy chair. It wasn't even on a par with what kids sat on at Captain Meriwether, but I guessed I was more comfortable than Stan Stewart.

After another brief look around, I flicked off the flashlight and stilled my body and mind.

Correction. I *tried* for stillness.

But, you know how it goes when you can't move or make a sound beyond breathing in and out.

First my nose itched. Then a spot in the middle of my back joined in. Then a tooth in need of dental work began to throb. Then I remembered we were almost out of mayonnaise and I forgot to put it on the grocery list. Then one eyelid twitched. Then I wondered if maybe I did make a note of the mayonnaise but forgot about the peanut butter. Then I weighed the merits of various brands of peanut butter and whether it's better on artisan white bread or whole wheat, better on warm toast or in a chilled sandwich with gobs of raspberry jam. Then I wondered, while trying to take my mind off the itch on the bottom of my heel, how many peanuts it takes to make a small jar of peanut butter, and whether more were necessary for smooth than for crunchy.

Time passed while I scratched a series of ever-more annoying itches and rode a thought train to Randomville. How much time? I have no idea. But I know what got me off that train—a faint scuff of sound. It was repeated again and again. It was the sound of someone climbing the carpeted stairs.

I longed to lean forward, closer to the door, but feared the step stool might squeak or drag on the linoleum floor. So I turned my head, aiming my right ear at the door, and wondering all the while if my left ear might be superior. I couldn't recall if I'd ever had my hearing tested, and I couldn't recall ever noticing a difference. I was right-handed. Did that mean my right ear would distinguish sounds better? Did it mean my right nostril would distinguish scents with more precision?

The scuffing was replaced by a muffled slapping.

Shoes on carpet?

I held my breath.

The sound passed me by along the hallway that led straight from the head of the stairs. With it went a pale and bobbling light, splintered into lines by the lower louver on the door.

I breathed again, slowly and carefully.

Time marched on.

Well, actually it didn't march. It moved like Michael Jackson doing the moon walk, giving the illusion of moving while staying just about in the same place.

The muffled slapping returned. The dim light came with it. The stealthy creeper passed the door, and turned the corner into the shorter hallway.

261

I tried to remember what was down that way. A sewing room? Definitely. And a small sitting room not nearly as stripped down as other rooms upstairs. I recalled walls painted in pastel green, embroidered cushions on a low sofa with curved legs, scented candles in silver candlesticks, a tall silver vase filled with huge paper flowers, an easel near the window, and—

The footsteps came back.

They paused outside the door to the linen close.

The light swayed back and forth along the louver, casting lines of light and dark on my shoes.

I pressed my tongue to the roof of my mouth and breathed around it. Short, shallow breaths.

A click.

A swish.

A beam of light stabbed my eyes.

The door banged against my knees.

I yelped.

The man in the hall shouted an obscenity, kicked my right kneecap, and ran.

Chapter 27

I fell sideways, clutching my knee with both hands and shrieking, "Stop him."

Feet pounded down the stairs.

"Stop," Stewart shouted.

Something thudded against a wall.

Glass broke.

My sister yelled.

More glass broke.

A door slammed.

And then, for a long moment, I heard nothing but moaning—not all mine, by the way.

Penelope called out, "Are you all okay?"

"Just banged up," I answered.

Iz howled something unintelligible.

Stan Stewart said nothing.

I struggled to my feet and hopped from the closet to the top of the stairs.

A light came on in the hallway. I peered over the railing and saw Penelope leaning over Stewart. He wasn't moving. Neither was the silver vase beside him.

I gripped the railing with both hands and started a one-footed descent.

"He's breathing," Penelope called to me. "His heart seems fine. But he's out cold."

"What about Iz?"

"I can't move." The cry came from the front of the house.

Moaning in dismay, Penelope darted in that direction.

I hopped as fast as I could without toppling over, reached the bottom of the staircase, and dug my phone from my pocket.

I tapped it to life as Stewart groaned, opened his eyes, and rubbed his forehead. "Did you get the license of the truck that hit me?"

If he could crack a joke, he'd probably live. I shook my head, put my phone back in my pocket, and hopped off to check on my sister.

Penelope had hit every switch, lighting up the room like a landing strip. Iz lay a few feet from the open front door in a nest of shattered glass, springs, gears, and the faces of clocks that had ticked their last. The remains of an antique table, its spindly legs snapped like twigs, formed a cradle around her. Using a doily as a whisk broom, Penelope brushed away shards of glass and urged Iz to stay still so she wouldn't cut herself.

Iz fixed a baleful glare on me. "Don't say it."

"Say what?" I attempted to hold back a smirk. I failed miserably.

"It was a good plan," Penelope insisted in a quiet voice.

"I almost had him," Iz said. "I would have had him, except he shoved me against this sorry excuse for a table."

I didn't mention the sorry excuse for a table—now good for little more than kindling—was probably 200 years old and, minutes earlier, would have been worth several hundred dollars or more. I also didn't bring up the value of the clocks and porcelain figurines.

Stewart emerged from the hallway wobbling like an inflatable beach toy in a gusting wind. "Did he get away?"

"No," a familiar voice said from beyond the doorway. "He's right here."

Chapter 28

"You followed me," I accused.

"And I was as disappointed as the day I discovered there's no Easter Bunny," Dave said. "I thought you'd make it more of a challenge."

He stepped inside, shoving the intruder before him. The man's face, with its thick brows, thin lips, and heavy jowls, seemed custom-made for the scowl he directed at the cuffs around his wrists. The pockets of his camouflage vest bulged. Two tiny porcelain ladies peered out of one. A silver candlestick poked from another.

"I took a picture of that candle holder thingie this morning." Heedless of glass shards, Iz scrambled to her feet. "It was in the sewing room upstairs."

"Was not," the man claimed. "I brought it from home."

I laughed. Even on a day when my imagination stayed in bed, I could have come up with a better excuse for having a piece of stolen property in my pocket. "Did you bring the figurines from home too?"

"Uh, yeah, I always— Hey!" He pointed at Stewart with both hands. "You can't take my picture."

"I just did." Stewart stepped around behind the man and peered at his hair. "There it is. The gray patch. This is the same guy who was visiting Mavis Dupree earlier tonight. I bet he's ripping her off too. And who knows how many other seniors."

266

He mimed spiking his camera and did a dance that would have made a running back proud. "This is it. This is the story that will get me out of Reckless River."

Lights flashing, a patrol car pulled up out front and Dave turned to escort the scowling man to his ride to jail.

"Where are you taking him? He doesn't have the money for the ferry," a voice cried from along the hallway.

I turned to see Perry Walker shuffling toward us, his arms extended, half dollars glinting on his palms. "He needs coins for the ferryman. He—"

Perry halted and stared at the intruder. "You're not a ghost." He dropped the coins and tears streamed down his face. "You're not my son."

To my amazement, my sister was the first to rush to console him.

As Stewart said, it was a great story. Papers all over the country picked it up, and he's been nominated for a number of awards. The day the first installment appeared in the *Reckless River Roundup*, the newspaper's owner gave him a raise he described as "substantial." He also got the crime beat all to himself and a reprieve from covering city government except when his pursuit of wrongdoing led him there. And, this being Reckless River, and some politicians being prone to do stupid stuff, I had no doubt he'd be no stranger to city hall.

If he got an offer from a big paper, he never said a word about it to me. In fact, he said so little, and changed the subject so frequently, I suspected he'd decided he liked being a big fish in a small pond and intended to stay. In case you're wondering, he had his pocket mended and his jacket dry cleaned, but that was all the wardrobe upgrade he went for.

The arrest also turned out to be good for Dave's career. Perry and Mavis were two of more than a dozen elderly victims in the area. The sum of their losses totaled well over a million dollars. Before the case went to trial, however, much of their property was recovered. The intruder—Bill "Spotty" Muller—had fenced only a few things, been disappointed at his cut, and worried about dumping too much loot in one area. He'd stockpiled the rest in a storage unit, planning to transfer it to a rental truck at the end of the summer and drive across the country from pawn shop to pawn shop. Instead, he'll most likely be going to a place where he won't need a driver's license for many years.

Speaking of driving, thanks to the instructor Dave hired, Allison is doing much better. Of course, "better" is a relative term, so I'm not ready to volunteer to be in the passenger seat when she merges onto the freeway during rush hour. She still has focus issues and still tends to blame mistakes on other drivers or the angle of the sun, but the instructor doesn't let her get away with that. He insists she silence her cellphone and stow it in the glove box when she starts a lesson. He's a stickler about not using the rearview mirror to check her hair when she's at a stoplight. And he's making sure she gets lots of practice executing tight turns, starting and stopping in narrow lanes, and getting close enough to the service window to grab a bag of burgers without scraping a fender.

Did I mention Allison's driving instructor is Harvey Goodspeed?

Harvey's also doing a great job with Ardie's program. He handles crowd control, and presents a daily session called "How Crooks Got Caught" that draws on actual cases and plays on the crime-doesn't-pay theme. Those sessions also allow him to paint himself as a crime-fighting hero second to none. Ardie

268

tells me kids take his ego-inflated claims with enough grains of salt to fill the average shaker.

Harvey's still keeping an eye on Sybil, but so far either she hasn't backslid or he hasn't caught her. And she's been a hit with the kids, staging short plays and dramatic readings, all involving colorful costumes she and Ardie whip up. She even persuaded Harvey to take part in one of them, casting him in the role of a tree in Sherwood Forest—a tree with a very thick trunk.

And the adventure worked out for Iz in several ways. First, figuring prominently in the newspaper story and the TV coverage it generated, gave her ego a boost. Iz with a boosted ego is less likely to dump on others, so I benefited as well.

Second, she was able to use a few key facts of the case to leverage her way to the highest possible evaluation from Sharlene. As it turned out, Bill "Spotty" Muller was good at listening and Sharlene, when she'd had a cocktail or two, was good at talking about herself and her clients. Enough cocktails, and she revealed confidential details such as names and addresses, to the nice man who often sat next to her at the bar and generously paid her tab, expecting nothing in return. When her unwitting role in the crimes became clear, she resigned and took a job on a chicken farm as a form of self-punishment.

Third, the program director, embarrassed by Sharlene's behavior and perhaps hoping—in vain—that Iz would splash a little whitewash on the story, gave her sterling grades and a glowing recommendation for future jobs.

And fourth, an advocate for senior citizens suggested to Iz that she should consider a job investigating reports of crime and abuse targeting older residents. That dovetailed with Dave's hopes for expanding the responsibilities of his office. They might work together on a project—if they can figure out

269

how to do that without showing all the negotiating and compromising skills of two Tasmanian devils thrust together in a cage barely large enough for one.

To my delight, Iz was so positive about the adventure and the possible course of her future, that she stepped up and took one for the team—she volunteered to fly to Missouri and spend a weekend with our parents. As I dropped her at the airport on my way to yet another visit to the dentist, I took in her freshly dyed orange and green hair and the pockets of her cargo pants bulging with who knew what, and I wondered how my parents would react. Would the shock bring them out of their gated community and back to the larger world? Or would it send them to the hospital?

As for me, well, I guess Dave figured that proving he could outsmart and outmaneuver me was far better than delivering a lecture. Or perhaps he figured previous lectures hadn't had much effect and he might as well tag along.

I didn't ask.

And he didn't tell.

We'll find out the next time I undertake a USUIE mission.

You can trust me on that.

Carolyn J. Rose grew up in New York's Catskill Mountains, the setting for her Hemlock Lake mystery trilogy. She graduated from the University of Arizona with a degree and a tan, and stayed on for graduate school. Thanks to boredom and a public service announcement on late-night TV, she abandoned literary studies for two years with Volunteers in Service to America in Little Rock. From there a series of coincidences and chance encounters led her to the land of TV news and 25 years as a researcher, writer, producer, and assignment editor in Arkansas, New Mexico, Oregon, and Washington. She's now a high school substitute teacher in Vancouver, Washington. Her subbing experiences, and her sometimes rocky relationship with the dogs in her life, led her to create the canine character Cheese Puff and the Subbing isn't for Sissies series. Other than writing, her interests are reading, swimming, walking, gardening, and NOT cooking.

Also by Carolyn J. Rose

The Catskill Mountains Mysteries
Hemlock Lake
Through a Yellow Wood
The Devil's Tombstone

The Subbing isn't for Sissies series
No Substitute for Murder
No Substitute for Money
No Substitute for Maturity
No Substitute for Myth
No Substitute for Mistakes
No Substitute for Motives
No Substitute for Misinformation
No Substitute for Momentum
No Substitute for the Munchies

And others
Nightfall Bay
An Uncertain Refuge
Sea of Regret
A Place of Forgetting

With Michael A. Nettleton
Death at Devil's Harbor
Deception at Devil's Harbor
The Hard Karma Shuffle
The Crushed Velvet Miasma
Drum Warrior
Sucker Punches

www.ingramcontent.com/pod-product-compliance
Lightning Source LLC
Chambersburg PA
CBHW061554170626
46811CB00001B/206